No Phones
in Heaven

GREGORY HAYDEL

PAGE PUBLISHING, INC.
New York, NY

First originally published by Page Publishing, Inc. 2019

ISBN 978-1-64544-341-4 (Paperback)
ISBN 978-1-64701-005-8 (Hardcover)
ISBN 978-1-64544-342-1 (Digital)

Printed in the United States of America

CHAPTER ONE

It is a warm fall day with a blue sky in September. The weather is perfect for playing outside. Jerry is kicking a soccer ball with his little sister, Janet, in the backyard. Jerry is nine years old with black hair and blue eyes, and Janet's seventh birthday will be in two days. Her hair is long and black, and she has brown eyes. Penny, their mother, is planting lilies in the flower bed near the fence in the backyard. Penny is a brunette with brown eyes, a very pretty twenty-nine-year-old who teaches fourth grade at the school where Jerry and Janet attend.

Jerry kicks the soccer ball hard while Janet runs to catch the ball, but before Janet can get close, the ball hits their mother. Penny grabs the ball and gives it to Janet and warns both children not to kick the ball near the flower bed, because it could hurt or kill her plants. Jerry and Janet both say they are sorry and continue to kick the ball around the yard, trying to avoid the flower bed, while their mother continues to plant different flowers. James is the father of Jerry and Janet, a twenty-nine-year-old handsome, black-haired, blue-eyed man with an athletic body. James is on his way home from his office where he is the CEO of a law practice, driving a black Mercedes Benz listening to the radio with music by Blake Sheldon, singing along.

There is a preacher in a white truck running late for a wedding across town. The name of the preacher is Pastor Mathew, a tall man at six feet four inches at the age of fifty but looks to be in his late thirties. The reason Pastor Mathew is running late is he was trying to finish building a dollhouse for an orphan girl and didn't realize how late he was. Now rushing through traffic, Pastor Mathew decides to take a shortcut through the subdivision where Janet and Jerry are playing kick ball. Janet kicks the ball too hard, and Jerry can't respond fast enough to the ball before it crushes one of the freshly planted flowers

Penny has put into the ground. Penny yells at Jerry for not catching the ball and tells them to stop playing in the backyard.

After grabbing the ball from the flower garden, Jerry shouts at Janet, "Let's go in the front yard where we can't get in trouble."

Janet smiles at Jerry and complains, "You are too slow to catch my rocket kicks. You need to get faster if you want to stop my kicks." Then she hugs her brother as they walk to the front yard.

Meanwhile, the phone rings in the house, and Penny takes off her gloves that she was wearing while planting flowers and runs into the house. It is James asking how everything is at home. Penny is a little short of breath from running inside and tells her husband she had to yell at the kids for crushing one of her freshly planted flowers. James asks Penny to calm down and says it will be okay.

"I'm a few minutes away."

He asks if there's anything she may need at the local store. Penny takes a breath and tells James, "No, honey, nothing is needed from the store. I love you." She hangs up the phone and heads back to the flower garden to plant more flowers.

Penny is planting flowers when she remembers the talk she had with Janet last night as she was getting her ready for bed. Out of the blue, Janet asks her mom, "Where do the people that die go to?"

Penny is surprised by the question from her daughter and asks, "Why would you bring that up?"

Janet says to her mother with a tear in her eyes that her friend at school just went to a funeral for her grandmother and really misses her loving voice and the times they spent together. Penny gives her daughter a big hug and says that all the people that loves and do their best to live like God's Son, Jesus, will go to heaven forever and ever. Janet looks at her mother and smiles.

"How old do you have to be to get into heaven?"

Penny says, "When your heart beats for the first time, you are old enough to get into heaven. God knows your love for him and will welcome you into heaven."

Janet hugs her mom and whispers, "I love you, Mommy, and I love Jesus too," and closes her eyes.

CHAPTER TWO

Penny is almost finished planting her flowers and smiles at the flower garden that looks so pretty. Meanwhile, James decides to stop at local grocery store to buy an apple pie for dessert for tonight thinking that everyone would enjoy a pie for certain.

Pastor Mathew is driving a few miles over the speed limit through the neighborhood trying to get to the wedding he will be officiating, but knows he is already late. The father of the bride is calling him on Pastor Mathew's mobile phone. Pastor Mathew answers the phone, and after hearing the concerned voice of the father of the bride asking if he is going to arrive soon because everyone is waiting on him so they can start the wedding, Pastor Mathew says in a calm, reassuring voice that he will be at the ceremony in just a few minutes.

"I'm on the street where your home is located.

The father says back to Pastor Mathew, "Thank goodness. You can't miss the house where I live. They have many balloons in the front yard. Please park in the driveway. We have an open space reserved for you so you don't have to park on the street."

Pastor Mathew responds and tells him, "That's terrific, because there are many cars parked on both sides of the street that must be for people attending the wedding."

Jerry and Janet are kicking the ball to one another. Janet tells Jerry that they have a lot of cars parked on the street today. Jerry runs to kick the ball back to Janet and says, "Yeah, there is a wedding today down the street, and people are parking anywhere they can." Jerry kicks the ball hard, and the ball goes over a parked car onto the street.

Janet yells to Jerry, "That was a bad kick, big brother," and runs after the ball that has already landed in the yard across the street.

et runs in between the parked cars without looking for any traffic it may be coming down the road. She darts onto the street right front of the truck Pastor Mathew is driving. Pastor Mathew slams n his brakes, but it's too late. Janet is hit by the truck and thrown against another car that is parked on the street. Janet is bleeding from her head and screaming in pain for her mommy. Pastor Mathew gets out of his truck and runs to the little girl while Jerry runs to her screaming, "Janet, Janet, are you okay!" Pastor Mathew is praying to Jesus, "Please let her be okay, God," crying with tears coming down his face.

Jerry is crying seeing the blood coming out of Janet's head and yelling, "It's all my fault. I shouldn't have kicked the ball into the street." He then asks Pastor Mathew, "Sir, is my sister going to die?"

Pastor Mathew responds with a trembling voice, "No, she will be okay," but deep down Pastor Mathew knows that the little girl is hurt very badly as he uses his handkerchief to press against the bleeding to stop the blood flow.

Pastor Mathew asks Jerry, "Son, are your parents home?"

Jerry cries back, "My mother is in our backyard."

Pastor Mathew tells the little boy to run to his mother to have her call 911 and explain what has happened. Jerry runs to his backyard screaming, "Mommy, mommy!" As he gets to the backyard, Penny gets up from her knees with a concerned look on her face, asking Jerry, "What's wrong, son, calm down, tell me what has happened."

Jerry is crying and tells his mom to call 911. "Please hurry, call 911. Janet has been hit by a truck. She's bleeding from her head and crying." Penny runs inside to call 911, nervously talking to the operator, telling the address of her home and crying, "It's my little girl, she has been hit by a truck in front of our house, please hurry."

The 911 operator calmly asks Penny, "Where is the girl now, and how bad is she hurt?"

Penny is shouting to the operator, "I don't know. My son came running to me in our backyard crying that his sister ran out into the street after a soccer ball, and was hit by a truck, and she is bleeding from the head, and crying in pain. I have to go take care of my daughter, she needs me, please hurry with help, please hurry."

Penny runs crying out of the front door with Jerry, screaming at the top of her voice, "Mommy is coming baby, mommy is coming."

Jerry is crying too, "Janet, we are coming."

Penny is shocked to see the swelling of her precious little girl's head and the blood-soaked handkerchief that Pastor Mathew is holding firmly on Janet's bleeding head. Pastor Mathew is crying telling Penny, "Your little girl just ran out into the street between the parked cars, and I tried to stop, but dear God I couldn't stop in time, it happened so fast."

Penny grabs Janet into her arms and cradles Janet whispering, "It's going to be okay, baby."

Janet tells her mom that her stomach hurts and it's hard to see clearly. Penny is crying along with Pastor Mathew who is kneeling and praying. Jerry cries to his mom, "It's all my fault, I kicked the ball too hard, and the ball went into the street. Mommy, I'm sorry, Mommy, please forgive me."

Penny looks at Jerry with tears in her eyes. "Jerry, I forgive you. I love you, son. Janet's going to be okay. Please pray to God to keep her well."

James is walking out of the store not far from his home when he sees and hears fire and rescue trucks with sirens and lights flashing speeding down the road heading toward the neighborhood where James's house is located. James bows his head and says a short prayer for anyone who might be hurt that the rescue people are going to help, not knowing it's James's own daughter they are going to help. James is going down the street when he has to pull over to let an ambulance pass his car.

James says another prayer for whoever the ambulance is going to. James continues down the street to his home when he is stopped by a police officer who is standing in front of his police car.

The policeman walks up to James car and tells him that he has to keep the street clear of traffic because there has been an accident down the street, James asks the police officer what kind of accident. The police officer with a sad face tells James that a little girl has been hit by a truck and she is hurt badly. James looks worried and tells the police officer, "I have a little girl. My address is 209 Maple Street."

The police officer says to James in a concerned voice, "That is the location of the accident."

James is frantic. He runs as fast as he can toward his home praying aloud to Jesus. "Let my little girl be okay. Please, God, heal her. Please, God, watch over my little girl."

The police calls fire and rescue that is on the scene that the father of the child that is hurt is running toward the accident, and be aware he is very upset. They respond to the police officer they will try to calm him down when he arrives. James runs as fast as he can toward his home, and as he gets closer, he sees the ambulance's flashing lights with his neighbors standing around with very concerned expressions on their faces. James, who his breathing hard after running a few hundred yards, holds Penny who is crying while watching paramedics try to help Janet who is still crying and in a lot of pain. Pastor Mathew is giving a statement to police officers, doing his best to keep it together, but everyone sees that the pastor is mentally and physically shaken.

Jerry is crying telling his dad that it was his fault for kicking the ball in the street. James consoles his son and tells Jerry, "It was an accident, son, we know you didn't mean for any of this to happen. Son, please don't blame yourself for this."

The paramedics do all they can do to stabilize Janet by starting her on an IV and putting on a neck brace and are now ready to transport Janet to the emergency room. Penny asks paramedics if she can ride in the ambulance with her daughter to try to keep her as calm as possible. The paramedic says that would be a good idea, knowing that the little girl's vitals are showing weakness and time is running out for Janet. James kisses his little girl and tells her to be strong as the paramedics load her in the ambulance. James kisses Penny to reassure her that everything will be okay.

"Jerry and I will be following the ambulance on the way to the hospital."

The ambulance sirens are turned on as it leaves the scene of the accident, speeding down the street. When it passes in front of the house where Pastor Mathew will be performing, the father of the bride is standing in the front yard waiting for Pastor Mathew. With a concerned expression on his face, he calls Pastor Mathew on his mobile phone but gets no answer. James and Jerry are running back to his car when the father of bride walks to him to ask what is going on with the ambulance. James slows down just enough to tell him, "My little girl was hit by a truck, and she is hurt badly. We have to go to the hospital."

The father of the bride wishes James good luck with his little girl and hopes she will be okay. The police at the scene have finished their investigation of the accident and told Pastor Mathew he is free to go. Pastor Mathew thanks the police officer and gets in his truck to go to the house down the street where the wedding is being held. The father of the bride walks over to Pastor Mathew as he is getting out of his truck and says, "You finally made it. Better late than never I guess."

CHAPTER THREE

Pastor Mathew is walking with his Bible in his hand and begins to tell the story of the accident with the little girl and how her head was swelling and bleeding and was in a lot of pain. The father of the bride is shocked by the news and asks Pastor Mathew, "Will you be okay performing the wedding ceremony?"

Pastor Mathew looks at him with tears in his eyes and says, "I will do my best to make this a happy occasion, but I will have to leave right after the vows are said to go the hospital to be with the family of the little girl." The father of the bride agrees that would be the best thing to do.

The ambulance driver is doing his best to get to the hospital as fast as possible. He calls the hospital and lets the nurse on duty know they are five minutes from arriving and the little girls vitals are getting worse and to be prepared for critical care. The ambulance arrives at the hospital with a police escort that helps to save time. The nurses and doctor on duty meet the paramedics at the entrance of the emergency room and immediately start taking Janet's vital signs and examines her body for bruises, cuts, and any other abnormalities that are visible.

Penny introduces herself to the doctor in charge as the little girl's mother with tears coming down her cheeks. The doctor looks at Penny with confidence and tells Penny, "I'm Dr. Monroe. We will do our best to take care of your little girl, and make her well. Try to calm down please, and I will let you know how she is doing as soon as possible."

The nurse and doctor take Janet behind closed doors for further exams. Dr. Monroe is very concerned with the swelling of Janet's head and asks Janet, "Where are you hurting, sweetheart?"

Janet has never stopped crying since being hit by the truck and tells the doctor that she can't see clearly.

"My stomach hurts so much. I want my mommy!"

The doctor introduces himself as Dr. Monroe.

"This is Nurse Sarah, and Nurse Jane. They are very smart, and we will do our best to make you feel better, but first, we have to take some x-rays to look inside you to see exactly what may be wrong with you that is causing you to have all this pain. Is that okay with you?"

Janet tries to be strong, but she is really scared. Nurse Jane says, "Janet, I'm going to give you some medicine to stop the pain so I can fix the cut on your head so you will not bleed anymore. I'll be done in just a few minutes, sweetie."

Nurse Sarah holds Janet's little hand and tells her, "I'm here to help you be brave."

Janet tries to smile through the pain and tells the nurses, "My daddy told me to be strong, and everything would be okay."

The nurses know that the little girl is in serious trouble physically but do their best to smile and reassure the little girl that everything will be okay. James and his son, Jerry, arrive at the emergency room to find Penny in the waiting room sitting down with her head in her lap sobbing.

James runs over and kneels in front of her to hold her. Penny looks up with eyes red from crying so much and leans on to James saying in a shaken voice, "James, our little girl is so fragile. She was hit by that big truck. God, please watch over and heal her broken body."

Jerry runs to his mom and hugs his parents as tight as he can, crying, "Daddy, will Janet be okay?"

James doesn't look up but says to Penny and Jerry, "All we can do now is pray that the doctors here can fix whatever is wrong with Janet. God help them, please, God help them!"

Dr. Monroe orders an MRI for Janet to know exact seriousness of internal damage in her head and abdominal areas of her body. Dr. Monroe is joined by another doctor at the MRI examining room. Dr. Jones is a very good surgeon, and as the doctors look at the results of the MRI, the concern on their faces tells the story of despair. The prognosis is not good at all for Janet. Dr. Monroe notices that the swelling of the brain is causing pressure on Janet's optical nerves, causing blindness, and tells Dr. Jones, "We have to operate ASAP so there are no ruptures of the vessels that give her sight."

Dr. Jones agrees, but then he points at the abdominal area on the graph, which shows major damage to the spleen, kidneys, liver, and small intestines.

Dr. Monroe says in a worried voice to Dr. Jones, "The truck's bumper had hit her very hard to do all this damage, and I have concerns if she will survive the surgery of the abdominal cavity, it's so torn up inside there."

Dr. Jones tells Dr. Monroe, "I have to concur with those findings, but we have to do something now, or she won't survive the night."

In the waiting room, Penny has calmed down enough to walk around, while James is nervously pacing the floor. Nurse Jane walks in the waiting room to ask if there is anything she can get for them. Penny walks over to Nurse Jane and asks, "What is taking so long, why has the doctor not come to tells us what is happening with our little girl?"

James goes near Penny to hold her in his arms. Jerry watches Nurse Jane tell them that the doctors are looking at all the test results. "He will be here any minute to give the plan to make your little girl well again. Please be patient."

Penny complains to James that something is very wrong. "Our little girl is in trouble. What are we going to do if Janet dies?"

James holds his wife tightly and reassures her, "Our little princess will be okay. She is strong and brave. Please don't say she is going to die."

At that moment, Dr. Monroe and Dr. Jones arrives at the door of the waiting room and approaches Penny and James. Dr. Monroe introduces himself and Dr. Jones to Janet's parents then explains the injuries to them and what they plan to do to fix them. Dr. Jones explains the swelling of Janet's head and how that swelling is causing pressure on optic nerves, causing her to have trouble with her vision.

"We will have to perform surgery on that part of the brain to release the pressure so the blood vessels cause no further damage. Now that is a serious surgery, but not as serious as the problems we have with her abdominal areas." Dr. Monroe asks James and Penny to please sit down.

CHAPTER FOUR

Dr. Monroe sits down next to James, looking at their faces, seeing hopefulness mixed with anxiety.

"Dr. Jones and I are very concerned about the injuries to Janet's vital organs. The MRI showed damaged to the kidneys, liver, spleen, and small intestines, but we have to look inside to know exactly what is right and what is damaged."

Penny starts to tremble as James holds her hand.

James asks, "When will the surgery begin?"

Dr. Jones, who has been on his phone during part of the conversation texting, speaks up, "We are getting everything ready now and should be ready within the hour. Nurse Sarah will be bringing by a consent form for the surgeries that will outlined in detailed description what we plan on doing with the surgery and what could go wrong. All surgeries are a risk, but we promise to take the best care for Janet."

James asks Dr. Monroe, "Can we see our little girl before her surgery gets under way?"

Dr. Monroe smiles to reassure Penny, James, and Jerry. "Of course, the nurse will be here in a few minutes, then all of you will give Janet hugs and kisses."

Both doctors walk out of the waiting room. Jerry walks over to his mom and dad, and they do a group hug for a few minutes till Nurse Sarah interrupts them with the consent forms.

"These are the consent forms for the surgeries. Please read them carefully before signing. It describes in detail what the surgeries will try to fix and what could go wrong, if there are any complications during or after surgery."

James thanks Nurse Sarah. Penny, James, and Jerry sit down to read the consent forms as Nurse Sarah smiles and tells the family, "I'll be back in a few minutes, and I will take you to see Janet in her room till they are ready to take Janet to surgery."

James is reading the consent form and feels distraught after reading the terrible outcome if surgery takes a turn for the worst. Penny starts to cry as she reads and tells James, "It has to be okay. We can't lose our little girl."

Jerry hugs his mom, trying to comfort her the best he can. "Mom, the doctors are smart. They will fix Janet, you'll see. Please don't cry."

James signs the consent forms then hands the forms to Penny to sign, but her hands are shaking so bad her signature looks like chicken scratch. Nurse Sarah returns to the waiting room and asks if there are any questions about the consent form.

James hands the clipboard with the consent form on it to the nurse and says, "No questions, except when can we see our little girl?"

Nurse Sarah smiles. "Good news. Janet is waiting now and has been asking for you all."

They follow Nurse Sarah to Janet's room where Nurse Jane is trying to make Janet comfortable. Jerry is the first to see Janet and is shocked to see his little sister's head swollen around her eyes with a large bandage wrapped around her head where she was bleeding. Penny walks over to Janet's bedside and gives her a kiss and hug.

Janet asks, "Is that you, Mommy? I can't see clearly since the accident. My stomach hurts me so much, Mommy."

Penny is fighting back the tears trying to be strong so Janet will know everything will be okay. "The doctors have told us that they are going to make you feel better real soon, so don't you worry."

James stands close to Janet and gives a soft kiss on Janet's cheek. Speaking softly, he says with a tear rolling down his cheek, "Sweetheart, please don't you worry. You'll be all better in a little while. We love you, and the doctors and nurses promised to take very good care of you."

Janet tries to smile and says, "Thanks, Daddy. The people here are so nice to me. Where is Jerry?"

Jerry walks around the bed and with a shaky voice says, "Here I am, Janet. I am so sorry this happened to you. It was all my fault. I should have never kicked the ball so hard, and you wouldn't have run out into the street to get that ball. Please forgive me."

Janet turns to Jerry and starts to cry. "It's not your fault, Jerry. I should have looked for cars like Mommy taught us before crossing the street."

Mommy leans over to wipe away Janet's tears with a tissue and says lovingly, "It was an accident, and everything is going to be okay. Janet is going to have to be brave, and we have to be strong to support our little princess so she can get better soon."

James speaks up and says, "Your mom is right. It's no one's fault. We need to pray and believe that God will give the nurses and doctors the wisdom to fix everything that's wrong with Janet, and our little girl heals quickly."

James asks everyone to hold hands and starts to pray. "Heavenly Father, we love and praise you. We believe in you to hear our prayers. We ask you to put your mighty hand on Janet and heal her in your son Jesus's holy name. Thank you, Lord, for hearing our prayer, and, Lord, keep us all strong so we can support each other through this difficult time. Amen."

Penny continues to hold Janet's little hand while James and Jerry look at each other with sad expressions, each wondering what will happen in the next few hours. There is a soft knock on the door of Janet's hospital room, and Nurse Jane and Nurse Sarah walk through the doorway.

"It's time to go and make this little girl all better," says Nurse Jane as she starts disconnecting wires that monitor Janet's vital signs.

Nurse Sarah walks over to the other side of the bed as Penny and James watch the nurse get the bed Janet is lying in ready to move. Jerry is watching all the lights go dim as they pull the plugs on the different monitors.

Nurse Jane smiles at the parents and speaks kindly, "Please don't worry. We will take good care of Janet."

Jerry speaks up in a concerned voice, "Please make my sister all better. She is the only sister I have, and I love her so much."

Nurse Jane is unlocking the bed so it will move easily and smiles at Jerry and says, "She is in good, caring hands. Don't you worry."

Jerry smiles back. "I know she is in God's hands, and he is an awesome God."

Penny smiles at her son and tells Jerry, "We have to believe, we have to believe in God."

The nurses start to move the bed out of the room into the hallway.

Nurse Jane says to Penny, "You can hold Janet's hand till we get to the operating room."

Janet squeezes her mom's hand, crying, "Mommy, I'm so scared. What's going to happen to me? Is it going to hurt? Please, Mommy, tell me. I don't want to die."

Penny tries to hold back her tears, and she gets as close as she can to Janet's face. "Now you listen to your mommy, Janet. You will be okay. You will be just fine. Don't talk like that. You are not going to die. I want you to pray to God right now and until we see you after the doctors finish operating on you."

Janet stops crying and ask her mommy, "Are you sure I'm going to be okay?"

Penny says in a sturdy voice, "I know you will."

Janet tells her mom, "I love hearing your voice, Mom, lets me know I'm going to be okay. I love you, Mom, Dad, Jerry, and Jesus too."

The nurses get to the doors where you go through to get to the operating room.

Nurse Jane says, "We will let you know how the surgery is going in a few hours."

Penny, Jerry, and James give kisses to Janet as they move Janet's bed through the double doors, and all of them say "We love you" before the doors close, and start walking back toward the waiting room. Penny is crying as James tries to console her by hugging her.

Jerry speaks up and says, "Mom, Janet is a fighter, and she is strong. She will be okay, you just wait."

James kisses Penny on the cheek and says, "Honey, Jerry is right. Janet is strong. She'll be okay. We have to believe."

CHAPTER FIVE

It has been over an hour since the accident, and Pastor Mathew is just finishing the wedding ceremony. The bride and groom are signing the marriage certificate, then the two witnesses. Pastor Mathew is the last person to sign and date the document then hands it to the groom.

The groom shakes Mathew's hand and says, "Great job, Pastor, will you please stay and have some food and drink with us to celebrate?"

Pastor Mathew smiles at the groom, but underneath that smile he is full of concern for the little girl that is at the hospital.

"I have some place I really need to be, but enjoy the rest of the day, and God bless you and your bride."

The father of the bride walks up to Pastor Mathew and gives him a white envelope containing a couple hundred dollar bills and thanks him for the beautiful ceremony.

Pastor Mathew says, "You're welcome. It is very nice being here, but I must go to the hospital, because I am very concerned about the little girl that was hit by my truck."

The father of the bride's name is Aaron. He asks Pastor Mathew to please be careful driving to the hospital. "We all hope the little girl will be okay, and thank you for not saying anything about the accident. It would have put a damper on this joyous occasion."

Pastor Mathew smiled back at Aaron and says, "That's the last thing I would do. This is a special day, happy tears and memories. Now I must go. God bless all."

Pastor Mathew waves and says his goodbyes to the wedding guests as he walks to his truck parked out in the driveway. He looks at the bumper of his truck for the first time to see any marks where the little girl was hit by the truck. To his surprise there are no visible marks at all. He scratches his head and thinks to himself, Wow, I must have hit her body. Her head would have left some kind of mark.

Pastor Mathew gets inside his truck, driving down the street, and sees the little girl's blood on the street, bleeding from her head, and tears begin flowing from his eyes. He prays, "My God, please take care of that little girl and her family. I know they are all worried."

A few minutes later Pastor Mathew is parking his truck in the hospital parking lot, and he gets out of his truck still wearing the white collar. When a couple in their forties are walking away from the hospital entrance, the couple smile at Pastor Mathew.

The man speaks with a kind voice, "Good afternoon, Pastor. It is never a good sign when you visit the hospital. Someone must be on their deathbed."

Pastor Mathew looks at the couple with a tender smile and replies, "Yes, sometimes I visit to give last rites, but today I go to support a family who is in need of a miracle. Would you all pray for the needy today?"

The woman speaks in a caring manner, "Yes, Pastor, we will pray."

They walk away toward their car that is parked nearby. Pastor Mathew walks into the hospital looking for someone that may know where the little girl may be.

The secretary at the front desk looks at Pastor Mathew and asks, "Can I help you, Pastor?"

Pastor Mathew is looking down the hall when he asks the question, "Was there a little girl brought in a little over an hour ago? She may be six years old and had been hit by a truck, suffering from a cut to the head."

The secretary looks and smiles back at Pastor Mathew. "Let me look, and see." The secretary picks up her phone and talks to a nurse from the emergency room and gets the answer Pastor Mathew is looking for. Pastor Mathew looks the secretary in her eyes as she put the phone down.

She says, "Yes, the waiting room is on the second floor, Pastor, just to let you know the little girl has just gone into surgery. The little girl's family is in the waiting room, if that is who you are looking for."

Pastor Mathew thanks the secretary for the information and walks toward the elevator to go up to the waiting room on the second floor. The elevator doors open with no one inside, and Pastor Mathew steps inside the elevator, and after the doors close, Pastor goes to his knees asking God please let the little girl be okay. Pastor Mathew gets to his feet then pushes the number two on the panel in the elevator. The doors open to the second floor. Pastor Mathew walks over to the nursing station. The nurse at the station looks at Pastor Mathew and sees the white collar, surprised to see him.

"Did someone die, and no one told me?"

Pastor Mathew looks at the nurse. "I hope not. I am here to inquire about the little girl that is having surgery now."

The nurse responds with a relieved look on her face. "Oh okay, the surgery has just begun, but her parents are in the waiting room down the hall on the right if you like to go wait with them."

Pastor Mathew smiles at the nurse and says, "Thank you. I will do that."

James gets up from his chair where he was sitting next to Penny and Jerry and tells Penny, "I have to start calling our family about the accident. I know they will want to be here."

Penny says to James, still with a shaky voice, "I completely forgot about that, honey, thank you for doing that. I am too nervous to talk on the phone, and probably will cry so much no one could understand me."

James smiles back at Penny, who now is holding Jerry's hand as Jerry tries to comfort his mom. James walks out to the hallway in front of the waiting room and sees a man with a white collar on, but as the man gets closer, James somewhat remembers this man was talking to the police officer at the accident.

Pastor Mathew introduces himself to James, and James reaches out to shake his hand and ask, "Did someone call you for us, why are you here?"

Pastor Mathew is confused, thinking James would know that it was him that was driving the truck that hit James's little girl, so Pastor Mathew takes a step back and with tear-filled eyes begins telling James, "It was me driving the truck, and I got over here as soon as I could to help in any way I can. I was on my way to a wedding on your street when the accident happened. I am so sorry."

James looks surprised. Then he starts to remember Pastor Mathew more clearly at the accident scene. James remembers that the white collar was not around Pastor Mathew's neck at the accident, and that is why he didn't understand why he was at the hospital.

Penny hears the talking outside the waiting room, and Jerry and Penny get off their seats and walk to the doorway of the waiting room. Penny is wiping tears from her eyes as she looks at Pastor Mathew. Penny tries to smile, but with the anxiety she is feeling, it's almost impossible to make that happen. Before she can speak, Pastor Mathew asks her as kindly and with as much compassion as he can how their little girl is doing. Penny looks at Pastor Mathew with confusion overrunning with nervous tension.

"I really can't say. All we know is that the doctors are going to do their best to make her okay. The nurses are so nice here and said it will be hours before they can tell us anything about her condition."

Pastor Mathew asks if they could all hold hands and pray that the surgery fixes Janet as good as new. Pastor Mathew starts the prayers, looking down at the floor, "Heavenly Father, we pray to you now that your mighty healing hands take hold of your child Janet, and restore her body and mind as only you can do. Lord, we believe that all things are possible through you our God, and, Lord, watch over this family today and the days to follow to keep them strong in their faith for you, oh Lord, and heal their heartache, and, Lord, give this family the strength to lean on each other with the love you give, and their families, and friends. Amen."

Jerry says amen loudly then turns to his dad smiling. "Pastor Mathew says prayers a little better than you do, but, Dad, I like it more when you say the prayer."

James looks at his son and gives him a big hug and smiles. "I love you, son." And he gives Jerry a kiss on the cheek.

James excuses himself and says, "I have to make some calls to let our loved ones and friends know about the accident and where we are," and walks down the hallway just outside the waiting room.

Penny, Jerry, and Pastor Mathew find a seat in the waiting room and begin the hard task of watching the clock as Janet starts her surgery. James is on his cell phone, calling family member after family member, doing his best not to start crying on the phone as he explains about the accident and the hospital where the surgery is being done. James asks some family members if they can call other family members to let them know that they need all the praying that our loved ones and friends can do, and will let them know how Janet is doing as soon as they know anything. The response from every person he calls is the same: they are so sorry to hear the sad news. "And yes, we will pray for Janet, and all of you, and we will try to be at the hospital as soon as we can to offer support in any way we can."

CHAPTER SIX

The anesthesiologist, whose name is Robert, is waiting in the operating room when the nurses bring in the hospital bed where Janet is lying. Nurse Jane is a trained anesthetist and will be assisting Robert with the anesthesia.

Janet asks, "Where are the doctors that will operate on me?"

Nurse Sarah smiles at Janet and says, "They are washing their hands very well now and will be in here in a few minutes."

Robert looks at Janet and says, "In a few seconds, I want you to count to twenty for us, and you will go to sleep for a little while, so the doctors can operate to try to make you better. Can you do that?"

Janet says, "Yes, but can I say a prayer first."

Robert looks at Nurse Jane and smiles. "Yes, Janet that would be okay."

Janet closes her eyes and says, "Jesus, I love you, please watch over my mom, dad, Jerry, and all the people I love. Jesus, watch over me too."

Janet's eyes begin to get heavy as she starts counting to twenty, but before she gets to the number nine, she is under the influence of the anesthesia. Robert keeps a close eye on all the monitors that are hooked up to Janet's little body to ensure that all her vital measurements are safe and strong to continue the surgery. Dr. Monroe and Dr. Jones enter the operating room together.

Dr. Jones, the neurosurgeon, asks Robert, "How is our little patient doing?"

Robert says back with confidence that all vitals are strong and holding steady.

Dr. Monroe says to Dr. Jones, "Start time on the first surgery is 5:30 p.m."

Dr. Jones makes his incision on the frontal lope to inspect the insides of Janet's brain. Hopefully with precise cutting, he will help relieve pressure on Janet's optic nerve that is causing Janet to have blurred vision. Dr. Jones notices after careful inspection that he can reduce the swelling to save the vision on Janet's eyes. Dr. Monroe is looking at the job Dr. Jones is doing and compliments him at the great job he is doing.

Nurse Sarah is the assisting nurse and also says, "Awesome skills with the scalpel, Dr. Jones."

Dr. Jones smiles at both of them and responds with a smile on his face, "I'm doing my best. This little girl is so pretty we have to make her perfect."

Robert speaks up, "All vitals are good. We are looking good on time."

Dr. Monroe says, "Time is 6:15 p.m., and all is well."

Dr. Jones is inspecting for any other problems that may cause any damage to Janet, and after looking very thoroughly, he sees that it is time to close up the opening in the skull and begins to sew with expertise needle and thread. Nurse Sarah compliments Dr. Jones on the perfection in the closing of the wound.

Dr. Jones responds, "This little girl is so pretty. I want her to have no physical scarring whatsoever."

The doctors look at each other after checking again with Robert on vitals.

Robert tells the doctors, "It is clear for us to begin with the next surgery."

Dr. Monroe asks Nurse Jane for the scalpel, and Nurse Jane hands Dr. Monroe the scalpel.

Dr. Jones looks at a clock on the wall in the operating room and says, "The time is 6:30 p.m. Starting on the abdomen surgery."

Dr. Monroe takes the scalpel and begins to make the incision to open up the area where most of the damaged organs showed up on MRI. The doctors closely inspect the inside of Janet's abdomen with Dr. Monroe speaking first after noticing that the spleen is very badly damaged.

"Well, this spleen has to be removed. We will just have to watch her white cell count for any infections that can occur."

Dr. Monroe starts to cut away the spleen. He then applies a sutured technique to stop any bleeding around the spleen that has been removed. Dr. Monroe asks Nurse Jane for more suction around the area he is applying stitches to make sure that suture is done properly.

Robert looks at his monitors and sees Janet's blood pressure results and relays them to the doctors, saying, "Her blood pressure is dropping slowly and is now at 90 over 60."

Dr. Monroe does his last couple of stitches on the spleen removal area and checks for any bleeding that may be visible, and after careful inspection, Dr. Monroe says to everyone that sutures are looking good.

Dr. Jones takes a look inside and says to Dr. Monroe, "I have to concur, Doctor, you have done an excellent job."

Dr. Monroe asks Robert on vitals, and Robert replies that blood pressure is in good condition now with heartbeat strong and body temperature at 99.5.

Dr. Monroe asks Nurse Jane for more suction, and both begin to inspect the liver and both kidneys. Dr. Monroe sees very minor damage to both kidneys, but the liver has been damaged. Dr. Jones also inspects the kidneys and says that they look healthy but says to Dr. Monroe in a disappointing voice that the liver has significant damage, and most of it has to be removed. Dr. Monroe takes his scalpel and begins a partial hepatectomy to cut away the damaged parts of the liver.

Dr. Monroe looks at Dr. Jones and says, "I believe I have all the damaged parts cut away and believes her liver will still be able to do its job without any issues."

Dr. Jones concurs with Dr. Monroe after looking carefully at the liver, seeing that the color is healthy. Nurse Jane is looking at Robert, who is keeping his eyes on vital signs, and says, "Doctors, vitals are still holding strong."

Dr. Jones looks at the clock and says, "Time is 7:00 p.m."

Dr. Monroe says, "Okay, let's get a look at her small intestines and hope for the best."

Dr. Monroe sees that the duodenum is damaged, but the jejunum and the ileum seem to be in good condition. Dr. Jones has checked the entire length of the small intestine and concludes six feet will have to be removed. Dr. Monroe start the process of cutting out the sections of small intestines while Nurse Jane and Nurse Sarah make sure no leaks contaminate inside the body cavity that will cause major problems such as infections, toxic repercussions, and an overload of bad bacteria in Janet's body. Dr. Monroe has successfully removed the damaged areas of small intestine and has reconnected and spliced the ends where the cuts were needed to fix damaged tissue.

The alarms for the monitor start signaling Robert that blood pressure is dropping fast. Dr. Jones looks for the reason. It seems the liver area is bleeding, and the cause may be the stitches have broken loose. Dr. Monroe pushes aside the small intestines that he has just finished repairing and does his best to stop the bleeding. Dr. Jones is ordering Nurse Jane to add two units of blood so the blood pressure will hopefully go back to a safe level.

Dr. Monroe is having a difficult time trying to suture the liver that was accidentally torn while Nurse Sarah was cleaning around small intestines. Minutes pass by as Dr. Monroe gets a handle on the bleeding, and after a few more minutes all is well, the bleeding has stopped, and blood pressure is back to normal. Nurse Sarah tells everyone she is sorry for causing issues.

Dr. Monroe looks at Nurse Sarah and says, "Listen, we came close to losing this little girl, but we didn't. It looks like she will be okay."

Dr. Jones says, "Let's make sure everything is clean inside and all sutures are holding good and tight with no clotting, or any leaks."

Nurse Jane has cleaned everything up very well, and Dr. Monroe asks Robert how the vitals are.

Robert says, "That vitals are all strong."

Dr. Monroe looks at everyone and says with relief in his voice, "Let's start closing up the wound, and then we go see the family and give the good news."

The doctors are stitching up the opening, and Dr. Monroe asks Nurse Jane to let Janet's family know that the surgery is finished.

"Dr. Jones and I will be out in twenty minutes to talk to them."

Nurse Jane says, "Yes, sir, Dr. Monroe." As she is walking out of the operating room, she says to everyone, "Awesome job, and thank God it's over."

Robert starts talking to Dr. Monroe. "You know, Doctor, that was a miracle the way that little girl came back after losing all that blood, and with her blood pressure going down to flat line levels, how is that possible?"

Dr. Monroe is just finishing the closing of all suturing and looks directly at Robert and says, "God works in mysterious ways, that's for sure."

Nurse Jane is walking into the waiting room, and to her surprise it is full of people that know Janet's family. Also there are Janet's grandparents, who look worried but are anxious to hear how the surgery has gone. Nurse Jane speaks up loud and clearly so that everyone in the waiting room can hear her news.

"The surgery has finished, and Janet is resting peacefully. The doctors that performed the surgery will be here to talk to Janet's parents in about fifteen minutes. Till then thank you for being so patient. The doctors will answer all of your questions and when you can see Janet. The nurses are watching Janet closely now in the recovery room."

Nurse Jane looks directly at Penny and James and says with a smile, "It will be about thirty minutes before I can ask the doctors when you can go into the room where Janet is resting."

CHAPTER SEVEN

Everyone is smiling in the waiting room after hearing the good news from Nurse Jane. Penny is kissing Jerry and hugging him tightly, telling Jerry, "I told you not to be worried. It's all going to be all right. Thank God for his healing powers."

James is waiting to give Penny a kiss and a huge hug. Penny turns around to James and looks into his blue eyes, smiles at him, then kisses him, and they hug each other as their parents look on and smile for the family unity they show. The waiting room is full of joy, and some in the room start calling other family and friends, letting others know the good news of Janet's surgery results and how good she is doing.

Dr. Monroe and Dr. Jones are walking and talking down the hall on their way to the waiting room when Dr. Monroe asks Dr. Jones, "Do you want me to give the prognosis?"

Dr. Jones says, "Yes, you can, and if you need some help with any questions, I'll try to help you with the answers to explain to the parents so they will understand clearly what we have done during surgery and what we can expect in the future."

Pastor Mathew is all smiles as he heard the news from Nurse Jane and notices the doctors walking toward the waiting room while he stands next to the entrance of the waiting room. Pastor Mathew walks toward the doctors with his right hand extended to shake hands with both doctors. Pastor Mathew shakes hands with Dr. Monroe first and then Dr. Jones then says with a smile on his face, "God bless you all for the tremendous job that was successfully done for that precious girl. We all have been praying so much for you all and her."

Dr. Jones smiles back at Pastor Mathew and says, "Don't stop believing, Pastor. We all want that little girl to have a long, healthy life."

Pastor Mathew responds in a joyful voice, "Amen to that, Doctor."

Dr. Monroe says to the Pastor Mathew, "Please excuse us. We need to talk to Janet's parents."

Pastor Mathew says, "Of course, Doctor, they are waiting to hear from you all. They are in the waiting room with their friends and family."

Dr. Jones is the first one to walk into the waiting room, followed closely by Dr. Monroe. James looks at the doctors and starts to walk over to shake hands with both doctors, and as he does, Penny walks over too. Penny gives a heartfelt hug to both doctors, thanking them for doing the best they could do for Janet.

Dr. Monroe smiles back at Penny and says, "Thank you. We would like to talk to you and your husband about the surgery and what we have done to make Janet healthy."

Dr. Jones asks family and friends in the waiting room if they could have a few minutes alone with the parents to explain the surgery and Janet's recovery of. The group of people in the waiting room all look at Dr. Jones as he speaks, and the people are smiling at the doctors, and thanking them for doing a great job on the surgery as they all walk past exiting the waiting room."

Dr. Monroe walks in the waiting room toward a row of chairs, and ask James, and Penny to please have a seat. Penny sits down first, then James next to her holding Penny's hand."

Jerry who is standing at the door looks at his dad and says, "Can I stay, Dad?"

James looks at Jerry and says, "Son, please stay with your grandparents for now, and we will let you know everything about your sister in a little while. Jerry smiles at his dad and says, "Okay, then turns to walk outside the doorway of the waiting room, and disappears in the hallway. Dr. Monroe starts to explain the surgery that was performed on Janet beginning with her head. Dr. Monroe speaks directly at James, and Penny looking at their faces as he talks trying to reassure them that Janet is doing well, but not out of the woods yet, Janet has to go through some days of healing, and we will keep a close watch on her during this time."

Dr. Monroe looks at Dr. Jones and says, "Dr. Jones is a very good neurosurgeon who did the surgery on Janet, I'll let him explain how that went. Dr. Jones looks at Penny and James to explain the procedure that he performed, and starts telling them that without getting to fancy with all the medical terms of the surgery I open up her little head with the smallest incision I could make, and found the problem that was causing the swelling of her head, and causing her vision to be impaired. Dr. Jones then explains that there was significant bruising of her frontal lope, or right above her eyes that had too much pressure on her optic nerve and to reduce, or relieve that pressure I had to cut into some tissue, and Dr. Jones looks at Penny as she starts to cry softly holding James hand even more tightly."

James does his best to comfort his wife with words that speaks from his heart, and compassion and says, "Honey it will be okay, our baby girl is going to be just fine, please don't cry."

Dr. Jones looks at Penny says, "I'm not trying to upset you I just want you all to know that we have taken care of the damage, and we assume that Janet's vision will be fully restored, and she should not have any headaches."

Dr. Jones looks at James and says, "We should know soon how Janet's vision is by asking her a few simple questions about any blurred vision, colors, and focus on near, and far objects. I believe that your little girl will recover just find from her head injury, now do you have any questions for me concerning what I just explained to you all. Penny Looks at James, and then ask Dr. Jones will Janet have any visible scars that can be seen. Dr. Jones responds with a smile, no, not unless she loses all her hair, the place where I had to cut will be covered by your daughter's beautiful black hair just as soon as it grows back, which shouldn't take that long, we just have to make sure that the wound heals perfectly so there will be no complications, and by that I mean no infections, any other questions. James ask Dr. Jones how long will that be for the wound to heal completely."

Dr. Jones smiles back at James and says, "Completely healed that will take at least three weeks, by then Janet should be able to start growing her hair fully, and look just fine."

Dr. Jones looks at James, and Penny and says, "Now Dr. Monroe will tell you about the surgery he performed on Janet. Dr. Monroe speaks to James and Penny softly, but loud enough to be heard, I will try to explain what I found after looking at the MRI, and what I saw was damage to the small intestines. Penny begins to cry softly as James tries to calm her down by rubbing her arm, and saying to her it's okay, honey, let's just listen to the doctor. Dr. Monroe continues to speak, now this may sound difficult to understand, but this is what had to be done, I had to make an incision to gain access to the organs that are under Janet's belly, much like if I was doing a C section on a pregnant woman. I immediately found after careful inspection that the spleen was severely damaged, and had to be removed, there was no saving that organ, but the good news is a human body can function well without a spleen much like the appendix. Dr. Monroe smiles for a brief moment looked very serious, I also found that the liver which is very important to the human body also had damaged to it, but when I looked all around the liver, Dr. Jones, and I both noticed only a small section of the liver was not going to survive, so I decided to remove the damage area, and after removing the damaged part of the liver we started looking for any other damage, and what we found was the large intestine, stomach, and both lungs were in great condition. I start looking at the ribs, and though they are bruised, none are broken, but when inspecting the small intestines, we both see significant damage. The small intestine is approximately twenty feet long, and I had to remove six feet, but Janet should have no issues with her digestive tract, and recover to live a normal life."

Dr. Monroe looks at Penny and James, and now I will try to answer any questions you might have. Penny ask when can we see our daughter, and when will she be able to go home?"

Dr. Monroe says to Penny, "We will have to keep Janet in ICU for at least twenty-four hours, and then when we know that her recovery from these two surgeries are at good levels we will move Janet to her own private room, then when we see if her vitals are holding strong, and getting stronger, then after a few more days we may discuss discharging her from the hospital, but Janet will be under strict orders to stay in bed for a few more days until all her wounds heal, and that may take up to a few weeks. James ask Dr. Jones do you know if Janet's eyes will be okay."

Dr. Jones looks at James and says, "I believe we relieved the pressure in time to ensure that her vision will be normal, but we won't know till we examine her after she wakes up which should be in a few minutes. Nurse Jane walks past the small crowd of family and friends of Penny and James to go into the waiting room, and when she enters Nurse Jane smiles at Penny, and ask her how are you? Penny stands up and gives a smile back, I'm nervous, and mentally drained, but I need to hold my little girl, and tell her she will be okay, and not be frightened."

Nurse Jane holds Penny's hand and tells her, "We have Janet in ICU, and you and your husband may see her for a little while. James stands up, and Dr. Jones and Dr. Monroe also stand up to walk out of the waiting room."

Dr. Monroe says to James, "We will be in to check on Janet in a little while, you all have a nice visit."

The family and friends of James and Penny are curious about Janet's health, and some ask James questions.

James says, "The doctors told us about the surgery, and right now I want to go see my baby girl. We can talk later on, and I'll let you all know what was done."

Nurse Jane leads the way to ICU. Penny, Jerry, and James are following close to Nurse Jane, and she turns to Penny and speaks softly, "Please do not be surprised to see all the tubes and wires that are hooked up to your little girl."

Nurse Jane says, "We have to keep a close watch on her so if anything would happen we will be quick to respond to help improve her condition, but Janet is doing fine and should be waking up in five minutes or so."

Penny is the first to walk into the ICU room where Janet is lying with Jerry next to her side and with James just behind them. Penny sees her daughter and begins to cry. Jerry starts to cry softly, trying to be strong, but Jerry can't hold his tears back, especially when he hears his mom sobbing. James tries to hold Penny up knowing she is weak and doesn't want Penny to faint.

CHAPTER EIGHT

Nurse Jane asks Penny, "Please take a seat next to Janet's bed till you regain your composure." James helps Penny to the chair next to the bed and makes sure Penny is okay.

Jerry is looking at his sister Janet and sees that Janet is moving ever so slowly and tells his mom in an excited voice, "Look, Mom, Janet is moving, she may be waking up."

Nurse Jane walks closer to Janet and looks at her face and says, "Yes, she is waking up."

Nurse Jane asks, "Please try not to get Janet upset in any way, because that will interrupt her recovery."

Penny stands up slowly and leans over Janet, doing her best not to cry, and whispers to Janet, "Hey, sweetheart, it's Mommy. Mommy is right here, and you are going to be okay."

Janet slowly moves her head side to side and says, "I hear you, Mom."

James stands next to Janet just across from Penny and gently gives Janet a kiss on her cheek and says, "Hey, baby girl, Dad's right here. Are you doing okay?"

Nurse Jane has been looking at Janet's monitors, and all the vital signs for Janet are at good levels.

She says, "I'll be back in a few minutes, and call me if you need anything."

James smiles at Nurse Jane and says, "We will, and thank you so much," then turns back to Janet who is now looking around the room.

Penny asks Janet, "How is your vision, can you see clearly now?"

Janet looks directly at her mom and says, "Yes, I can see very well now, Mom."

Jerry gets closer to his sister and says, "Are you hurting anywhere?"

Janet gives her brother a smile and says, "No, I am not hurting anywhere. The doctors must have fixed me."

James and Penny let out a laugh and smile at each other.

James tells Janet that the doctor has given her some medicine that is strong. "So you will not hurt too much, but if you do feel any pain, let us know, and the nurse will give you some more medicine to take away the pain, okay?"

Janet smiles at her dad and says, "Okay," and then she says, "I wish they would have given me this medicine at the accident, because I was hurting really bad at that time, but I'm feeling okay now."

Penny asks Janet if she is thirsty, and Janet answers, "No, not right now, I'm okay."

James ask Janet, "Do you remember what happened?"

Janet looks at her dad and begins telling the events that led up to the accident. Jerry gets closer to Janet so he can hear her story.

Janet says, "Jerry and I were playing kickball in the front yard, because Mom had planted some flowers in backyard, and we didn't want to hurt Mom's flowers. Jerry kicked the ball hard, causing the ball to go out of the yard and into the street."

Janet begins to cry slowly and says, "It's my fault, Dad. You always taught Jerry and I to always look both ways before crossing the street, but I didn't, Dad. I just ran in between the parked cars and out into the street." Janet is now crying more now as her mom tries to console her.

Janet says, "That's when the truck hit me in my side and knocked me flying into another car, and I hit my head, then I couldn't see well, and I starting crying for my mom."

Penny wipes the tears from Janet's face and says, "You are okay now, baby, please don't get upset."

The nurse says, "You have to stay calm, and get your rest, okay?"

Janet looks at her mom and says, "Okay, Mom, I'm sorry this happened, and I'll try to stay calm."

James says softly to Janet, "Listen, baby girl, you get some rest now. The doctors that operated on you will be visiting you soon to ask you some questions about how you are feeling. You do your best to answer their questions truthfully, because it's very important that you let them know so they can help you get better quickly, okay?"

Janet smiles at her dad and says, "I'll do my best to help them, Dad."

Nurse Jane walks into the ICU room and asks, "How is everyone doing, and especially this brave little angel?"

Janet speaks up first before anyone else does and says, "I'm not an angel. Angels are in heaven."

Nurse Jane walks closer to Janet and says, "You are right, angels are in heaven, so how are you doing, can I get you anything, would you like some water or juice to drink?"

Janet smiles at Nurse Jane and says, "Yes, I would like some water please."

Nurse Jane holds a glass of water with a straw.

Janet drinks the water and says thank you to Nurse Jane. Dr. Monroe and Dr. Jones walk into the ICU room together as Nurse Jane is putting the glass down and walks to the side of the room close to Janet so the doctors can ask Janet some questions. Dr. Monroe looks at Janet and looks at her monitors, noticing that all is well, then asks Janet if she is feeling any discomfort in her belly area.

Janet answers, "Not very much pain there now, but I'll let you know if it does so you can give me more strong medicine."

Dr. Monroe smiles at Janet and says, "Well, you are very smart at your age to ask for that. By the way, how old are you?"

Janet smiles and says happily, "I'm six, but in two more days I'll be seven years old."

Dr. Monroe says as he looks at Penny, James, and Jerry, "Well, we are going to try to get you better so you can have your birthday at home."

Dr. Jones moves closer to Janet and asks, "How good can you see, and do you have any pain anywhere in your head?"

Janet looks at Dr. Jones and says, "I have no pain, and I can see very well."

The doctors look at each other with relief on their faces.

Dr. Monroe says, "That's terrific. Now we want you to get some rest. It's very important that you get stronger so your body can continue to heal."

Dr. Jones says to Nurse Jane, "We're going to give Janet some medicine to help her get some much-needed sleep, and when you wake up, we will let your parents talk to you some more."

The doctors say goodbye to Janet's family and walk out of the room.

Penny gives Janet a big hug and a kiss and says, "We will see you soon. I love you. We will be right down the hall."

James and Jerry hug and kiss Janet and say, "We love you too. Get some rest, and we'll see you soon," and walk out of the room.

Nurse Jane smiles at Janet and says, "Your family really loves you, so now I'm going to give you some medicine that will make you sleep for a few hours, and then you can see your mom, dad, and brother."

Janet says, "Okay," and slowly drifts off to a peaceful sleep.

James, Penny, and Jerry walk back toward the waiting room to find their loved ones and friends that are waiting anxiously for any news on Janet's condition. Penny is approached by her mother who gives her a big hug and a kiss then asks Penny, "How are you doing? You look stressed out, honey."

Penny tells her mom, "I am stressed out. My baby is in ICU and went through some difficult surgeries, but Janet is doing okay, and now we just have to make sure she heals slowly but surely."

James smiles and tells everyone, "The good news that Janet is holding her own and resting peacefully."

James gives his mother a hug and says, "Mom, this is tough on all of us, but I believe Janet is going to be just fine. We have to believe that God is going to heal her without any issues." James looks at his watch and looks at Jerry and asks, "How are you doing, son, are you hungry?"

Jerry says to his dad, "Yeah, Dad, time has passed by worrying about Janet, I completely forgot about eating, but now we know Janet is doing well, I could eat some food."

James says to Jerry, "Let's go get something to eat." James asks Penny if she wants to join them.

Penny says, "I'm going to stay close to our daughter, but you can get me a burger and fries. I really need to get something to eat so I can be strong for our baby girl." Penny walks over to her friends that are in the waiting room and thanks everyone for being there and for all the prayers. The friends and close family all ask if there is anything they can do for her.

Penny smiles at everyone and says, "Yes, just keep praying for Janet." Everyone in the waiting room gives hugs and kisses to Penny, James, and Jerry before leaving the hospital.

James gives Penny a hug and tells her, "Jerry and I will go get some burgers, and be back as soon as possible."

Penny smiles at James and gives a kiss to Jerry before they leave the waiting room. Nurse Sarah walks into the waiting room and sees that Penny is all alone, sitting looking at pictures on her smartphone.

Nurse Sarah takes a seat next to Penny and smiles and says, "I just want to let you know that Janet is resting and she is doing well, but I'd like to know how you are doing."

Penny puts her phone down and says, "I was just looking at some of Janet and Jerry's pictures. They grow up so fast." Penny speaks with a smile on her face. "I am feeling better now." Penny stands up and walks toward the window and looks at the sky and says, "You know, Nurse Sarah, I am doing okay, but I will feel better when my little girl is back home and running around like most kids do."

Nurse Sarah walks over near to Penny and says, "Janet will be up and running around in a few months, so all we have to do is be there to help her through the healing process." Nurse Sarah asks Penny, "Is there anything I can get for you?"

Penny says, "No, thank you, my husband and son have gone to get us some burgers to eat, and then we will try to rest till we can see Janet again."

Nurse Sarah says, "Okay, if you need anything, just ask. I'll let you know if there are any changes on Janet's condition, and you get as much rest as you can."

Penny says, "I'll try, I have to."

CHAPTER NINE

James and Jerry enter the waiting room where they see Penny sleeping in the chair. James walks over and gently touches her shoulder, whispering, "Honey, we are back with the burgers."

Penny rubs her eyes and says, "I must have dozed off for a few minutes, but I'm glad I did. I feel much better now that I took a power nap."

Jerry hands his mom a burger and says, "You will feel even better when you eat this burger, Mom."

Penny says, "It sure does smell good, thanks son I love you."

Jerry says, "I love you too, Mom."

James smiles at Penny and says, "These burgers hit the spot. I didn't realize how hungry I was."

Penny says, "Yeah, they are good, and I needed something to give me some energy." Penny takes a bite of the burger and says to James, "Nurse Sarah stopped by and told me to try to get some rest, and that Janet is resting well, and will let us know when we can see her again."

James says, "Well, I'm glad to hear that, and we should do our best to get some rest so we can be there for Janet when she needs us." James is throwing the paper bag that contained the burgers into the garbage can in waiting room when Nurse Sarah enters the waiting room.

Penny rises quickly when she sees Nurse Sarah and says excitedly, "Is Janet okay?"

Nurse Sarah smiles and says, "Yes, she is doing well. I just wanted to let you know it may be best for all of you to go home, and try to get a good night sleep in your own bed, and if there is any change in Janet's condition, I'll let you know, or if you must, you can stay in this waiting room."

Penny looks at James and Jerry and says to Nurse Sarah, "I think it will do us good to go home, and we will be back up here first thing in the morning, but let us know if any changes happen."

Nurse Sarah says, "I promise I will." Nurse Sarah leaves the room.

Penny says, "Let's go home, James," and holds on to Jerry's hand as they walk out of the waiting room.

The next morning Jerry is the first to wake up and knocks on the door to his parents' bedroom.

James rubs his eyes and says "Come in" and asks Jerry, "Why you up so early?"

Jerry says, "I woke up thinking about Janet, and I want to go see her."

Penny hears Jerry and asks, "What time is it?"

Jerry says, "It's 6:00 a.m."

Penny says, "Oh, baby, that is too early. I want to go see your sister too, but we will wait another hour, and I will call the nurse and find out when we can see Janet."

Jerry says, "Okay, Mom, I'll go eat some cereal and get dressed, and be ready when it's time to go." Jerry walks out of the door while saying, "I hope Janet got some rest during the night."

James gives Penny a hug and looks at her. "That boy loves his sister."

Penny gives a small kiss to James and says, "Yes, he does, but he is feeling guilty about the accident, and I am too, because I told them to stop kicking that soccer ball in my new flower garden, and that's why Janet and Jerry were in the front yard playing."

James gives Penny a hug and says, "Listen to me, honey. It was an accident, and if we try to explain why, and how, well, you can blame me, because I bought the soccer ball for them to kick."

Penny takes a deep breath and says, "I hear what you are saying, but I don't know why this happened. I just hope Janet is going to be okay."

James smiles at Penny and says, "We all want that," and gets out of bed and walks to leave the room, asking, "Can I cook you some breakfast?"

Penny says, "You know I am hungry. Can you make some French toast?"

James says, "Sure, sweetheart, it will be ready in ten minutes."

Penny and James are finishing up their breakfast.

Jerry says, "I'm ready to go see Janet."

Penny tells Jerry, "We will be ready in twenty minutes, so be patient."

Penny calls the hospital to find out when will be a good time to visit Janet. The nurse tells Penny that 8:00 a.m. will be a good time for a visit. Penny thanks the nurse.

James walks in as Penny is saying goodbye to the nurse on the phone and says, "What's up, honey?"

Penny says, "The nurse tells me that 8:00 a.m. will be okay to visit Janet, so if we leave now, we should be there on time."

James says, "Great, let's go see our girl," and gives Penny a kiss.

James, Penny, and Jerry arrive at the hospital, and go to the nurses' station to ask if they can see their daughter Janet. The nurse says, "I will send a nurse to let you know, but for now please go to the waiting room. It should be only a few minutes."

Penny follows James and Jerry to the waiting room and takes a seat, looking nervous. James sees that Penny is anxious and says, "Honey, it will be okay, just a few minutes we will be able to see our little girl."

Nurse Jane enters the waiting room smiling and says, "Good morning. I have good news. I just went take a look at Janet, and she is doing well." Penny rises from her chair and asks if she is awake.

Nurse Jane says, "Janet should be waking up soon, so if you all want to go in to visit, then follow me."

Penny walks up to Janet's bedside and using her fingers brushes back Janet's hair behind her ear. Janet slowly opens her eyes when she feels her mom's warm hand.

Penny smiles at her daughter and says softly, "Hey, sleepyhead, how are you doing?"

Janet looks around the room and sees her mom, dad, and Jerry and says, "I missed y'all."

James and Jerry gets closer to Janet's bed and says, "We missed you too. I was up early this morning telling Mom and Dad let's go see you, but we had to wait till 8:00 a.m."

James asks Janet, "How did you sleep?"

Janet says, "I slept well, but I had a strange dream."

Penny asks Janet, "What was so strange about your dream?"

Janet looks at her mom and begins to tell her dream. "I dreamed I was in heaven, Mom, and I saw Jesus, and he looked just like the picture of Jesus in the Bible."

Penny is getting teary-eyed and says, "Well, you are right here with us, so don't you worry."

Jerry speaks up with curiosity and says, "Janet, did they have angels with wings flying around in heaven?"

Janet looks directly at Jerry and smiles and says, "Yes, they had plenty of angels flying, but they also had many people that were walking too."

Janet looks at her dad and smiles and says, "Dad, they also had animals. The animals were very friendly, and they smelled very clean."

Penny looks at Janet while wiping a tear from her eye. "Sounds like your dream of heaven was perfect."

Janet looks at her mom and says, "It was perfect, but I was sad, because I looked everywhere, and I couldn't find you all anywhere, and Jesus told me that it would be okay, and Jesus made me feel good even though I was missing y'all."

Penny looks at her daughter, gives her a kiss on the cheek, and says, "We love you, baby, and heaven will have to wait, because we need you here with us. So are you hurting anywhere on your body this morning?"

Janet points to her stomach area and says, "It feels funny, like a tickle down there. Sometimes it feels painful."

James asks, "How does your head feel?"

Janet says, "I'm okay. I can still see clearly."

James asks, "Any headaches?"

Janet smiles at her dad and says, "No headaches, Dad, I feel okay, but, Dad, when can I go home?"

Dr. Monroe walks into the ICU room just before James can answer Janet's question. Dr. Monroe walks up to Janet's bed and smiles and says, "How are you feeling this morning?"

Janet speaks softly, "I feel a tickle in my stomach."

Dr. Monroe looks under the cover to examine the sutures to make sure all is well and finds that there is the normal redness around where the incision for surgery was made. Penny asks Dr. Monroe with concern in her voice, "Is everything okay?"

Dr. Monroe looks at Penny with a serious expression but tries to reassure Penny and says that the pain medicine is being slowly reduced and Janet will feel small measures of soreness in that area where the surgery occurred. "There's nothing to be concerned about. All of Janet's vital signs are looking very good, and I expect a full recovery."

James asks how long Janet will have to stay in ICU.

Dr. Monroe looks at James and says, "I will stop by late this afternoon, and if I find that she is doing well, I can have her moved into a private room as soon as tonight." Dr. Monroe asks, "Janet, how clear is your vision today?"

Janet says, "Very well."

Dr. Monroe asks Janet, "Are you having any headaches, or any other pains anywhere else?"

Janet looks at the doctor and says, "No, just feels like a tickle on my stomach."

Dr. Monroe says, "That is normal, but be sure to let the nurse know if you feel any discomfort so we can fix it quickly," and with that Dr. Monroe looks at James and Penny and says, "I will talk with you all late this afternoon." He smiles at Janet and says, "Now you relax and get some rest so your body can get stronger." Dr. Monroe waves goodbye and leaves the ICU room.

Penny says, "Are you feeling tired, my baby?"

Janet says, "A little, but I don't want to be alone, Mom. Can you stay a little longer?"

Jerry says to Janet, "I want to hear more about your dream of heaven. What else can you tell us?"

James speaks to Jerry and says, "Now, son, Janet will tell us more about her dream tomorrow. We need to let your sister get some rest. Give your sister a hug, and we will be in the waiting room if you need us, okay, baby girl?"

Janet smiles and says, "Okay, Dad."

James gives Penny a kiss and says, "We will be waiting for you."

Penny says to James, "Okay, sweetheart, I'll see you later."

James and Jerry leave the ICU room and walk down to the waiting room where they find Pastor Mathew sitting in a chair. Pastor Mathew sees James and Jerry walk into the waiting room and gets up with his right hand extended to shake hands with James. The two men shake hands, and Pastor Mathew asks James how Janet is doing.

James lets go of Pastor Mathew hand and smiles and says, "The doctor was just in her ICU room a few minutes ago and tells us Janet is doing well, and may put her in a private room tonight if she continues to recover without any complications."

Pastor Mathew smiles with relief and says, "I was on my knees last night for hours praying for her. I am so happy to hear that she is doing so well." Pastor Mathew asks if there is anything else he can do.

James says, "Just keep praying for our little girl."

Pastor Mathew tells James that he has asked his church to pray for all of them, so there are hundreds of prayers going up to heaven for healing and strength. James thanks Pastor Mathew for stopping by.

Pastor Mathew says goodbye to Jerry and James.

Penny is in the ICU room with Janet, and Nurse Sarah walks in to check on Janet and asks Janet if there is anything she can get for her.

Janet says to Nurse Sarah, "Can I have something to eat?"

Nurse Sarah smiles and says, "Well, darling, that is a good sign, that you are getting stronger, but we will have to keep you on this IV for at least twenty-four more hours, then we will begin to give you some real food, is that okay?"

Janet smiles and says, "I guess, I just can't taste what that IV is giving me."

Penny smiles at the nurse and says that girl is something else and tells Nurse Sarah Dr. Monroe says he may be able to put Janet in her own room tonight.

Nurse Sarah looks at Penny and says, "That's great news. That means Janet is doing excellent in recovery time."

Penny holds Janet's hand, and Janet's eyes seems to be getting heavy. Nurse Sarah speaks softly to Penny, "Looks like Janet is getting tired."

Penny asks the nurse, "Would it be okay if I stay here till she falls to sleep?"

Nurse Sarah says, "Of course it is, and I'll let you know if there are any changes."

Nurse Sarah checks the monitors for Janet's vital signs one more time then walks out of the room. Penny looks at her little girl as Janet closes her eyes to drift off to sleep. Penny kisses her daughter's cheek and whispers, "I love you," and walks out of the ICU room to go to the waiting room. Penny walks into the waiting room to find Jerry and his dad looking at some outdoor magazines, and when they see Penny, they both get up from their chairs to ask how is Janet doing.

Penny smiles at both of them and says, "She just went to sleep, and she told the nurse she wants to eat some real food because the IV has no taste," and they all laugh for a few seconds."

James tells Penny, "Pastor Mathew was waiting in here when Jerry and I walked in, and told us that he has hundreds of people that go to his church praying for Janet and us."

Penny looks at James and says with some joy in her voice, "That's very sincere for him to be here and to ask his church members to pray for us."

CHAPTER TEN

The time is now 5:00 p.m., and James, Jerry, and Penny are just returning from eating at the hospital cafeteria, and they are in the waiting room. Penny and James have been making and taking calls from family and friends throughout the day letting them know the good news of Janet's recovery. All the family and friends are happy to hear how well Janet is doing and will keep praying for the family.

Dr. Monroe walks into the waiting room and shakes hands with James and Penny and smiles at Jerry and says, "I have some good news. I just went to check on Janet, and she is doing well enough to be moved out of ICU and into a private room."

Penny is so happy she gives Dr. Monroe a big hug then says, "I'm sorry, Dr. Monroe. I am so happy to hear the good news I lost control for a moment."

Dr. Monroe is a little surprised at the hug given by Penny and says, "That's quite all right." Dr. Monroe then explains that Janet will still need plenty of rest so that she can heal slow and steady. Penny asks if it would be okay if she could stay in the room with her.

Dr. Monroe smiles and says, "I was hoping you would ask that, because I know that would give great comfort to your daughter and help her recovery tremendously."

James asks Dr. Monroe, "When can we see her?"

Dr. Monroe says, "You can follow me now to her room. It's right down the hall from here."

Dr. Monroe walks into the room first where Janet has just been moved and says to Janet, "Would you mind some visitors?"

Janet says, "What visitors?"

Dr. Monroe moves to the side of doorway, and Penny, James, and Jerry walk into the room and stand next to Janet's bed with big smiles on their faces. Janet's face is full of joy, and she begins to talk excitedly, "Mom, Dad, Jerry, I missed you all so much. I must be getting stronger. The doctor gave orders to move me into my own room."

Penny gives Janet a hug and says, "Yes, sweetheart, you are doing great, but you still have to get your rest."

Dr. Monroe walks next to Janet's bed and says, "Listen, Janet, we will try to give you some food to eat starting tomorrow, and see how you will do with solid food, if that is okay with you."

Janet says to Dr. Monroe, "That sounds great."

Dr. Monroe says, "You all have a good night," and walks out of the room. Everyone wishes Dr. Monroe a good night before he walks out of the door. James walks close to Janet's bed and gives Janet a kiss on her cheek and asks, "How are you doing?"

Janet tells her dad that she still is feeling a little tired, but happy they all are here.

Jerry says to his sister, "How would like if Mom spent the night with you in this room?"

Janet's face turns to her mom and excitedly says, "For real, Mom, you can stay in my room."

Penny has a small tear go down her face and says, "Yes, baby girl, the doctor gave me permission to stay with you as long as I want."

Janet starts to tear up. She says, "Oh, Mommy, that makes me so happy. I will feel so much better knowing you are here with me. I get scared. Knowing you are close by, I will feel safe."

Penny wipes Janet's tears away and says softly, "You don't have to be scared at all. Mommy is here to watch over you."

Nurse Jane comes into the room and has a chart with information of Janet's readings and asks Janet, "How are you doing?"

Janet speaks with a grin on her face, "I still have a tickle in my stomach, but other than that I feel okay."

Nurse Jane writes down on Janet's chart all the readings that she finds on the monitors and notices that Janet's body temperature is slightly above normal. Nurse Jane looks at the bandages on Janet's stomach area and then puts the cover back on Janet.

Nurse Jane then says, "I'll be back around midnight. Till then try to get some rest."

Jerry says to his dad, "I'm getting tired."

James tells Jerry, "Okay, son, we will be leaving. Go give your sister a kiss good night."

Jerry walks over to Janet's bed and gives his sister a kiss on the cheek.

Janet says, "I will see you tomorrow."

Jerry smiles at his sister and says, "Okay."

James gives a kiss on Janet's cheek and says, "I love you, baby girl, and try to get some rest."

James turns to Penny and gives her a big hug and a kiss on the lips and says, "Is there anything I can get you before I leave?"

Penny smiles and says, "I'm okay, honey, and, Jerry, you make sure to brush your teeth before bedtime."

Jerry gives his mom a hug and says, "I will, Mom," and Jerry and James walk out of Janet's room.

The next morning at seven o'clock Nurse Sarah walks into Janet's room where she finds Janet still asleep, but Penny is awakened by the presence of Nurse Sarah.

Penny says, "Good morning, nurse."

Nurse Sarah speaks with a smile on her face, "Good morning, how did you sleep?"

Penny smiles and says, "Very well for being on a couch in a hospital room. I know I was exhausted too, and that helps."

Nurse Sarah is writing down the information on Janet's chart and notices the elevated temperature and sees that Janet's body temperature has risen a few degrees more since midnight when it was checked last.

Penny says to Nurse Sarah, "I noticed that Janet is warm to the touch. Why is that?"

Nurse Sarah says, "I will let Dr. Monroe know about her rise in temperature, but Janet's temperature is not too high to be concerned, because she is recovering from surgery."

Nurse Sarah looks at the bandages around Janet's stomach and says, "Everything else looks good."

Nurse Sarah begins to walk out of the room and says to Penny, "Dr. Monroe should be stopping by to check in on Janet soon."

Penny says, "Thank you," and the nurse leaves the room. Penny is looking at her daughter sleep when her cell phone rings, and Janet is awakened by the phone and smiles at her mom.

Penny says, "Hello."

James says, "Hello, how are you all doing?"

Penny says, "Our little girl is just waking up, and she's a little warm. The nurse says that's normal after a surgery, but she says she will let Dr. Monroe know. The doctor should be in to check on Janet before eight this morning."

James says, "Well, Jerry and I will try to be there before the doctor to hear what he has to say."

Penny tells James, "I really would like you to be here when the doctor is looking at Janet. Be safe on the road, and I'll see you all in a little while."

Penny smiles at Janet and says, "Are you hungry?"

Janet grins at her mom. "Yes, I am. Can I eat some food today?"

Penny smiles. "Well, I don't know, today is your birthday. I will try to convince the doctor to let you eat some birthday cake."

Janet looks at her mom a little confused and says excitedly, "Wow, Mom, I forgot my birthday is today."

Penny says, "Yes, sweetheart, you are now seven years old. Happy birthday, sweetheart. You know, I almost forgot too with all that is going on. I will ask the doctor if it would be okay to have some family to sing 'Happy Birthday' to you."

Janet is looking at her mom and says, "Oh, Mom, you're the best mom in the whole wide world. I love you."

Penny says, "I love you too."

James walks into the room at eight o'clock with Jerry and goes directly to Janet's bedside carrying some balloons that have writing on them with very colorful words that spell out "Happy Birthday." Janet is in tears with joy and smiles at her daddy.

"You remembered it was my birthday, I love you, and the balloons are beautiful. Thank you, Dad."

Penny is smiling at James and walks over to him to give a big hug and kiss and says, "Honey, that is so sweet of you to get those balloons."

James says, "It was Jerry's idea. I just agreed and bought them downstairs at the gift shop."

Penny gives a big hug to Jerry and tells him, "You are such a good brother, thank you."

Jerry asks his mom if they can sing to Janet for her birthday."

Penny says, "Let's sing." So they all start singing "Happy Birthday" to Janet.

Dr. Monroe walks into the room just as they finished singing and says, "Who has a birthday today?"

Janet smiles and says, "It's mine. I am seven today."

Dr. Monroe smiles at Janet and says, "Happy birthday. Now let's take a look at you."

Dr. Monroe looks at the bandages and finds they look good. He looks at the monitor to see that blood pressure is normal, but her temperature is above normal and tells Penny, "We will take some blood from Janet and send it to the lab to understand why Janet has a fever." Dr. Monroe asks Janet if she has any pain.

Janet says, "I have some pain around my stomach, but it's not too bad."

Dr. Monroe says, "Well, I will be back later this afternoon, and if you still want to eat some food, I will give you permission to eat some soft foods that are easy to digest."

Janet says, "I like ice cream."

Dr. Monroe smiles and says, "Yes, ice cream is very good for a soft-food choice." Dr. Monroe walks out of the room, and James follows the doctor into the hall and asks how Janet really is doing.

Dr. Monroe says, "When I get the results back from the lab, I will know if her white blood cell count is low, and if it is low, that proves that she has an infection, which we will fight with antibiotics."

James asks if it would be okay to have a few family friends visit for a little while for Janet's birthday.

Dr. Monroe says, "Yes, for a little while, but Janet needs to get her rest. She still has a lot of healing to do."

James thanks Dr. Monroe and walks back into the room.

CHAPTER ELEVEN

James walks back into the room and asks Penny to call her parents to stop by this afternoon around three o'clock.

"I'll call mine to bring some chocolate cake for a small birthday party for our little girl."

Penny asks James, "Is that okay with Dr. Monroe?"

James says, "Yes, I went into the hall to get permission, and he said it was okay, but to remember that Janet is not to get too excited, because she has a lot of healing to do."

Janet smiles at her dad and says, "Thank you for asking for that. I love you, Dad."

James gives his little girl a hug and says, "I love you too."

Nurse Sarah walks into the room and notices the balloons and looks at Janet and asks, "Is today your birthday?"

Janet smiles and says, "Yes. Dr. Monroe says I can have chocolate ice cream today."

Nurse Sarah says, "Well, I'll take some blood from you for the lab, and I'll get an orderly to bring you that chocolate ice cream, is that a deal?"

Janet grins at Nurse Sarah and says, "That's a deal."

Nurse Sarah is finished taking the small amount of blood and wishes Janet happy birthday and walks out of Janet's room after saying goodbye to James, Jerry, and Penny. It's three o'clock in the afternoon, and Janet and Jerry's grandparents are in the room celebrating Janet's birthday. Everyone sings "Happy Birthday" to Janet.

James tells Janet, "When you are well enough to have a birthday party at home, we will invite all your friends, and have a better party than this one."

Janet says to her dad, "Thanks, Daddy, but this birthday party is awesome, because I have the most special people I love here with me."

Penny's mom and dad, and James's mom and dad smile and get teary-eyed. Then they all take turns giving Janet hugs and kisses. The grandparents say their goodbyes and say, "We will visit you soon, Janet. You try to get some rest so you can get strong enough to go home, and we love you."

Janet smiles back at her grandparents and says, "I love you too, and thanks so much for the chocolate birthday cake. It was delicious."

Penny walks over to Janet and touches her forehead and says, "You are still a little warm, darling, how are you feeling?"

Janet tells her mom, "I'm feeling tired. Can I go to sleep now, Mom?"

Penny softly whispers to Janet, "Yes, my baby, go to sleep. I'll be here when you wake up."

Jerry and James take a seat on the sofa and watch Janet sleep for an hour.

James looks at his watch and tells Jerry, "Son, it's five o'clock. I guess we will be going home for the night. Kiss your mom good night."

Penny gives Jerry a kiss on the cheek, and before Penny has a chance to talk, Jerry says to his mom, "I will brush my teeth before bedtime."

Penny smiles at Jerry and says, "You are growing up to be a smart little man. I love you, son."

James walks over to Penny and says, "I love you, honey," then looks at Janet and tells Penny, "She sure is sleeping peacefully. I guess we wore her out with our small birthday party."

Penny says, "Yes, she was tired. I hope she can sleep all night."

James tells Penny, "I will call you later tonight. Do you need anything?"

Penny says, "No, my sweetheart, I'm feeling a little tired myself. I believe I'll take me a nap too," and with that being said, James and Penny hug, and James and Jerry walk out of Janet's room.

Penny looks at Janet and smiles then walks over to the sofa and sits down and drifts off to sleep.

The alarms are sounding loudly, and Penny wakes up surprised, and as she looks around the room, she sees flashing lights on the monitor.

Nurse Jane, who has just come on duty for her eight-hour watch, rushes into Janet's room. Nurse Jane is looking under the covers at Janet's bandages, and they look okay, but Janet's abdominal area is swollen. Nurse Jane takes off the alarm on the monitor and sees that Janet's blood pressure is dangerous low, and her temperature has risen to 106 degrees. Penny is standing up close to the bed with a shocked expression on her face and asks Nurse Jane, "What's going on with my daughter? She was sleeping so peacefully an hour ago. Please tell me what is going on."

Nurse Jane tells Penny in a nervous voice, "Your daughter's blood pressure has dropped to a life-threatening level, and her temperature is way too high. We have to get her back to normal now."

Nurse Jane is on the intercom asking for help in room 207, code blue stat. Dr. Monroe and another nurse rush into Janet's room and immediately are trying to get Janet's blood pressure back to normal, but fail to get Janet's pressure to rise.

Penny is now at the point of top-level anxiety, and Dr. Monroe asks Nurse Jane to please take Janet's mom outside of the room. Penny does not want to leave her daughter's side, but Nurse Jane finally convinces Penny to wait outside in the hallway, and as they walk out of the room, Penny screams at Dr. Monroe, "Please don't let my little girl die."

Dr. Monroe turns for a moment to look at Penny and says with a deadly serious expression on his face, "I'm going to do my best."

Dr. Monroe is telling the nurses that are assisting him that she has to be bleeding internally. "I've tried everything I can to get her pressure to stabilize, and it's not working." Dr. Monroe tells a nurse, "Call the OR. We will have to open her up to see what is bleeding, and hopefully we have enough time to stop the bleeding." Janet's temperature is now at 107 degrees.

Dr. Monroe says, "We have to get her temperature down right now, or risk brain damage. Let's move her quickly to OR and get some ice on her body stat."

The nurses help move Janet's hospital bed out of the room quickly and down the hall. Penny is in tears leaning on the wall in the hallway when Janet's bed passes by. Penny looks at her daughter and is frightened of the way Janet is looking. Her color is reddish pink, and her stomach is unusually swollen. Dr. Monroe looks at Penny as they pass each other and stops for a moment to tell Penny, "Your daughter is in critical condition. I will have to operate now. Janet is bleeding internally, and I have to get the bleeding stopped," and then he says with as much compassion as he can, "You need to get your husband here to be with you," and then Dr. Monroe runs down the hall to the operating room to start emergency surgery on Janet to try to save her life.

Dr. Monroe is finishing scrubbing up and has the nurse put on his latex gloves. As he walks into the OR, Janet's little body is covered with bags of ice, which has dropped her body temperature to 102 degrees.

The anesthesiologist tells Doctor Monroe that Janet is ready for surgery. "Blood pressure is ninety-five over sixty-five and holding. We have put two units of blood in her in the last ten minutes with five units standing by."

Dr. Monroe says to his nurses in the OR, "Now let's open her up to find where she is losing all this blood."

Dr. Monroe starts his incision and immediately asks the nurse for suction to remove all the blood that is flowing inside Janet's body cavity. Dr. Monroe is doing his best to find where the bleeder is but sees another life-threatening problem. Janet's small intestine has rup- tured, and liquids are pouring out, contaminating the body cavity.

Vital signs are now going down, even as more units of blood are being pumped into Janet's bloodstream.

The anesthesiologist tells Doctor Monroe, "We are losing her. Blood pressure is eighty over fifty, and she is going into tachycardia. Heart rate is thirty beats per minute, and dropping."

Dr. Monroe is doing his best to stop the bleeding, but then the monitor signals alarm that the heart has stopped.

Dr. Monroe looks at the monitor and says loudly, "No, no, no, we can't let her die." Dr. Monroe looks at everyone in the operating room and is distraught.

The nurse looks at the clock in the operating room and says sadly with tears falling down her face, "Time of death, six o'clock."

Penny has been on the phone since the nurses rushed Janet into the operating room, calling James and her parents. James and Jerry arrive at the hospital so quickly that Penny can't believe her eyes when they run into the waiting room out of breath. James holds Penny in his arms doing his best to support her knowing that she would be very nervous; she would be weak. Penny never stopped crying since Janet left her side in the hallway going to the OR. James is doing his best to hold it together. Jerry's crying was just as loud as his mom.

James asks Penny to be strong and tell him what happened. Penny wipes her tears away with a tissue and tells James that she was sleeping when the nurse rushed into the room. The nurse was calling for help from the other nurses.

"I watched their concern when the nurses were doing all they could do to try to help Janet. Dr. Monroe came in the room and immediately told one of the nurses in the room to get the operating room ready, we have to hurry."

Penny then begins to cry again and tells James, "Janet's skin color was so red because of her high fever. I am so worried, James. I have tried to find out what is going on, but no one has come to tell me any news."

Jerry stops his crying and hugs his mom and tells his mom Janet is going to be okay; she just has to be. James asks Penny to try to sit down.

"I'm going to find out what is happening with our little girl."

James walks into the hall and notices a nurse come out of the operating room, but when the nurse looks at James, she turns her head. James went to ask the nurse at the desk if anyone can tell him why no one is letting them know about their daughter, Janet. The lady behind the desk tells James that she has been trying to get some information for his wife Penny but no one is giving her any news. James is getting upset and can't believe why no one is telling them anything and turns to go back to the waiting room when he sees Penny's father and mother walk into the waiting room. James goes into the waiting room, and as he walks closer to Penny, he can feel the love of Penny's parents as they try to comfort her with hugs and words of faith.

James walks next to Penny, and he tells her, "Sweetheart, I did my best to find out any news, but no one will tell me anything."

Jerry walks to the doorway of the waiting room and looks down the hall and notices Dr. Monroe walking toward the waiting room.

Jerry runs to his dad with excitement and shouts out the words, "The doctor is coming, Dad." Everyone in the waiting room turns to the doorway of the waiting room. Dr. Monroe walks into the waiting room holding his hands together.

Penny rushes over to Dr. Monroe and looks into his eyes and says, "How is my daughter, when can we see our daughter?"

James walks over to Penny to hold her close to his side and looks at Dr. Monroe eye to eye. "Please tell us some good news."

Dr. Monroe takes a deep breath and looks at James then looks at Penny, and before he can speak another word, Penny has tears in her eyes running down her face hitting the floor.

Dr. Monroe's voice starts to crack as he says, "I did everything I could, God knows I tried everything, but I couldn't save your little girl."

Penny begins to lose the ability to stand, and James uses all his strength to hold her up. Penny's mom goes to Jerry and sits him down in a chair in the waiting room, holding him as he begins to cry and say with conviction, "It's my fault. I'm sorry, Mom, it's my fault."

Penny's dad kneels down next to Jerry and tries to quiet him down by telling Jerry, "It's not your fault."

Jerry looks at him and says, "Papa, if I hadn't kicked that stupid soccer ball in the street, none of this would have happened."

Penny's mom tells Jerry with tears coming down her face, "It was an accident. That's all it was. Please don't blame yourself," but

Jerry continues to cry, and the grandparents do their best to console Jerry.

James, who now has tears running down his cheeks, is asking Dr. Monroe what happened. "When I left my daughter two hours ago, she was doing fine."

Dr. Monroe asks Penny and James to please sit down and begins telling what happened to cause Janet's death. Dr. Monroe wipes a tear from his face and says, "I was called an hour ago with a code blue in your daughter's room, and this is what happened next."

CHAPTER TWELVE

Dr. Monroe looks at Penny, who looks weak and pale, and decides that Penny is in need of a sedative to calm her nervousness down before she goes into a convulsion because of the anxiety she is going through. Nurse Jane is passing in the hallway in front of doorway of the waiting room, and Dr. Monroe calls out to Nurse Jane.

Nurse Jane stops when she hears Dr. Monroe and goes to him and says, "Yes, how can I help?"

Dr. Monroe asks Nurse Jane, "Could you please bring a few pills of Valium and some water for Janet's mom?"

Nurse Jane says, "Right away, Doctor." Nurse Jane leaves the waiting room but is back within two minutes. Nurse Jane gives two pills of Valium to Penny and a bottle of water.

Nurse Jane tells Penny with compassion in her voice, "I'm so sorry for your loss."

Penny takes the pills and drinks from the bottle of water and thanks Nurse Jane for all she has done for Janet. Nurse Jane asks Dr. Monroe if there is anything else he may need.

Dr. Monroe says, "Not now, but stay nearby in case I would need something."

Nurse Jane says to the doctor, "I will be right down the hall," and leaves the waiting room, doing her best not to cry.

Dr. Monroe tells Penny in a soft, calming voice, "The Valium will help you stay calm," and then begins to tell what has happened to Janet. Everyone in the waiting room is looking at Dr. Monroe as he starts to tell the events that happened to Janet.

Dr. Monroe looks at James and says, "When I saw Janet, she had a temperature of 106, and her blood pressure was very low. I immediately asked the nurse to get the operating room ready for surgery. I looked at Janet's stomach and noticed that it had swollen considerably, and that led me to believe that Janet was bleeding internally. We rushed Janet into the operating room, and once I was able to see inside her body cavity, I noticed two things right away. Janet had an artery that was leaking blood fast, and a part of her small intestine had ruptured in a different area where I repaired it a few days earlier. I tried my best to stop the bleeding and was giving her units of blood to try to hold her blood pressure stable. I didn't have enough time to repair the artery, and her vital organs began to shut down, and she died at six o'clock this evening."

Penny is starting to feel the early effects of the Valium and tells James, "What are we going to do, James, our little girl is gone."

James thanks Dr. Monroe for explaining what happened and tries to give Penny as much attention as he can. Dr. Monroe says he is so sorry he couldn't save Janet and then stands up and walks out of the waiting room feeling like he lost his own child.

James looks at Penny with tears in his eyes and says, "Honey, this is going to be difficult for us to cope, but we have each other and family."

Penny looks at James and hugs him and tells him, "We have the strength of God to carry us when we get weak and the pain is unbearable. Lord Jesus, keep us strong in your grace and love."

Nurse Jane walks into the waiting room, and everyone can tell she has been crying for Janet's passing. She asks Penny and James if they would like to see Janet. James looks at Penny, and Penny nods yes. Nurse Jane asks James and Penny to follow her to the OR.

Penny tells Jerry and her parents, "We will be back in a few minutes."

Jerry runs to his mom and hugs her tight and says, "I love you so much, Mom."

Penny says, "I love you too."

Nurse Jane leads James and Penny to the bed where Janet's body is lying and says, "I have to ask you because time is of the essence. Would you like to donate any or all usable organs from Janet to help others in need?"

Penny looks at James and says, "Yes, we would. We both have donor hearts on our driver license."

James smiles at Penny and says, "Janet would have wanted to do that."

Nurse Jane says, "Thank you. A team of nurses and a doctor will be in here to do that in five minutes, but till then I will leave you all alone with your daughter."

James says "Thank you" as Nurse Jane goes to inform the doctor that Janet will be an organ donor. James slowly lifts the white sheet away from Janet's head, and immediately the tears start falling from Penny's eyes. James holds Penny tight to help support her in case she gets weak in the knees.

Penny's voice is broken as she tries to say, "Our precious little girl is in heaven at the tender age of seven. Oh my god, why did this happen, James?"

James, who is looking at Janet's beautiful face, is doing his best to console his wife, but the anger is overpowering his grief, and he has no words that will comfort Penny. James then takes hold of Janet's little hand, and even though Janet has been dead for fifteen minutes, there is still warmth in her hand.

James starts to cry and tells Penny softly, "I'll never get to walk my baby girl down the aisle for her wedding."

Penny looks down at Janet after she kisses James on the cheek. "I know. She would have loved that from her daddy, and she would have been a very beautiful bride."

A few moments of silence pass as James and Penny just look at Janet's face. Then Nurse Jane walks in and says, "I'm sorry to interrupt, but the doctor and nurses will be here in a minute to retrieve the organs from your daughter."

James says, "Okay, we will be saying our goodbyes," and both James and Penny kiss Janet on the cheek then leave the OR.

Penny and James walk hand in hand back toward the waiting room where Penny's parents have been joined by James's parents who both looked astounded at the awful news of Janet's death. James's mom gives James a hug as soon as he enters the waiting room and then hugs Penny and whispers, "We are so sorry to hear that Janet has passed. Is there anything we can do?"

Penny, who now has the full effect of the Valium in her bloodstream that she took twenty minutes ago, has the calming voice of a nun and tells her mother-in-law with a smile, "It will be okay. Janet is with Jesus now."

The news of Janet's passing goes through the hospital halls quickly, and Nurse Sarah is just starting her eight-hour shift when she hears the sad news.

Nurse Sarah goes to the waiting room hoping to see James and Penny to offer her condolences. Penny and James are starting their way out of the waiting room when Nurse Sarah approaches the couple with compassion and says, "I was shocked to hear the awful news about Janet. I don't understand what happened. Janet seemed to be doing so well."

James and Penny both give Nurse Sarah a gentle hug. Penny says calmly, "We donated all of Janet's organs to help others in need of them."

Nurse Sarah realizes right away that Penny has to be on Valium to be so relaxed in the moments of losing her little girl less than an hour ago. James, on the other hand, is clearly distraught and eager to leave the hospital with what is left of his family and says as kindly as he can to Nurse Sarah, "Thank you for all you did for us and Janet."

James turns to Jerry and says with a slight tone of authority, "Come on, son, we need to go home. We have to get your mom home so she can rest."

Nurse Sarah steps to the side of the room so they can exit the room easily and speaks with loving compassion to Penny and James, "If I can help you with anything, please don't hesitate to call anytime."

James looks at Nurse Sarah and smiles and says, "Thank you, we will," and as he holds Penny by the hand, he knows that he will be hearing those same words hundreds of times in the next few days from family and friends and even strangers he has never met before.

Penny's parents and James's parents follow James, Penny, and Jerry out of the hospital after James signs legal documents to have Janet's body transported to the funeral home not far from their residence. James's dad has called the funeral director on behalf of his son to schedule picking out a casket for Janet and other protocol for Janet's funeral for tomorrow morning at eleven o'clock.

In the parking lot of the hospital, James asks his parents and Penny's parents to follow them to his house just to have loved ones close under this difficult time. The parents agree to visit with James, Penny, and Jerry. James is driving onto the driveway of their home, and to their astonishment, Penny sees flowers, balloons, greeting cards that are speaking loudly with words "Rest in peace, Janet."

Penny looks at James and says, "My god, how fast does bad news travel nowadays."

The parents follow James and Penny to the front door and stand closely and watch as James and Penny start to read some of the notes on the flower arrangements.

James smiles at Jerry and Penny and says, "My god, we are blessed with loving and compassionate friends and family."

James tries not to cry as he reads some of the cards, and his mom gives him a hug and says with a soft, loving voice, "Son, it's okay to cry a little in front of loved ones."

James hugs his mom and says with choked-up words, "I know, Mom, but I have to be the strong one now to help my family get through this tragedy."

James opens the front door, and everyone walks past the gifts that their friends and relatives have delivered while James and his family were at the hospital just an hour ago.

Penny says to her mom, "I'm going to make some tea. I believe that will be more soothing than coffee."

Penny's mom says with a smile after wiping a tear from her face, "Let me help you with that, my dear," and they both go into the kitchen followed closely by James's mom, who also is wiping tears from her face.

Penny says to both of them as she reaches for the tea, "Can you all believe the outpouring of love that is displayed out by the front door?"

James's mom smiles at Penny and says, "It just goes to show that love is still on the planet, and most people are decent and compassionate."

James is sitting on the couch with his dad and father-in-law while Jerry is staring out of the window looking at a delivery person bringing more flowers to put down by the front door.

Jerry looks at his dad and says excitedly, "Dad, some man is bringing more flowers."

James tries to smile at Jerry and says, "Yes, son, I'm sure they will have plenty more out there when we wake up tomorrow morning."

Penny's dad, who is in shock of Janet's death, tells James, "Whatever you need, we will all pull together to help you for as long as it takes."

James reaches over to extend his right hand, and the two men shake hands and smile at each other.

James says, "I appreciate that, because I know we will all need someone to lean on to make it day to day."

James then looks toward the kitchen and says, whispering, "I am mostly worried about Penny, and how she will cope with losing our baby girl." James then looks at Jerry and says, "I'm afraid Jerry will need counseling because he is blaming himself for kicking the soccer ball in the street, which caused Janet to run after it and get struck by the truck."

James's dad says to James, "Son, we will be here to support all of you."

Penny is walking into the living room carrying a tray with cups. Her mom is following Penny with the teapot.

James's mom is close behind them with cookies and says to everyone, "Have some comfort food and drink," trying to smile as she speaks.

James stands up and says, "Thanks so much. Let me pour the tea for everyone," and does so very carefully.

Everyone is drinking their tea and enjoying their cookies when there is a knock at the door.

Jerry stands up and says, "I'll see whose there," and walks to the front door and opens the door. Jerry is surprised after opening the door to see it is the pretty lady on Channel Three TV news station standing there with a man behind her holding a large camera. The lady speaks first and introduces herself as Mary Hebert of Channel Three news.

"May I speak to your parents?"

Jerry is smiling at the lady and says, "I know who you are. I see you on TV all the time," then turns to the living room and excitedly says, "Mom, Dad, it's that lady from the news program."

Penny is the first one to stand up and walks over to the front door still holding her cup of tea.

James puts his cup of tea down on the table, walks to the front door, and stands next to Penny. The parents of Penny and James also join them at front door.

Penny asks, "Can we help you with something this evening?"

CHAPTER THIRTEEN

The lady at the door introduces herself to Penny and asks if they would mind going on camera for a few minutes to talk about their beautiful daughter's life.

James looks at Penny and says, "Honey, let's talk about this for a few minutes before agreeing to this knowing this could be a good thing, or a bad thing."

James asks Ms. Hebert, "What questions will you be asking?"

Ms. Hebert says, "Our news station sent me here to do a compassionate story about your daughter. It will only be a minute or two about you holding a picture of Janet, and maybe you all could stand in front of all these flowers, telling our viewers how Janet loves going to school and being with her friends."

James looks at Penny, and Penny says, "Only if we can look at what you will show on the air before you put it on TV."

Ms. Hebert says yes to that, and the interview starts with Ms. Hebert standing in front of James and Penny's home. She then walks over to where the flowers and balloons are while talking. Ms. Hebert starts by saying, "I'm standing in front of the home of the little girl that we all have been praying for since she was accidentally struck by a truck two days ago. Her name is Janet Kingman."

The camera now turns to focus on James and Penny with Penny holding a beautiful picture of Janet that was taken only a few months ago. Ms. Hebert walks next to Penny and asks, "Can you tell us a few things about your daughter?"

Penny takes a deep breath and says, "Our daughter was a very happy little girl who always tried to help anyone she could. That's why when she passed away a few hours ago, my husband and I agreed to donate her organs to the people that could benefit from her generosity."

James then speaks up as he puts his arm around Penny and Jerry, "We are all donors, and we feel life is meant to be shared, and we will miss our little girl very much, but parts of her will live on in other people."

Ms. Hebert starts to cry on camera and says, "That is so nice to do that for complete strangers."

Penny smiles and says, "That's just who we are, and Janet was such a beautiful girl on the inside and outside."

James then says while looking directly into the camera lens, "If I may ask anyone that was thinking to give flowers or any other kindly gestures out of compassion for Janet, I will be setting up an account in Janet's name at First National Bank here in the town of Franklin to have all money donated to children's hospital."

Ms. Hebert asks Penny, "If I may ask, how old was Janet?"

Penny smiles with a tear running down her cheek and says, "Today is her birthday, and she is seven years old, and we miss her so much."

The camera now is focused on Ms. Hebert, who is doing her best to not break down into a full-blown crying situation and says, "Thank you for allowing us to talk with you about Janet, and let me remind our viewers to give to the children's hospital in Janet's name."

The bright lights of the camera are turned off, and the camera-man is wiping tears from his face as he walks away and back to the Channel Two news van.

Ms. Hebert smiles at Penny and says, "Thank you so much for giving us the opportunity to share your story. Would you like to see it on camera now?"

Penny says, "No. I know that it went very well and should raise money for the children's hospital. That place could always use the extra funding."

James asks Ms. Hebert, "When will this play on TV?"

Ms. Hebert says, "It will play on the morning, noon, and our evening news program tomorrow if that is okay with you."

James agrees, "That would be fine."

Ms. Hebert then says her goodbyes to everyone that is standing by the front door and walks back to the news van. Ms. Hebert looks at her cameraman and says, "Wow, that was tough. I couldn't hold back my tears."

The cameraman says, "Yes, Mary, I was crying too. I don't know how they will cope with this loss, but I pray to God that this family stays strong."

Jerry waves to the people in the news van as he turns to be the last one going back into the house.

Jerry says to his dad, "We are going to be on TV tomorrow. I can't wait to watch it."

James says, "Yes, son, for a few seconds we will be on TV, but then we will be forgotten like all the other news stories, but I hope the people that watch this story tomorrow give to the children's hospital."

James's dad walks up to his son and gives him a hug and says, "I know people from all over will give money, son, and I'm going to be one of them."

Penny sits down on the sofa and starts to drink her tea and says, "I'm feeling tired. It's been nice having you all here supporting us, but I believe I could use a nap to get some much-needed rest."

Penny's mom looks at her husband and then speaks to Penny, "You are right, sweetheart. We all are feeling exhausted." Penny stands up and begins to hug everyone before leaving to go to her bedroom.

James thanks everyone for being here and says, "We will talk with you all tomorrow."

Jerry asks his dad, "What would you like me to do with the flowers and all the other stuff outside the front door?"

James tells Jerry, "Son, let's just leave it there for now. We need to go to bed and try to rest."

Jerry hugs his dad and says, "I'm going tell Mom I love her."

Jerry goes to his mom's room, knocks on the bedroom door. Jerry asks, "Is it okay to come in?"

Penny says, "Yes, son."

Jerry goes to his mom, who is already in the bed, and gives her a kiss on the cheek and tells her, "I love you, Mom. I hope you rest well tonight."

Penny smiles at Jerry and says, "I should sleep well. I'm very tired, and I love you too, son, good night."

James walks around the house making sure all the doors are locked and looks at the flowers that are stacked at the entrance of the front door and says to himself, "God, there are some loving people in this world."

James stops in front of Jerry's bedroom door and sees Jerry on his knees praying, and as he listens, he can't help being so proud of his son. Jerry asks Jesus to watch over his sister to make sure she is cared for in heaven and to watch over his mom and dad.

"Because I know they are going to miss my sister so much that they will cry every day, but, Jesus, I will do my best to make sure they know that Janet is in heaven with you, and I will do my best to make life easier for them any way I can. I love you, Jesus, and keep all of my family and friends safe."

Jerry gets into his bed. James walks inside Jerry's bedroom and gives Jerry a kiss and says, "I'm proud of you, son, and I love you. Good night."

Jerry smiles and says, "I'm proud of you too, Dad, and so happy you're my dad. I love you and good night."

James walks into his bedroom quietly and sees Penny with the covers up to her neck fast asleep. James puts on his pajamas and slowly gets into bed, doing his best not to wake his beautiful wife.

The next morning at eight o'clock, James is the first to get out of bed and goes to the kitchen to make some fresh coffee. Jerry smells the coffee brewing and goes to the kitchen where he says "Good morning" to his dad.

James asks Jerry, "How did you sleep?"

Jerry looks at his dad and says, "I slept good."

Jerry asks his dad, "Is Mom up?"

James says, "No, she is still sleeping, but I will wake her up in a few minutes, because we have to go to the funeral home to pick out a casket for your sister at eleven o'clock this morning and make plans for the time and day of the funeral."

Jerry asks his dad if he could go.

His dad says, "Sure, we want you to be there with us."

James makes a cup of coffee for Penny and brings it to their bedroom, and Penny opens her eyes as soon as she smells the aroma of the coffee.

Penny smiles at James and says, "Thank you, sweetheart, for the coffee. I tell you I slept like a rock. I didn't hear you get in bed at all."

James says, "It must be the Valium the nurse gave you at the hospital that made you sleep so well."

Penny takes a sip of coffee and says to James, "Oh, honey, that's some good coffee," and gets out of bed.

James tells her, "We have to be at the funeral home at eleven o'clock this morning, and we will take Jerry with us if you're okay with that."

Penny smiles at James and says, "Yes, we are a family, and that's what family does."

James says, "I will call my office now and clear my schedule for the day, and when you are ready, we will go to the funeral home."

Penny puts down the coffee cup and hugs James tightly and says, "I'm so glad you are here, because I couldn't do this without you."

James says to Penny, "We got each other to lean on, honey, and Jerry will help us get through this too."

James gives Penny a kiss and says, "I heard him saying his prayers last night, and I am so proud of the little man our son has become."

Penny asks James what was Jerry's prayer, and James says, "He asks Jesus to watch over Janet in heaven so she wouldn't be lonely and to help you and me as he knows we will be crying every day missing his sister."

Penny has a tear come down her cheek, and she wipes it away and tells James, "Wow, our boy is really growing up fast."

James says, "Yes, he has a big, loving heart for his age. I told him how proud I was of him, and he told me he was so happy to have me as his dad."

Penny smiles at James and says, "He's a chip off the old block for sure, just like his dad."

James leaves the room to make a phone call to his office. Penny goes to her bathroom to take a shower and then gets dressed to go to the funeral home. James, Penny, and Jerry arrive at the funeral home at eleven o'clock, and the funeral director meets them as they walk into the front entrance. The funeral director introduces himself as Mr. Thomas and asks, "Could you all follow me to my office."

Mr. Thomas gathers information about the family so that the local newspaper and radio station can let the public know the time and date of Janet's funeral service. Mr. Thomas then sends a fax to the newspaper and radio station and asks James, Penny, and Jerry to follow him to where the caskets are kept. Jerry is looking around the room at the many different caskets, and Penny is standing next to a shiny silver casket.

James looks at Penny and says, "Is this the one you are thinking about?"

Penny starts to cry, and Jerry goes over to his mom and says, "It's okay, Mom. That is a very pretty one."

Penny wipes her tears and says, "Yes, it is, but I'm so sad that we have to be doing this. My god, this is so hard to do."

James looks at Mr. Thomas and says, "This silver casket will be just fine for our daughter."

Mr. Thomas asks Penny, "Can you bring a dress for Janet to wear in the casket?"

Penny smiles and says, "Yes, I will."

Mr. Thomas says, "Thank you, and that will conclude our meeting this morning I have all the information I need and will call you this evening to confirm everything will be on schedule."

Mr. Thomas says he is so sorry for their loss of Janet. James, Penny, and Jerry arrive back home at twelve o'clock, and Penny puts on the TV to watch the news. There is the story with Mary Hebert telling the story of Janet and interviewing James and Penny last night. James and Jerry hurry to sit down and watch it with Penny. Penny looks at James when the news story is finished, and James is wiping a tear from his face.

Penny smiles and says, "That was a nice story for Janet."

Jerry smiles at his dad and says, "We look pretty good on TV if I do say so myself."

James says, "Yes, we do. It just gets to me seeing that we are in the news."

Penny's phone starts beeping with many texts coming through, and as she reads them, James asks, "Who is texting you?"

Penny says, "Wow, it's like twenty different texts from our family and friends saying they just saw the news and saying how sorry to hear the news about Janet, and want to help any way they can."

James's cell phone starts to ring. James answers the phone, and it's the bank manager where the account was set up for the children's hospital in Janet's name. James talks to the bank manager for a few minutes and smiles as he says goodbye. James tells Jerry and Penny that the bank is taking so many calls from people wanting to donate money it's hard to believe.

"The bank manager had to get extra help to take all the calls that are coming in."

Penny says in a joyful voice, "Praise God, our daughter is doing good things even though she's in heaven."

James looks at his phone again, and it's a text from the funeral director saying that everything is on schedule for the services tomorrow evening at five o'clock for immediate family members to visit with Janet, and then friends and other family members will be able to go to the wake at six o'clock till nine o'clock.

James returns the text and thanks Mr. Thomas for all his help in getting this done so quickly and says, "I will be bringing Janet's dress very soon," and puts his phone away. James tells Penny that all is well with arrangements.

"I will bring Janet's dress to the funeral home soon."

Penny says to James, "Thanks, sweetheart, I know tomorrow will be extremely difficult."

James says, "If you would like, I can get you a few more Valium to help you cope for the next few days of pain and sorrow."

Penny says, "Yes, do that for me. I'm sure I will need it to get through these next couple of days."

James calls Dr. Monroe's cell phone and asks if he could prescribe some more Valium.

Dr. Monroe says, "Sure, I will call your pharmacy to get ten more pills. How is Penny coping with her grief?"

James says that she slept all night and has had a few moments that were tough to watch, but for the most part, she has been strong. Dr. Monroe asks how Jerry and him are doing.

James says, "We are trying our best to be strong and support each other because we know the next few days are going to be extremely difficult to get through."

Dr. Monroe tells James that he personally knows a lady doctor that is very helpful in counseling anyone that have lost a family member, and when they are ready to talk with her, he would contact her to set up a session for Penny, Jerry, and him.

James says, "Thank you, Dr. Monroe, we will call you soon for that," and says goodbye.

James tells Penny about the conversation he had with Dr. Monroe and says, "I'll go pick up the Valium now just in case you need it tonight to sleep, and bring Janet's dress to the funeral home."

Penny kisses James and thanks him for being so kind. James returns from the pharmacy, and Penny takes only one Valium instead of the two that is recommended.

Penny says, "I believe I will go lie down and try to read a good book."

James says, "That's a good idea, sweetheart, and that may take your mind off the pressures of tomorrow."

The alarm clock rings at eight o'clock in the morning, and James turns the alarm off.

Penny wakes up and says to James, "Is it morning already?"

James rolls over to face Penny and says, "Yeah, it is."

Penny says, "Wow, I slept so well last night. It was amazing. That one pill of Valium really made me sleep all night."

James says, "Well, we have a few hours to get ready before we have to be at the funeral home, so we are not in any rush."

Penny says, "James, just hold me for a few minutes and tell me it's going to be okay."

James holds his beautiful wife in his arms in their bed and says, "With Jesus we will be okay. We will get through this and be stronger than ever."

Penny tells James, "That's what I need to hear."

They hold each other for ten minutes, not saying another word till they get out of bed. James is dressed in a black suit just like Jerry, and Penny is in a black dress as they walk to the entrance of the funeral home. Penny's and James' parents are standing next to the entrance. James asks if they would give them a few minutes alone with Janet before coming in.

James's dad says, "Son, you all take as long as you need. Just send Jerry to get us when it's good to go in."

James hugs his dad and mom, and Penny hugs her dad and mom before walking into the funeral home. Mr. Thomas, the funeral director, greets James, Penny, and Jerry as they walk in and tells James, "If you need anything, just let me know."

James thanks Mr. Thomas, and Jerry holds hands with his dad and mom as they walk to Janet's casket. Jerry speaks first after looking at Janet for a minute and says, "It looks like she is sleeping. Mom, look how pretty she is."

Penny is looking at her daughter and moves Janet's beautiful black hair a little to the side of her face and says to Jerry, "Yes, my son, she does looks like she's sleeping," but then Penny begins to cry, and James holds Penny tight by his side to make sure she doesn't fall.

Penny continues to cry and says in a broken voice, "She's not sleeping. She's not sleeping, son. Our little Janet is gone. She's gone to heaven, and we can't wake her up."

Jerry and James both start crying when Penny finished talking, and after a few more minutes of tears falling inside Janet's coffin, they all step back and look at all the pretty flower arrangements that are positioned on the left and right of the casket.

James starts to read a few cards aloud then returns in front of his daughter's casket. James bends over to gently kiss Janet on her cheek and says, "My heart is broken, baby girl, but I know you are in a much better place."

Penny is rubbing James's shoulder and crying.

James says, "We will miss you every day but will live for Jesus to make sure when we die all of us will spend eternity together in heaven." James kisses Janet again on the cheek before asking Jerry if he would like to say something to his sister.

Jerry looks at his sister and smiles after wiping his tears from his face and says, "Janet, I want you know that I will miss all the times we played together. I hope you have fun in heaven, and, sister, don't you worry about Mom and Dad. I will do my best to take care of them."

Jerry then looks at his dad and mom and says, "Janet, I wish we could talk to you and hear your voice one more time to tell you that we all love you." Jerry steps away from the casket and hugs his mom.

Penny hugs Jerry and says, "That was very sweet what you said to your sister, son, but we are going to take care of each other so we can pick up each other when one of us falls."

Jerry looks at his mom and says, "Okay, Mom, I can do that."

James asks Penny, "Are you ready to let our parents come in now to see Janet?"

Penny says, "Yes, I am."

James asks Jerry, "Please go get your grandparents who are waiting outside."

Jerry says, "Okay, Dad."

The grandparents walk in, and they take turns looking and talking to Janet. Penny is sitting down on the sofa and asks James, "Would it be all right to take one Valium? I'm feeling some anxiety now."

James gives Penny one pill and a bottle of water to wash down the pill. Penny thanks James. He smiles back at Penny and says, "Pray to Jesus to give you strength, my sweetheart. That's what I'm doing, and it's helping me."

Penny says, "I will and do my best to keep it together."

The funeral director walks over to James and says that it is almost six o'clock. "Is it okay to let friends and family in to make a line to see your daughter?"

James is sitting next to Penny and stands up and says, "Yes, we are ready to greet our family and friends."

Mr. Thomas says, "Okay, I will let them in, and just to let you know there are hundreds of people waiting to come in."

James helps Penny to her feet. They stand to the left of the casket.

Penny says, "I'm ready, James. I feel the Valium helping me relax, and I'm ready to hug our friends as they walk past Janet in her casket."

There are many tears falling as family and friends, both young and old, walk by Janet, and everyone hugs James, Penny, and Jerry and says how heartbroken they are for the passing of Janet, their beautiful daughter, and ask if they can help in any way and to just call and they will do whatever they can. Jerry was getting tired of standing up for over an hour now and asks his dad if he could go to the room where they keep the snack food and sit down and have some food.

James looks down at his son and says, "Sure, son, go take a break, and eat some food."

Jerry says, "Thanks, Dad, I'll be back in a little while."

Jerry is in the room eating a sandwich and chips, and people are talking in the room. Jerry knows some of the people there, but some are complete strangers. Jerry finishes his meal and walks down the hall where he hears a phone ring in a room just across from the restrooms. Jerry looks around and sees no one around and walks into the room and picks up the phone and says hello.

Jerry is astonished by the voice that is coming out of the phone. Jerry says, "Who is this?" And on the phone is Janet's voice, his sister. Jerry says, "How could you be talking to me now? I know this is my sister talking to me, but, Janet, there are no phones in heaven."

Janet is asking Jerry, "Run and get Mom and Dad so I can talk to them. I don't have a lot of time to be on this phone. It's long distance."

Jerry screams into the phone, "Hold the line, Janet. I'll be right back."

Jerry runs as fast as a ten-year-old boy can run through the funeral home, bumping into people and saying, "Excuse me, I have to get to my mom and dad, please excuse me."

Pastor Mathew has made his way to the casket after standing in line over an hour and looks at Janet and starts to cry. He has told himself he would be strong and hold back his emotions, but when he kneels down to say a prayer for Janet's family, the tears just cannot be stopped.

He prays loudly so that others close around him can hear his words of remorse and says the words, "Heavenly Father, please forgive me for the pain I have put upon this family and all the persons that know this beautiful little girl. I am so sorry for taking away the life of the girl that brought so much joy to anyone that had the privilege to know and love Janet, and, Lord Jesus, please give the parents of this child the peace in knowing that this child is in heaven with you now safe in your loving arms. Amen." Pastor Mathew stands up and wipes his tears from his face using a handkerchief, and James walks over to Pastor Mathew and says, "Thank you for that prayer, Pastor."

James then hugs Pastor Mathew and says, "We know it was an accident, and we forgive you, and God bless you."

Jerry runs into the room where his mom and dad are standing, out of breath, and his mom says, "What's wrong with you, Jerry, why are you running like you've seen a ghost?" Jerry is mumbling words that don't make any sense.

James says to Jerry, "Breathe, now speak to us slowly what you need us to hear."

Jerry takes a deep breath and says the phone was ringing in the room across from the restrooms and no one was around. Jerry says, "It kept ringing, so I went in to answer the phone, and the voice on the phone was Janet's voice."

James looks at Jerry and says in a serious tone, "Now come on, son, it may sound like your sister because you want it to, but it can't be your sister."

Jerry says to his dad, "Please, Dad, I know what I'm hearing. I didn't believe it at first, but you know how Janet can be when she wants her way. Please, Dad, Janet said to hurry, it's long distance."

Penny looks at James and says, "My god, that sure sounds like our little girl."

James grabs hold of Penny's hand and in a loud voice says, "Please excuse us, please let us get through."

James and Penny are moving through the crowded room, making their way to the small room where Janet is waiting on the phone. The room is loud with voices, some saying "What is going on?" and others saying that the little girl in the casket is calling from heaven.

Everyone is confused because how could this be true? Some are saying it is a sign from God Almighty, and some are in disbelief. James and Penny get inside the room with Jerry standing next to them. James pushes the button on the phone that allows the phone to go on speaker and says hello.

The voice on the other end of the line responds, "Daddy, this is your little girl. I love you."

Penny almost passes out, but James holds her up and then puts her in a chair next to the desk where the phone is sitting on.

Penny says loudly, "Janet, my baby girl, is that you?"

Janet says, "Yes, Mommy, it's me, please don't cry. I am all right now. I was frightened when I first got here, but Jesus talked to me and walked with me. He showed me around heaven, and, Mom, it is so beautiful and peaceful here."

Jerry speaks up, "Janet, is it true that the streets are made of gold?"

Janet says, "Yes, my brother, they are made of pure gold."

Pastor Mathew is one of the many people standing at the door of the room where the phone is, and like everyone beside him that can hear the voice, he is having a hard time believing that it really is Janet.

Penny asks Janet, "Do you remember the time we went fishing and you caught your first fish? What kind of fish was it?"

Janet says, "Mom, don't you remember, that was a three-pound catfish."

Penny smiles from ear to ear and says, "You are right, my baby."

James says, "How is this possible that you can call us from heaven?"

Janet says, "I told Jesus that I just had to let my family know I was all right, and you know with Jesus all things are possible, so I convinced Jesus to let me call you all from heaven, so life for y'all would not be full of grief and sorrow. Now I have to go because Jesus says so, but remember, I love you all, and so does Jesus."

Penny raises her voice and says, "Just a few more minutes, Janet, please can we talk just a few more minutes, tell us about heaven."

Janet says, "I have to tell you I'm not a little girl in heaven. My age is your age, thirty years old. I have to go, Mommy, but believe me, Heaven is the most beautiful place I have ever been, and it's real, and, Mommy, Jesus wanted you and Daddy to know he appreciates you all for donating my organs to the hospital for others to live longer. Jesus says I have awesome parents. I told him I already knew that, and Jesus laughed. I have to go now. Goodbye, and I love all of you."

The phone goes silent, and James and Penny hug and kiss each other. James says, "Our little girl is in heaven, praise Jesus."

The crowd at the door and in the hallway are excited and start singing "Glory Be to God." James and Penny make their way back to the casket and look at Janet's face and are surprised to see a smile on Janet's face. Everyone in the funeral home are now talking of the miracle that was witnessed by many, and a few people that was close enough to the phone recorded the conversation on their cell phones.

Penny looks at James and says, "Our baby girl is safe, James. I can rest peacefully now and not be sad. Yes, I will miss her very much, but I know she is in heaven, and that gives me joy."

The time on the clock is eight forty-five, and the funeral director begins to ask family and friends to give privacy to Janet's immediate family. The people in the funeral home have been talking about the phone call from heaven nonstop since it happened, and everyone in the funeral home feels a holy sensation in their soul that can only be explained by divine intervention, and smiles are on all that were there that evening. James and Penny smile down at Janet as she is in the casket.

James says, "Sleep well in heaven, my baby girl." Then he leans over and kisses Janet on her cheek.

Penny smiles at James and says, "Our little girl is something else. She convinced Jesus Christ to let her call us." Then Penny leans over the casket and tells Janet, "You watch your manners in heaven and always be respectful," then kisses Janet on the cheek.

Jerry hugs his mom and says, "Will Janet be okay in here all alone?"

Penny hugs Jerry and says, "She will be just fine son. Now let's go home. We have a busy day tomorrow."

The next morning is beautiful. The weather is warm and sunny.

James is getting dressed for the funeral, and Penny is putting on her makeup and tells James, "You know I slept so good last night, and didn't even have to take a Valium."

James smiles at Penny and says, "I know I heard you snoring off and on last night and was so happy to see you sleep peacefully."

Penny finishes putting on her makeup and puts on her black dress with black two-inch-high heels. James walks in and stares at his beautiful wife then says, "Wow, sweetheart, you look great."

Penny looks at James in his tailor-made black suit and walks over to straighten his tie and says, "You clean up very well too, honey."

They give each other a long hug when Jerry is yelling down the hall, "Mom, Dad, you have to see this."

Jerry runs into the room holding his iPad and says, "It's gone viral. Look, Mom, someone took a video of the conversation of Janet calling from heaven and posted it on YouTube, and it has over two million views and more every minute."

James looks at the video and is shocked by the overwhelming views. Penny is equally shocked but disturbed that this private conservation is now being watched by people all over the world.

Penny says to James, "Well, so much for privacy, but in a way I'm glad that it's out there because people will know there is a heaven."

James smiles at Penny and holds her hand and says, "Yes, there is a heaven, and our little girl is there with Jesus. Glory to God."

Jerry says to his mom and dad, "Well, all I know now is we are all famous."

James looks at Jerry and says, "Son, this will be news for a few days, and then something else in the news will take its place."

Jerry gives a serious look at his dad and says, "I'm not sure about that, Dad, because how many times have you heard on the news that someone calls from heaven?"

Penny looks at James and says, "Jerry has a very good point."

James looks at both his son and Penny with compassion and says, "I know one thing that is certain. Our lives will forever be changed by that phone call, and all we can hope for is that we can handle the situations that we will encounter from all sorts of people."

Jerry laughs and says, "You're right, Dad. There will people claiming this is a hoax and others that will forever be changed by knowing there is a heaven and start living a Christian life to make sure their soul makes it to heaven."

Penny hugs Jerry and says, "Well said, my son, you are so smart."

Jerry says smiling at his parents, "I get all that intelligence from living with the best parents on this planet."

James rubs Jerry's shoulders and says, "Okay Professor let's get ready to go to the funeral home."

James is amazed at the cars that are parked on the side of the street that leads to the funeral home.

Penny says to James, "What is going on with all these cars parked everywhere."

Jerry says, "I told you, Mom, the news is out about Janet calling from heaven, and people from all over are curious. It's about to get real."

James says, "Yeah, real crazy, where am I supposed to park?"

A police officer is on the street and notices James's vehicle and was told by his superior officer to direct James to a parking space reserved for his car. James thanks the officer. James parks his car in the designated parking area and gets out of the car and asks the officer, "Where are all these cars coming from?"

The officer responds after scratching his head, "They are coming from all over, some as far as Florida and Colorado driving all night long."

Jerry looks at his mom and says, "It's already started, Mom, the curious and crazy people are here. God help us."

Penny tells Jerry, "We are here to bury your little sister's body and not to be part of some circus act. We will be on our best behavior, son, and not let all this attention upset us."

James says, "That's right, son, be nice."

CHAPTER FOURTEEN

The police officer introduces himself to James as Tommy Peterson and says, "I've been ordered to stay by your family during the entire funeral service to protect you all from any persons that may disturb any of your family."

James thanks the officer for his assistance, and the officer says, "I was told to take you all in a private entrance into the funeral home to bypass all the people that are standing around the property of the funeral home."

Penny says, "This is surreal. I hope we can bury our daughter in peace."

The officer stands to the side of the room as James, Penny, and Jerry walk next to the casket that has Janet in it. Penny has tears running down her beautiful face when Jerry grabs some tissues from a box that sits on a table near the chairs and gives his mom the tissues to wipe away her tears.

Penny says to Janet in a soft, loving voice, "My baby, my precious little girl, we're going to miss you laughing and running around the house. Oh my god, what are we going to do without you?"

James hugs his wife, who is shaking alongside of him, and says, "We will be strong for our little girl today, and thank God for the comfort of knowing Janet is in heaven. Remember that, my darling, by the grace of God we will be all right."

Jerry looks over at the police officer that is standing by the wall and sees the tears running down his face. Jerry grabs some more tissues and walks over to the officer and gives him some tissues.

The police officer thanks Jerry for the tissues and says, "I'm so sorry this has happened to your family."

Jerry looks at the police officer and says, "Thank you, sir, we are all so sad Janet has gone away but happy she has made it to heaven."

The officer says to Jerry that is the best news anyone could receive. The funeral director approaches James and Penny to let them know that he will be opening the door to let family and friends view Janet one last time in fifteen minutes.

James shakes hands with the funeral director and says, "Thank you, and we will be ready at that time."

The funeral director says to James and Penny, "I was just outside, and there are thousands of people waiting to come in. I have never seen this many people in thirty years of doing this. I will do my best to have the crowd of people moving along in line as quickly as possible to try to stay on schedule for the service."

James thanks Mr. Thomas and says, "We will get through this just fine."

The doors of the funeral home open, and the line of people waiting to go in reaches for over hundreds of yards. Many people, complete strangers that just want to see the body of the little girl that has called her family from heaven.

James is glad to have the help of the police officer to keep the line moving as quickly as possible. The funeral service is on schedule, thanks to the funeral director helping all the people to get in and out of the funeral home after passing the casket to view Janet.

The family now is at Janet's grave site. The casket is removed from the white hearse. The pastor says many words of comfort to James, Penny, and Jerry, but Penny is not paying attention to his words because she is only looking at the small casket that is directly in front of her chair. The pastor finishes his compassionate speech, and James helps Penny to the casket.

Penny is leaning on the casket like she is giving a hug to her little girl for the last time. Penny stands up straight and says loudly so that the people around can hear her clearly.

Penny says, "My little girl, Janet, is in the best place. We all could pray to go when we pass away. God bless all of you that has shared this special day with us." Penny rubs the casket.

James is on one side of Penny, and Jerry is on the other side of his mom, walking away from the grave site with tears coming down all of their faces. The family, friends, and complete strangers watch as Janet's family walks away, and most of these people had tears of sadness streaming down their faces. You could hear someone say "Please, God, give this family the strength to endure this loss and the courage to live another day with you, oh Lord."

James, Penny, and Jerry arrive home after the funeral services to find many letters of encouragement from people they have never met on the front steps next to the front door, and when reading some of these cards and letters, Jerry says to his mom, "There are a lot of people in this world going through the kind of the situation we are going through except…" There was a pause.

James looks at Jerry and says, "Except what, son?"

Jerry says, "Well, Dad, at least we know for sure our Janet is in heaven, but if you read these cards and letters from everyone that sent us mail, they are not sure if their friend or relative is in heaven."

Penny gives Jerry a hug and says with a smile, "I guess Janet was not going to give up bothering Jesus till she got her way."

Jerry starts laughing and says, "Yeah, Mom, Janet was very good at getting her way, especially down here on Earth."

They all laugh while walking through the front door of their home. The phone rings as the front door closes. James answers the phone, and the person on the phone is telling James that the donations are still adding up to many thousands of dollars for the children's hospital, and they would like to give an all-expense-paid dinner at the restaurant of his choice. James smiles while Penny and Jerry look at him talking on the phone.

James says to the man on the phone, "Thank you, and we'll call you back when we would like to go," and says goodbye.

Penny looks at James and says, "Who was that, sweetheart?"

James walks over to Penny, gives her a kiss, and says, "It seems that a lot of money is still being sent in to the children's hospital fund that we put in Janet's name, and they want to give us a free dinner anywhere, anytime, in appreciation of our kindness."

Jerry smiles and, while rubbing his stomach, says, "Let's eat somewhere fancy where the food is awesome."

Penny says, "Okay, son, but not now, maybe in a few days. I just want to rest now."

The next day Penny and Jerry are going through clothes in Janet's room, and in the closet Jerry finds a shoebox. Jerry gives the box to his mom. Penny opens the box and inside, the pictures of Jerry, Penny, James, and Janet. The photos are of times they went to amusement parks, water parks, and camping trips in the last few years. Penny looks on the back of the photos and reads what Janet wrote. One photo of them camping, Janet wrote "The best days of my life with the best family this side of heaven," and Penny struggles to hold back her emotion as a tear slowly runs down her cheek. Jerry shows a picture of Janet and him going down a waterslide and on the back Janet wrote "Having a great time with my big brother. I love him so much."

Jerry hands the picture to his mom and says, "I really miss my sister, Mommy. How are we going to do this?"

Penny says, "Do what, son?"

Jerry starts to cry and says, "Go on living without her. My heart is hurting so much, and I can't stop thinking about Janet being gone."

Penny wipes away Jerry's tears and says, "Son, we will take it day by day, and as long as we live, we will always remember your sister and the joy that she gave to us."

Penny puts the pictures back in the box and says to Jerry, "We have memories of videos and pictures of our family, and when we need to, we can enjoy looking at them to keep those times fresh in our heart. The pain of not having Janet around will be difficult for all of us, but time will pass, and hopefully the heartache of missing your sister will not hurt as it does now. We have to pray to Jesus to help give us strength to get through the sadness and be strong."

Jerry hugs his mom and says, "Mom, can we pray now because I really need that strength from Jesus right now.

Penny smiles at her son and says this prayer: "Heavenly Father, we pray to you now that you give us strength and courage to go through the heartache that my son and I are feeling now. We pray that you take away our grief and give us joy and peace as we try to live without Janet. We ask this in your son Jesus Christ's holy name."

Jerry says, "Amen."

Penny then asks Jerry, "How do you feel now, son?"

Jerry says, "I'm still sad, but it makes me feel better knowing God is with us, and with God all things are possible."

Penny hugs Jerry and says, "I love you."

Jerry says smiling, "I love you too, Mom."

A few days have passed since the funeral, and James is getting ready to go to work, drinking some fresh coffee in the kitchen with Penny when the phone rings. Penny answers the phone, and on the line is the TV news reporter Mary Hebert who interviewed them earlier before the funeral. Penny puts the phone on speaker so James can listen in on the conservation.

Penny asks, "Why are you calling us besides giving your condolences?"

Ms. Hebert begins telling Penny that the overwhelming response of the video of her daughter calling from heaven has gone worldwide.

James speaks up to cut off Ms. Hebert's next sentence and says, "What is it that you need from us, Ms. Hebert?"

Ms. Hebert is heard clearing her throat and says, "If you could give our TV station a short interview of how you all are doing with the excitement of the phone call from heaven, our viewers would be very interested in your thoughts, and before you, answer if you will allow us to do this interview in our TV station, we'll be happy to donate twenty thousand dollars in Janet's name to the children's hospital."

Penny speaks up and says, "We will think about this, and give you an answer tomorrow."

Ms. Hebert thanks Penny and James and says, "I'll wait for your call."

Penny puts the phone down and looks at James, who is scratching his head.

James says, "Let's look at the pros and cons of this interview."

Penny says, "Let's sit down on the sofa and discuss this with common sense. We know that the video has gone viral and millions of people have seen and are talking about our divine intervention with our daughter."

James says, "Yes," but Penny says, "No one knows how we feel about this experience."

Penny pauses for a few seconds then says, "We could tell anyone who watches this interview that we always believe in heaven, and now we are certain without any doubt there is a heaven."

James says, "Yes, we could, but do we want more attention brought to our family?"

Penny says, "The news of this happening to us will last for a week or two then will fade away. I believe this happened for a special reason, sweetheart, and I don't know, maybe this will bring millions of souls toward God. You know the Bible says God does work in mysterious ways."

James smiles at Penny and says, "Okay, we will do the interview if you are ready to tell our story."

Penny hugs James and says, "I know Janet would want us to tell this miracle."

The next day James calls the TV station, and an interview with Ms. Hebert is scheduled. Ms. Hebert has talked to the funeral director to ask if the interview can be done where the phone call from heaven actually happened. Mr. Thomas agrees to the request knowing that this would be great advertisement for his funeral home and gives them permission to use the room where the phone call was taken.

James, Penny, and Jerry meet Ms. Hebert and the cameraman for the TV news station at the funeral at four o'clock in the afternoon. Ms. Hebert walks into the room where James is standing looking nervous. Penny and Jerry are sitting at the desk where the phone is.

Ms. Hebert asks how everyone is doing, and everyone says "Fine" at the same time, and it sounded kind of funny. Ms. Hebert says, "I know you all are nervous, but this will be a short interview, so before we start, let's go over the questions I will be asking so that you will not be surprised, and be more comfortable when the real interview is being recorded."

James says to Ms. Hebert, "That's a good idea, because we don't know what you will ask us, and we don't know exactly what we will say."

Ms. Hebert says, "Great. Now let us position ourselves around this desk so the cameraman can easily have all of us in his viewfinder."

Ms. Hebert asks the cameraman, "How do we look?" and the cameraman says, "I have everyone looking great in my viewfinder, and we are ready for recording."

Ms. Hebert says, "Thank you. Now, everyone, let's just practice these questions while the camera is rolling. I have let y'all look at the questions and gave some time to collect your thoughts on how y'all will answer them. Are we ready?"

Penny, James, and Jerry all nod yes. Ms. Hebert counts down to the cameraman: "Three, two, one."

"Hello, this is Mary Hebert from Action News TV Three. We are sitting here in the very room where this family was only a few days ago attending the funeral of their beautiful little girl, Janet. It was here that they received a phone call, but not just a phone call from anywhere, but from heaven, and the person calling was none other than their daughter who passed away a few days earlier." Ms. Hebert introduces the family by saying, "This is the father, James, this the mother, Penny, and this is the brother Jerry of Janet who called from heaven."

Jerry waves at the camera and smiles and says, "I am the one that heard the phone ringing, so I answered it."

Ms. Hebert smiles at Jerry and says, "Okay, Jerry, let's start there. You were walking by, and what happened?"

Jerry sits up straight and looks directly at the camera and says, "I went to go get something to eat, and when I walked out of the room where the food is, I heard this phone ringing, and to me it had a special ringing noise. I can't describe it, but it had me listening to it, and I couldn't walk away."

Ms. Hebert looks at Jerry and says, "What happened next?"

Jerry says, "The phone wouldn't stop ringing. I looked around, and no one was walking by, so I took it upon myself to go into this office and answer the phone, and when I said hello, I heard the voice that sounded like my sister, Janet."

Penny looks at Jerry while he is telling his story and rubs his hand. Jerry continues by saying, "Hello, who would you like to talk to?"

Ms. Hebert then asks Jerry, "This is the phone that was ringing that day you answered it."

Jerry says, "Yes, that is the very phone."

Ms. Hebert says to Jerry, "Please continue what happened next."

Jerry says, "I heard the voice say 'It's your sister Janet and I want to talk to Mom and Dad,' and she then says go run and get them. I told her that it can't be you, Janet, you're in the casket in the other room, and besides, there are no phones in heaven." Jerry pauses for a few seconds and says, "This made Janet upset, and she told me I better go get Mom and Dad now because this phone call was long distance and she didn't have very long to talk."

Now Penny, James, Ms. Hebert, and even the cameraman start to laugh at how that sounded. Ms. Hebert asks Jerry, "So what happened next?"

Jerry says, "I told her to hold on and I'll be back, and I ran as fast as I could to where Mom and Dad were in the funeral home."

Ms. Hebert says, "Thank you, Jerry," and then looks at James and Penny and asks what happened next.

Penny speaks up first and says, "We saw Jerry running through the crowd of people as fast as he could, and he started telling his dad and me about a phone that was ringing by the restrooms and how it wouldn't stop ringing. James told Jerry to calm down and take a deep breath."

Penny continues, "Then Jerry tells us when he answered the phone, the voice on the phone sounded exactly like his sister, Janet." Penny looks at James for a second, smiles, and says, "I looked directly in Jerry's eyes and told him that it can't be Janet, and that's when Jerry told us that Janet said for him to tell us to hurry because it was long distance and she couldn't talk long."

Ms. Hebert looks at Penny and says, "That's kind of funny."

Penny says, "Yes, it is funny, but that's what my Janet would say so at that moment. I looked at my husband because we knew it was Janet, and we ran with Jerry back to this room and talked on this very phone with our daughter from heaven."

Ms. Hebert looks at James and asks what happened next.

James clears his throat and says, "I put the phone on speaker mode so we all could listen and be part of the conversation."

Penny then speaks up and says, "I asked Janet how she was doing and Janet responded that she was scared at first when she got to heaven, but Jesus told her that everything was going to be okay and not to be scared. Then I asked a question that only Janet would know about when we went fishing that one time, and Janet knew the answer about how big and what kind of fish it was that she caught."

Ms. Hebert says, "So you ask the person on the phone that question to confirm it was your daughter."

Penny says, "Yes, because she would be the only person that knew that."

Ms. Hebert asks Penny, "What did you feel when your daughter answered that question?"

Penny looks at Ms. Hebert, and tears begin to roll down her face. Penny smiles as she wipes her tears away. "I knew right then and there that my daughter was talking to me from heaven, and though I was astonished, I was very happy to hear my beautiful daughter talking to me."

James speaks up now after holding Penny's hand and says, "We ask Janet some questions on how this could be that you could call from heaven." James smiles. "That's when Janet told us that she kept bothering Jesus until he let her call us. She told Jesus that she didn't want her family to be worried about her while she was gone."

Jerry speaks up and says, "If you know my sister, then you know she always gets her way. I asked her if the streets in heaven were made of gold, and she told us that they were made of pure gold and everything in heaven was so beautiful."

Ms. Hebert asks James what happened next.

James smiles and looks at Penny and says, "Then Janet told us that Jesus asks Janet to tell us thank you for donating Janet's organs to the hospital so other people could use them to live a longer, healthier life."

Ms. Hebert looks at James and asks, "How did that make you feel?"

James says while looking directly into the camera, "We are all donors, and we knew Janet would be happy to help other people with her organs so that they could live."

James then says, "We are Christians, and that's what we believe all Christians should do."

Penny smiles and says, "Yes, and then Janet told us that she had to go because Jesus was calling her, and she told us not to worry because everyone in heaven is so nice and that she loves us, and the last thing she told us before we were disconnected was that she would be waiting for us when we arrived in heaven."

Ms. Hebert clears her throat and wipes a tear from her cheek as she thanks Penny, James, and Jerry for sharing those precious memories with her and all the people watching.

Then Ms. Hebert says, looking at the camera, "I am a believer, and God bless." Ms. Hebert then continues, "Reporting live from the room where the call from heaven was taken, I'm Mary Hebert from TV Three News."

The cameraman takes the camera off from recording mode, and Mary asks him to replay the interview, and after watching the interview, she says, "I believe that it went perfect." James and Penny agree that they were satisfied with the results.

Ms. Hebert says, "Well, I thank you all for doing such a wonderful interview. We will let you know when it goes on air at the TV news station."

James looks at Penny and says, "That wasn't as hard as I thought it would be."

Jerry looks at his dad with confidence and says, "Yeah, Dad, it was like we've done this before."

Penny laughs and says, "Now, Jerry, we are just some naturals in front of the camera."

The next morning the phone rings around eight o'clock, and James answers the phone with Ms. Hebert from the TV news station on the line.

James says, "Good morning, Ms. Hebert."

Ms. Hebert says, "I have some really good news."

James says, "Hold on a second while I get Penny so she can hear this good news."

James walks to the bedroom where Penny is making the bed and says, "Honey, Ms. Hebert, is on the phone and has some really good news. I will put the phone on speaker mode so we can listen together."

James tells Ms. Hebert, "Okay, we have you on speaker. What is the good news?"

Ms. Hebert says excitedly, "The new director at the TV news station loves the interview we did yesterday and will play it at the 5:00, 6:00, and 10:00 p.m. news program today, and the best news is that he talked to the ABC News program that airs nationwide at five-thirty in the evening, and they want to air it today."

Penny looks at James and is stunned by the news and says, "You mean the whole nation that watches ABC News will broadcast the interview today."

Ms. Hebert says, "Yes, and we added if anyone would like to donate to the children's hospital in Janet's name that all funds would be greatly appreciated."

James says to Penny, "That should bring in thousands of dollars. Thank you for that, Ms. Hebert."

Ms. Hebert says, "Thank you all for giving us such a heartwarming and uplifting interview. I have to say goodbye for now, but again, thank you."

Penny says "You're welcome" as James disconnects the call. Penny looks at James and says, "What have we done, sweetheart? We will get our fifteen minutes of fame now."

James hugs Penny and says, "Let's hope that's all it is and not fifteen years of fame. I want to go back to being regular people and not in the limelight."

Penny says, "Well, time will tell what will happen next in our lives."

The time on the clock in the living room is five-thirty in the evening, and James and Penny ask their parents over to watch the interview.

CHAPTER FIFTEEN

James is getting coffee for everyone while they all sit in front of the television waiting for the news to begin. Penny and James have already watched the local news with the interview with Ms. Hebert on it and were happy the way it looked on TV.

Penny's mom says to everyone that she can't wait to see the interview, and just as she says that, the anchorman for ABC News talks about a miracle of a family that received a phone call from their daughter, but not just any phone call; this phone call was from no other place than heaven.

"Watch and listen to the call itself as it went viral on the internet only hours after first being played, and then the heartwarming interview with the family of the little girl named Janet who called from heaven."

The news anchor said after watching the interview that he felt something different but didn't know what it could be that moved him in a compassionate sensation. The interview only lasted a few minutes, but everyone in the living room has tears rolling down their face.

Jerry says to his dad, "Wow, Dad, it seems like we were right there in the funeral home talking to Janet."

James hugs Jerry and says, "Yes, son, it did."

James's mom says, looking at everyone, "Was it just me, or did everyone feel like a sensation touch your soul?"

Penny's mom says, "You know, you're right. I felt something inside me like a jolt of electricity go through my body."

Penny says, "Me too. I wonder if everyone that watched the news segment receive that feeling." Penny asks if anyone wanted more coffee, and everyone says no and that they had to be going back to their homes. James walks everyone to the front door while Penny picks up the coffee cups. James's and Penny's parents both say to James, "If you all need anything, if you need to talk, don't hesitate to call."

James hugs the parents and says, "We will call if we need anything."

Penny walks to the front door to say goodbye as they are walking out of the house. James closes the front door and says, "Well, let's hope our lives return to normal soon."

Penny says, "Yes, I do too, but I believe it will take weeks before this story fades away."

Jerry tells his mom and dad that the phone call from heaven has over sixty million views and is growing faster since it was broadcast on the ABC evening news. Jerry shows the views on his iPad to show what that means.

Penny says, "This is crazy, I mean who would ever thought this would get this much publicity."

James hugs Penny after looking at Jerry's iPad and says, "Let's hope we can get some much-needed rest and remember our daughter in peace."

In a small town in east Texas, a man was watching the ABC News segment when he felt something strange go through the core of his soul. That man's name is Trent, almost sixty-two years old with a full head of hair, and it would be very gray if it was not for the just-for-men hair color he puts in it after every haircut.

Trent is six feet tall and weighs around 180 pounds. He is in good shape for his age. Trent has five children. The oldest is Jackie, a five-foot-nine-inch mother of three boys, all teenagers one year apart, the oldest being fifteen. Jackie is thirty-five years of age in great shape with long black hair and green eyes. Trent's second oldest daughter is Kelly, a mother of two beautiful daughters, ages twelve and eleven. Kelly is thirty-four years of age and also has short black hair with blue eyes and is five feet ten inches tall. Leslie is Trent's third to oldest daughter who is thirty-three years of age and has a son who is ten years old and a daughter who is nine years old. Leslie is five feet nine inches tall and in great shape. Leslie has brown shoulder-length hair with hazel eyes. Trent's fourth oldest child is a son named Micah. He is thirty-two years of age with two sons that are ages eleven and nine years old.

Micah is six feet three inches tall, has a muscular body, brown hair, and green eyes. Trent's youngest child is Noah, a thirty-one-year-old son who is six feet four inches tall and has a slim, muscular body frame. He has black hair with blue eyes. Noah has not been married and has no children. Trent is watching the ABC News when he gets a phone call from Jackie. Jackie is asking him if he saw the story on the news about the little girl that supposedly called her family from heaven.

Trent tells his daughter, "Yes, I did, and I believe it's true."

Jackie tells her father that she believes it is some fake news because no one has ever called from heaven. Trent tells Jackie that may be true, but there is always a first time for everything.

Jackie says, "I love you, Dad, but that story is just too hard to believe, and if you want to believe it is true, well, you go ahead. There are millions like you that believe it too."

Trent asks Jackie, "Is that the only reason you called me today?"

Jackie says, "No, Dad, I want to stop by around six-thirty this evening."

Trent says, "I'll be here, honey, see you then. I love you."

Jackie says, "I love you too, Daddy, goodbye."

Trent looks at a picture of his family and touches the picture of his beautiful wife, Rebecca, who he was married to for thirty-four years until breast cancer took her life a couple of years ago. Trent looks at the picture with a tear in his eye and says out loud, "I miss you so much, sweetheart. I wish you were here to enjoy my retirement years. I worked so hard to build this family business, and now at sixty-two years old I'm retiring and all alone with no one to share this time with. Yeah, I know I have my children and grandchildren and plenty of friends, but I wish I had my best friend with me. I wish I had my wife with me."

Trent puts the picture down and walks to the kitchen and starts making a pot of coffee. The coffee is brewing, and the smell of the coffee is strong in the air.

Trent says out loud, "That smells good."

The doorbell sounds from the front door as Trent is putting two cups on the kitchen table. Trent walks to the door and looks through the peephole and sees it is his daughter Jackie standing there. Trent opens the door, and Jackie walks inside the house, gives her dad a hug and a kiss on the cheek, smiling as she puts her purse down on the sofa that is only a few feet from the front door.

Trent closes the front door and says, "I have some coffee on. Would you care to have a cup with your old dad?"

Jackie smiles at him as he walks by her while walking to the kitchen and says, "Sure, Dad, it does smell good. I would like a cup with a teaspoon of sugar."

Trent pours two cups of coffee. Jackie sits down.

Trent says, "What's the real reason you came by this evening?"

Jackie starts to speak, "Well, Dad—" The doorbell sounds again.

Trent looks at Jackie and says, "Now who could that be at my front door? No one called and said they were stopping by."

Jackie sips her coffee and says, "I don't know who that could be, Dad."

Trent walks to the door and looks in the peephole and says, "Now what is she doing here without calling me first?" Trent opens the door, and his daughter Leslie walks in with some kind of papers in a folder.

Trent says, "Well, just come right on in, Leslie." He closes the front door as she walks into the house. Leslie walks straight to the kitchen while saying, "Man, that coffee smells good. Dad, may I fix me a cup?"

Trent says, "Sure, honey, help yourself." Trent looks a little curious while looking at Leslie pouring herself a cup of coffee and smiles at his two daughters. "Now what is going on, why are both of y'all really here?"

Jackie takes a sip of her coffee and clears her throat. "Man, that's some good coffee, Dad."

Trent says, "Yeah, right, now spill the beans, what do y'all need?"

Jackie says while smiling at her dad, "Now we all know you will be turning sixty-two next week, and you have been talking about retiring for many years, so all the kids have put in some money for you to take a birthday trip."

Trent looks at Jackie and Leslie and says, "Oh really, so my children want me take a trip for my retirement. Where y'all sending me, to a nursing home?"

Leslie laughs and almost chokes on her coffee and says, "No, Dad, you have a long time before we put you in the old folks' home." Leslie then opens the folder with papers in it and shows her dad. "We want you to take a cruise, a Caribbean seven-day cruise, all-inclusive free drinks. Everything is paid for. Just show up and relax."

Trent smiles and says, "You know, I knew y'all two were up to something. I just had a feeling."

Jackie says, "Well, will you go, Dad? It's in two weeks, and we know you will have a great time."

Trent looks at the brochure and smiles then says, "Really, how you know I will have a great time?"

Leslie puts her coffee cup down on the table and says, "Because, Dad, it's a singles cruise where mostly everyone on the ship will be single."

Trent stands up and says, "Wait a minute, now I don't know if I'm ready to mingle with singles."

Leslie says, "Dad, it's been two years since Mom passed away, and it's time you have some fun."

Jackie stands up and looks her dad in the eye and says, "Yes, Daddy, it's time. We were all there with you when Mom fought her hardest to beat breast cancer, and for two years you watched her fade away like we did, and God only knows how difficult it was to watch as you held her hand and she took her last breath. All of our hearts were broken watching that, and we miss her so much, but to see you go through that time it made all your children sad."

Trent looks at Jackie and gives her a hug.

Leslie stands up and says, "Wait a minute, now I want my hug too, Daddy. After all we all made this decision to give our dad a trip he will remember for a long time, and who knows, you might just meet someone special that will get your motor running again."

Trent laughs and says, "There is nothing wrong with my motor, sweetheart. It's just been in the garage for a few years."

Jackie laughs and says, "Well, it's time to start that bad boy up and see if it still has what it takes to get to the finish line."

Trent smiles and hugs both of his daughters and says, "I guess I'll have to show y'all the old man still has it."

Jackie says after she kisses her dad, "So you're going on this cruise, right?"

Trent smiles. "Yeah, I will go."

Leslie says, "Awesome, Dad, because we already paid for it, and it's nonrefundable—no, Dad, just kidding. We would only lose our deposit."

Jackie says, "Great, Dad, I'm so excited that you are going."

Trent says with a smile on his face, "Me too, Jackie, but I'm nervous."

Leslie says, "Dad, you will be just fine. They will have so many men and women on this beautiful ship. I know you will meet some good people like yourself and have a great time."

Trent smiles as the three of them walk toward the front door.

Trent opens the front door and hugs and kisses his two daughters and says, "Y'all be safe driving home."

Leslie says, "Now we have your birthday party planned for next Saturday, so don't make any plans."

Trent says, "I'm looking forward to it, honey, just let me know what time and place."

Leslie smiles and says, "I sure will, Dad. Now go look at the brochure I left on the kitchen table and research what this cruise is all about."

Trent says "I will" and "good night" and closes the front door as he hears his daughters giggling leaving his house.

Jackie is standing next to her car in her dad's driveway talking to her sister Leslie smiling and says, "Man, that went so easy. I thought we would have to beg Dad to go."

Leslie says with joy in her voice, "Yeah, you're right. I'm so happy now. It's like Dad really is going on that cruise. I wish I could go just to spy on him and see how he handles all the women that will try to hook up with him."

Jackie laughs and says, "Girl, you're so crazy, but yeah, I would like to be a fly on the wall too. I know one thing, he will be nervous, but after a few days, he will be all right."

Jackie gets into her car while saying to Leslie, "I'll call you later to discuss Dad's birthday party."

Leslie waves goodbye as she walks to her car and says, "Okay, that sounds good."

The two sisters drive away in different directions as they return to their homes about a mile away from their dad's home. Trent pours himself another cup of coffee then picks up the brochure of the cruise line and starts to read all the destinations that will be visited during the seven-day cruise."

Trent talks to himself out loud while reading the brochure and says, "Man, this is a nice-looking ship, and look at that swimming pool, swim-up bar. It's huge. I could see myself having a good drink and hopefully meeting a nice pretty lady."

CHAPTER SIXTEEN

Trent takes a drink of his coffee and turns the page of the brochure, and smiles as he views the picture of the room he will be staying in for six nights and says out loud, "Wow, what a nice room, and look at the view. I hope we have good weather for this cruise." Trent then turns the page and sees that the entertainment for the cruise will have the rock and roll bands REO Speedwagon and Loverboy playing in the huge lounge at night. Trent also reads that they will have a DJ playing some good dance music on the nights that rock and roll bands are not playing. Trent then reads that the food on the ship will have some famous chef known around the world.

Trent says out loud, "I never heard of this cook, but I hope he knows how to put some seasoning on his food," and laughs to himself. Trent puts the brochure down and takes his last drink of coffee and walks to the kitchen sink to wash his coffee cup when his cell phone rings. Trent reads the name on caller ID, and it's his youngest child calling. Trent answers the phone saying, "Hello, son. How are you doing, Noah?"

Noah says, "Hey, Dad, what's up."

Trent says, "I was just looking at this brochure of this cruise my children paid for."

Noah says, "Really, a cruise, well, what you think about that?"

Trent says, "I am really blown away about the whole thing, big boat, nice room with a view, big pool, and some awesome rock and roll bands playing."

Noah says, "Hey, Dad, don't forget all the food and drinks you can consume. I hope you know it's all-inclusive. Even the excursions off the ship are included so try to make as many as you can. They are all paid for."

Trent asks Noah, "What are you saying? You mean that riding horses on the beach and scuba diving is paid for?"

Noah says, "Yes, Dad, if it's on the list of what's offered, we all paid for it. All you have to do is sign up for it on the ship and go have an awesome time."

Trent says to Noah, "I don't what to say, son. I really appreciate all of y'all doing this for me. I really do. I just wish your mom was here to enjoy this cruise with me."

Noah says, "Listen, Dad, we all wish Mom was here, but it's been two years since Mom went to heaven, and really, Dad, you have to stop grieving and enjoy what life you have left," laughing through the phone. "You are not getting any younger, you old dog."

Trent says, "You are right, son, I'm not as young as I used to be."

Noah says, "And, Dad, who knows, you might find some lady as pretty as Mom on that ship."

Trent says, "I doubt that. I'll never find a woman as beautiful as your mom, but there's always someone that is almost as pretty as your mom."

Noah says to his dad, "I know that, Dad, but just enjoy the cruise and have a great time."

Trent says, "I'll try, son."

Noah says, "Okay, Dad, talk to you later, have a good night."

Trent says, "Good night, son," and puts his cell phone on the table and gets ready for bed.

The next day was Saturday, and Jackie has called Noah and asks if all the siblings could meet at his house to discuss their dad's birthday party. Noah tells Jackie that would be fine. Everyone can stop by around 1:00 p.m.

Noah opens his front door to find his three sisters at the front entrance and his older brother just a few steps behind. Noah welcomes them into his home, which is one of the nicest homes in his neighborhood. Noah asks everyone to join him in the backyard, which has a large in-ground pool with a separate hot tub, an outdoor kitchen and huge grill.

Micah comments to his brother, "Noah, you really got it going on. This backyard is awesome."

Noah says, "Thanks, brother. It's almost paid for, and then I'll be looking for someone to marry and share it with me. I worked hard for all this paradise."

Noah's sister Kelly walks up to Noah gives him a hug and says, "Yeah, when you don't have any kids, you can afford to have a backyard like this."

Noah says, "Now, Kelly, all of y'all have nice homes, and y'all are welcome here anytime. Just call before stopping by."

Kelly gives her brother a kiss on the cheek and says, "I'm glad you said that, baby brother, because us sisters would like to ask you if it's okay to have Dad's birthday party here in your backyard next Saturday."

Noah looks at his sister and older brother and says with a smile, "Well, of course you can, just as long as everyone helps me clean up after the party."

Jackie says, "Of course we will help, and if it is okay, we would like to rent a fun jump for the kids. I mean, Noah, your backyard is so big, there is plenty of room."

Noah says, "On one condition, everyone has to play on it."

Micah says, "I can handle having some fun. I'm not that old yet to jump on a big air-filled fun jump." They all laugh and say it will be a great party.

Noah says, "I can grill some burgers and hot dogs."

Micah says, "I'll get the chips and watermelons."

Kelly says, "I'll get paper plates and other stuff to eat with."

Leslie says, "I'll get the birthday cake and ice cream."

Jackie says, "I'll get the ice and all the adult beverages and cold drinks for all our kids."

Noah smiles and says, "Well, that sounds like a plan we all can agree on. Now let's hope for beautiful weather for next Saturday."

Kelly says, "What time is this party going to start?"

Micah says, "How about 1:00 p.m.? That will give everyone time to get things together."

Jackie says, "I'm good with that."

Everyone smiles and agrees with that suggestion.

Jackie says, "Well, let me call Dad now and see if he's available." Jackie calls her dad on her cell phone and puts it on speaker mode so everyone can hear the conversation with their dad.

Trent answers his phone.

Jackie says, "Hey, Dad, how you doing?"

Trent says, "Fine, how are you, Jackie?"

Jackie says, "I'm good, Dad. Hey, listen. I have you on speaker phone now, and all your children are listening."

Trent says, "Okay, what's up."

Kelly speaks up and says, "Dad, we are all here at Noah's home, and we have made plans for your birthday party for Saturday at 1:00 p.m. Can you be here at Noah's for that?"

Trent says, "Okay, so let me get this straight. My birthday party at Noah's house at 1:00 p.m. next Saturday."

Leslie says, "Yes, Dad, can you be here?"

Trent says, "Sure, I'll be there. Will all the grandkids be there?"

Micah says excitedly, "Of course, all your loved ones will be here."

Trent says, "What do you need me to bring to the party?"

Jackie says, "Nothing at all. We have all this worked out. Just be here for 1:00 p.m."

Trent says, "I'll be there, and hey, you guys, I love y'all so much for doing this for me."

All his children say at the same time, "We love you too, Daddy."

Jackie tells her siblings, "It sounds like Dad is feeling good about his birthday party."

Noah says, "Yeah, it sure does, and I talked to him last night on the phone, and he is excited about the cruise we paid for." Noah then looks at his brother Micah and smiles. "Dad is somewhat nervous about meeting some single women though." Noah walks around his in-ground pool. "I need to tell him that what he needs is to find some other male friend on the cruise that can be his wing man and help him navigate the waters of search and conquer the love connection."

Kelly laughs at Noah and says, "Like you navigate, you thirty-one years old and still not married."

Noah walks back to the group of siblings and says with a big smile on his face, "Only because I want to be. As soon as I become debt-free, I will find a woman and get married."

Leslie says, "Well, you better hurry, Noah, you are not getting any younger."

Micah says, "Yeah, brother, or any better looking." Everyone laughs.

Trent gets a phone call from one of his best friends, Willis, whom he went to high school with.

Willis asks, "How have you been, old man?"

Trent says, "I'm doing fine, and, you, what you been up to?"

Willis says, "Old buddy, I've been working on some birdhouses in my workshop, and I have four of them built, all painted up and ready to put up one in my yard tomorrow if you have time to help me."

Trent says, "Sure, I'll help you, my old friend, what time you want to do this?"

Willis says, "How about eight o'clock if that's not too early."

Trent says, "No, that's fine. I have been getting up early for years. Just because I'm retired now doesn't mean I lay in bed all day."

Willis says, "I know that, but you are getting old," with a laugh in his voice.

Trent says with a chuckle, "What you talking about, Willis?"

Willis says, "You know, Trent, after a million times you say that and it's getting kind of old."

Trent laughs and say, "What you talking about, Willis?"

Willis says, "Okay, I see you around eight in the morning. Don't be late."

Trent says, "I'll be there, and, Willis, will you have some fresh coffee ready when I get there?"

Willis says, "Sure, I will. Have a good night."

Trent says, "You have a good night too."

The next morning Trent arrives at Willis's home, and they are drinking some coffee. Willis shows Trent the birdhouses that he built in his workshop.

Trent says smiling, holding one of the birdhouses, "I'm very impressed on the details you put into the craftsmanship of these birdhouses."

Willis says, "I took my time, Trent, and I have to agree. They came out very well."

Trent says, "I would like to buy the rest of these three if they are for sale."

Willis says, smiling, "Which one you want at your house?"

Trent says, "This one here is super-nice."

Willis says, "That one is your birthday present. The other two I will sell to you for fifty dollars each."

Trent shakes Willis's hand and says, "You have a deal and thanks so much for this beautiful birdhouse you really have a talent for building these birdhouses."

Willis says, "Thanks, man, now let's go put this birdhouse up, and if you need help putting up the birdhouse I gave for your birthday, just call and I'll be there to help you."

Trent says, "You got a deal," while reaching in his wallet to take out a hundred dollar bill and gives it to Willis smiling. Willis thanks Trent as they start putting up the birdhouse, and after ten minutes, the birdhouse is fifteen feet high on a pole.

Willis stands back with Trent looking at the birdhouse and says, "It sure looks better up there than on the shelf of my workshop."

Trent says, smiling, "What you talking about, Willis?"

Willis laughs at Trent and says, "You'll never stop saying that, old man."

Trent says, "Nope, I'll be saying that in heaven."

Willis says, looking at Trent, "You know, Trent, I believe you will. Now how about another cup of coffee, my old friend."

Trent says, "That sounds good. I have some news I want tell you about."

Willis says, "Some good news, Trent."

Trent says, "Yeah, I believe so."

Willis and Trent are drinking some coffee in Willis's kitchen when Trent says, "You'll never guess what my children got me for a birthday present this year."

Willis takes a drink of coffee and then puts the cup down on the kitchen table. "Well, old boy, let me guess, a watch, a real nice watch."

Trent says, "They know I don't care to wear anything on my body. That's just not me even though I have a couple good watches."

Willis says, "Well, I don't know, you seem to have everything you need, a nice boat, truck, motorcycle, sports car. Tell me, what is it?"

Trent pulls the brochure out of his back pocket and shows it to Willis. Willis looks at the brochure and reads out loud, "Seven-day all-inclusive Caribbean cruise."

Willis smiles at Trent and says, "Wow, dude, that's so cool. Man, who you taking with you?"

Trent says, "That's just it, my friend. This is a singles cruise where you meet other people of the opposite sex and, well, you know, have fun. Maybe get to know someone nice, and who knows, maybe I'll find someone."

Willis interrupts Trent and says, "Yeah, you old dog, maybe hook up with some lonely, desperate person like yourself."

Trent smiles and says, "What you talking about, Willis? I'm not desperate, but I'm lonely, and it's been two years since Rebecca passed away."

Willis pats Trent on the back as he puts his empty cup in the sink and says, "Well, I know this will be an adventure, and I am glad for you. I was getting concerned for you, because it's time you get back into meeting some females. I know you have been grieving, but it's been a while, my friend. I tell you one thing, if I was single, I'd be happy to get on that ship and have an awesome time together to see what kind of trouble we could get into."

Trent puts his empty cup in the sink and tells Willis, "Yeah, we sure would have some fun, but I'll be all right."

Willis says, smiling, as they walk to the front door, "Yeah, my friend."

CHAPTER SEVENTEEN

Trent arrives back at his home and carefully takes the three bird-houses inside and puts them on a table near the living room. Trent then walks to his backyard and looks around where he decides a great spot to put the birdhouse and says to himself out loud, "That's the place right there where the pole will go to support the birdhouse."

Trent goes back into his house and looks at the birdhouse, and after admiring it for a few minutes and says out loud, "Man, that Willis can build a cool-looking place for some lucky birds to sleep in."

Trent passes his time watching TV for a few hours then walks out to check on his little garden he has planted in the backyard. That's his therapy, which helps with his grieving and being lonely. Trent talks to his tomato plants and cucumber plants, bragging how healthy they are looking, smiles to himself, and says out loud, "Y'all going to be delicious in a salad." Trent goes back into his house and studies the brochure of the cruise again to try to visualize the excursions that are being offered for the seven-day cruise. An hour passes. Trent puts down the brochure and gets ready for bed after taking a shower and getting dressed in pajamas.

Trent walks over to the side of his bed and kneels down on his knees and takes a picture of his wife Rebecca off the nightstand. Trent holds the picture close to his face and smiles as he looks into Rebecca's eyes. Then a tear falls down his face as he speaks out loud, "Oh, my beautiful Rebecca, how I miss your smile, your smell, and most of all holding you close."

Trent wipes away the tear from his face. Trent then puts the picture down and closes his eyes as he puts his hands together and says, "Heavenly Father, thank you for all your blessings you have given me, and please forgive me for any and all wrongdoings I have committed today, and, Lord, if I should die before I wake, I pray to God my soul you should take. Help me, Lord, to be a righteous man, and to live a Christian life. Please, Lord, watch over my family to keep them safe, and, Lord, give healing and peace to those that are suffering, dear God, that only you can give. I ask all these things, God, in your son's holy name, Jesus Christ."

Trent picks up the picture of his deceased wife, Rebecca, again and looks at the picture and says, "Good night, my love, my angel in heaven. I miss you so much, sweetheart, but the pain gets easier every day." Trent puts back the picture on the nightstand and stares at it for a few minutes then says, "Our children have bought me a cruise to go on for a week, and to tell the truth I'm nervous about this adventure." Trent clears his throat, fighting back another tear from his eye and says, "But before you passed away, you made me promise that I would try to find someone to live and love so I would not be lonely. It's been two years since I held a woman or even kissed a woman, and I guess it's time. I know our daughters have been pushing me for months to date someone."

Trent turns out the light and stares at the ceiling. "I guess it's time I try at least to see what God has in store for me. Only God knows what will happen. Good night, Rebecca. I love you, honey, and always will."

The days went by quickly, and before Trent knew it, Saturday morning was here. Trent was sitting in the kitchen looking out of the window admiring the birdhouse he put up a few days earlier when his cell phone rang. Trent answers the phone, and on the other end of the line is his daughter Kelly.

Trent says hello, and Kelly asks if her dad was going to be on time for his birthday party today. Trent laughs and tells Kelly that he would be there at Noah's home at one o'clock and not to worry, that his memory is still good even though he's retiring. Kelly laughs and says, "Dad, I know you are still smart, and your brain works fine, but your children just want to be sure what time you are going to show up."

Trent says to Kelly, "Listen, sweetheart, I'll be there on time, y'all don't worry about the old man."

Kelly says, "Okay, Dad, that's fine. I'll let everyone know you'll be on time, and, Dad, you are not an old man. In fact, Dad, you still look young for your age, and that's the truth."

Trent says, "Well, thank you, Kelly. That's makes me feel great. I'll see y'all at 1:00 p.m. Love you," and hangs up the phone after Kelly says, "I love you too, Dad."

Trent finishes his cup of coffee and goes back to his room to change his clothes for his birthday party, which will be starting in just a few hours.

It's eleven o'clock, and all of Trent's children are showing up at Noah's home with gifts for their dad. The grandchildren are there also, and everyone is looking at the huge air-inflated slide that is being set up in Noah's huge backyard.

Kelly tells Jackie, "Wow, that whatever you call it is tall."

Jackie says, "It should be. It's the biggest inflatable water slide they have. It's forty feet tall, and we all going to have fun on it today."

Leslie says to Jackie, "You really believe Dad is going to climb up that thing and slide down into that pool at the bottom."

Micah says, smiling at everyone standing around the slide, "Heck, I bet Dad will not hesitate once he sees all his grandchildren having a blast sliding down into the water. The thing is how we get him to stop, that's the real issue."

Everyone is laughing when Micah finishes his statement. The two men that set up the inflatable slide are just putting the last heavy weights around the bottom of the slide that make sure if a high wind would blow it would not move and stay secured at the slide's original position. Noah and Micah walk over to inspect the weights, and one of the men says, "I promise, this inflatable slide and pool will be safe and secured."

Noah agrees and says, "If we have any problems, we will call you, but it seems everything looks good."

The man's name is Phillip, and he tells Noah, "I am the owner of this inflatable slide, and we have six more inflatable slides and fun jumps, but this is the biggest one we have, and if you have any problems, call me and I'll be right over."

Noah shakes hands with the owner and his helper and says, "Thanks, and I'll call you around six o'clock to let you know it's okay to dismantle the slide and remove it."

Phillip smiles at Noah and Micah and says, "Y'all have a great time, and I'll be waiting for your call. Goodbye."

The two men walk away with a few tools in hand and wave goodbye to everyone while some of the grandchildren say "Thank you" and wave goodbye. The children ask their parents if it was okay to go swimming in the pool, and they all agree that since it is so hot that would be fine. Noah tells the kids when the slide's pool area is full of water they can start having fun sliding down the tall slide into the water. The children all are excited when they hear that news and scream in joy, "Thanks, Uncle Noah we love you."

Noah smiles and yells back, "I love y'all too. Now be safe in the pool."

The three sisters—Jackie, Kelly, and Leslie—are putting tablecloths on the three long tables that are set up end to end under the covered patio while Noah is getting the grill ready to cook some burgers and hot dogs.

Leslie opens a box with party supplies and asks Micah if he and his wife can start blowing up balloons while Kelly's and Jackie's husbands put a long banner that reads "Happy birthday, Dad" on the wall next to the tables. Everyone is talking about how good everything looks while putting up balloons and other party supplies.

Leslie says when all the decorations are finished being put up, "Wow, gang, we did it. Y'all did an awesome job, and it didn't take long with all of us helping. Thanks so much."

Everyone stands back and admires the job they accomplished. They smile at each other and say, "Yeah, it does look pretty good." Everyone gives high-fives to each other.

Kelly starts taking a few pictures of the patio all decked out with the many colored balloons and says, "I know Dad will be surprised to see all this."

Jackie's cell phone rings as she is putting snacks and chips on the table. Leslie wants to know who Jackie is talking to, so she gives the sign language of "Who is it on the phone?"

Jackie in turn says, "Oh, hello, Uncle Danny, how are you?"

Jackie then says, "Are you still coming to my dad's birthday party?"

Jackie smiles and says, "That's great. We will see you then."

Leslie says, "Tell me, girl, what's up, is Uncle Danny going to make it here today?"

Jackie says, "Yes, he will. He's running a little behind schedule because of an accident on Interstate 10, but he says they are on their way."

Leslie says, "Wait a minute, they, who is they, who is Uncle Danny bringing? Woman, you better tell your sister what's going on with our uncle Danny, because you know he's our favorite uncle."

Kelly steps up to the two sisters after hearing some of the conversation and says, "Girl, you are crazy, that's our only uncle, but you are right. He is our favorite uncle."

Kelly says, "Speak up, Jackie, what's happening with Uncle Danny?"

Jackie says, "Uncle Danny told me he met a woman through a friend of a friend and has been on several dates with her."

Kelly says to Jackie, "Well, Jackie, what else did Uncle Danny say about this woman?"

Jackie says to Leslie and Kelly, who now are all ears, "Well, he did say she was a schoolteacher. She teaches in Lafayette."

CHAPTER EIGHTEEN

The time is almost 1:00 p.m., and the doorbell rings.

Noah tells everyone after looking at his watch, "Hey, listen. That has to be Dad. Everyone get ready to say 'Happy birthday' when we walk through the patio doors."

All of Trent's children and their children gather around to the side of the patio doors just out of sight and wait for Trent to walk through the doors with Noah.

Noah opens the front door and smiles at his dad and says, "Hey, Dad, you are right on time, come on in."

Trent looks around and sees no one and says, "Noah, where is everyone at? I could smell the BBQ from the front yard."

Noah shakes his dad's hand and says, "Happy birthday, you old light bulb."

Trent says, "Yeah, I'm sixty-two, but I'm still shining bright, son."

Noah laughs. "Yeah, you're right, pop. Hey, let's go to the backyard. I'm just finishing up all the food on the BBQ pit."

Noah lets his dad walk through the patio doors first, and everyone screams "Happy birthday!"

Trent looks around at all the decorations and smiles from ear to ear. Kelly is trying her best to take pictures of her dad's expressions. All the grandchildren run to their grandfather and say "Happy birthday, Grampsy, are you surprised?"

Trent looks around and sees all the work it took to make Noah's backyard look like Disney World with balloons, a huge inflatable water slide, and all the other banners that read "Happy birthday, Dad," and "We love you, Grampsy." Trent is smiling, but then a tear starts to fall down from his eyes. Jackie walks over to hug her dad with her sisters close behind.

Jackie says, "Now, Dad, this is a happy day, no tears today."

Kelly and Leslie says, "Yes, Dad, no tears today. We are going to have fun."

Trent says, "I'm not sad. These are tears of joy. I am so blessed to have the most loving children that a father could hope for. I love every one of you. I really do, and thanks each and every one of y'all for doing all this work for me."

Kelly gives her dad a kiss on his cheek and says smiling while wiping some of her own tears away, "Dad, you are the best, and it's us that are blessed to have a dad like you to love us." Trent looks around the patio and notices on a table by itself many presents stacked high with colorful gift-wrapping paper and beautiful bows.

Trent walks over and says, "Wow, that's a lot of presents, why did y'all get so many? Y'all already bought me a cruise."

Micah walks over to his dad and shakes his hand and smiles and says, "Happy birthday, Dad. Listen, we got the cruise for you, but your grandchildren bought these gifts for you, so after we eat, we will let each grandchild give you the present they bought for you. Us parents have no clue what they bought, so we will be surprised like you will be when you open up the presents."

Trent says "Wow" after looking at all the presents again.

Kelly says, "Dad, they used their own money to buy the gifts for you, so we know the gifts will be coming from them."

Trent says, "Well, let's eat. I could eat a horse."

Noah is taking the last of the burgers off the grill when Trent walks over smiling at his son and says, "Son, I really like your home."

Noah says thanks, smiling back at his dad while walking back toward the tables to put down the plate of burgers on the table.

Trent says, "Son, I am very proud of you," and hugs Noah. "You have worked hard with the business I started, and it has really paid off. You have a beautiful yard, pool, and a big house."

Noah speaks up quickly and smiles, "Dad, I know what you are going to say before you say it."

Trent smiles. "Yeah, what am I going to say next?"

Noah looks at his dad straight in the eye. "All I need now is a woman."

Trent laughs and says, "Yeah, you right, that's exactly what I was going to say."

Noah says, "You know your daughters have been trying to fix me up with a woman for years now, and when I find the right one, I'll know it, so till then I'll keep looking."

Trent says, "That is fair to say. Now let's get everyone together to eat."

Jackie's cell phone beeps, and she reads the message from her uncle Danny, which reads, "Arriving now, will be ringing doorbell soon."

Trent was telling all his grandchildren to join him by the outside sink to wash their hands before eating lunch, so all the kids got in line and took turns washing and drying their hands when the doorbell rang.

Jackie says to Noah, "I'll go see who it is."

Noah says, "Okay, sis, you do that."

Trent looks at Noah and says, "Are you expecting anyone else? I thought you said this was only family today."

Noah says back to his dad in a serious tone, "Yeah, Dad, only family today. It must be a delivery man or something."

Jackie walks to the front door and opens the door to see her uncle Danny standing there with a large box wrapped in gift paper. Standing next to him is a tall brunette, slender in shape, with brown eyes.

Jackie says, "Hello, please come in," and gives her uncle Danny a hug.

Danny says, "Hey, Jackie, you are looking as pretty as ever. Let me introduce you to my girlfriend, Lisa."

Jackie gives Lisa a hug and says, "Welcome, Lisa, so nice to meet you. Please come in and follow me. Everyone is at the back patio."

Lisa smiles and says, "Thank you, Jackie, it's very nice to meet you. Your uncle Danny has been telling me some nice things about his brother's children and their children."

Jackie continues to walk back to the patio through the house as Lisa admires the interior rooms. Lisa comments on the decor, saying, "Your brother Noah has very good interior-decorating skills."

Jackie stops in midstride and turns to look at Lisa and says, "Well, Lisa, he has been in many homes while working as a master electrician. He has found what he likes, and you are right. Noah does have a good sense of decorating."

Uncle Danny is following the two women, not saying a word until he walks through the patio doors. Danny sees everyone and says loudly, "Hey, my loved ones, Uncle Danny is here."

Everyone turns to see Uncle Danny, and smiles appear on everyone's face. Trent is surprised to see his only sibling there and walks quickly to him to take the present from him and set it gently on the floor.

Trent looks at his brother and says smiling, "Wow, brother, it's awesome to see you."

Trent and Danny give each other a big hug for at least ten seconds. Danny looks at Trent after the big bear hug and says, "Yeah, bro, great to see you too. I got a call from Jackie about your birthday slash retirement party, and well, here I am."

Trent smiles with joy in his heart and says, "Man, I'm so happy to see you. It's been at least eighteen months since I've seen you."

Danny says, "Yeah, I know, since Jennifer's funeral."

Trent asks with a compassionate voice, "How are you doing?"

Danny says, "I'm taking it day by day, and by the way, how are you doing? I know you've been dealing with Rebecca's passing too."

Trent says with a serious tone, "It's been tough, Danny, but time has a way of letting the heartache and grief slowly diminish, but I miss her so much, especially on a day like today, but hey, enough of this sad talk. It's great to see you."

Trent walks over to Lisa and smiles and says to Lisa, "Now what might your name be, and how did you hook up with my brother?"

Danny walks over to Lisa and takes hold of her hand and says, "Everyone, I'd like to introduce my girlfriend, Lisa. We met through mutual friends. She is a sixth-grade teacher at a private school in Lafayette, and please, everyone, be nice to her."

Kelly smiles at her uncle Danny and says, "We will, Uncle Danny. She is so pretty."

Leslie speaks up and says with a sexy voice, "Yeah, Uncle Danny, very pretty and young for your age."

Danny says, "Well, she is beautiful, but believe it or not, she has two grown children, and a grandchild that's three years old."

Jackie looks at Lisa and says, "That's hard to believe, Uncle Danny, but hey, Lisa, whatever you are doing to look so young, me and my sisters want to know the secret."

Lisa smiles at everyone and says, "Thank all of y'all for the compliments, and I'll let you know my secret for looking young after we eat. I'm starving." Everyone laughs.

Trent says with a loud voice, "Yeah, let's eat. All this good food is getting cold."

And with that everyone finds a seat at the table. Trent asks Noah to say grace over the food because it's his home. Noah begins by saying, "Heavenly Father, we thank you for the food you have blessed us with today. Lord, watch over everyone and keep them safe in Jesus's name we pray." Everyone says "Amen."

"Now dig in, everyone."

After about ten minutes, everyone had their fill of burgers, potato salad, garden salad, and chips of all kinds.

Micah stands up and asks to have everyone's attention. "I would like to say a few words to the man of the hour, to our father. A man I've looked up to since I was old enough to be taller than him." Everyone laughs at that remark.

Micah smiles and says, "No, seriously, I am taller than him, but really I love my father. Not because he gave me a job with his electrical business right out of high school, but like all my siblings would say loud and proud, because he is everything a father is supposed to be. He is loving, caring, kind, and an awesome dad." Everyone looks at Micah and smiles.

Trent says, "Wow, that is a good toast, son. I love all of y'all." Then Trent laughs and says, "Can I open my birthday gifts now?"

Everyone laughs, and the nine grandchildren line up with each one carrying the present they purchased for Trent, their grandfather.

The youngest gives his present first with the oldest grandchild giving his present last. The presents were all different. One was a powerful flashlight that look like a key chain; a pair of tennis shoes; one was a big book to read; one was a couple of silk ties; one was some tools, and so on—great gifts. Trent opens each gift and hugs his grandchild, thanking them by saying, "Thank you for taking the time to buy these wonderful gifts."

Each grandchild smiles at their grandfather and says, "You're welcome, Grampsy, I love you," and gives their grandfather a kiss on the cheek. The parents are smiling at this abundance of love, and they feel the compassion at that moment. Kelly is filming the whole thing on her cell phone.

Jackie says, "Kelly, we have to make copies of this on a DVD."

Kelly smiles at Jackie and says, "I got this, sister, and we will all get copies." Kelly continues to film.

Danny picks up his gift from the table and hands it to Trent and says, "I hope you enjoy the present, my brother."

Trent opens the gift, and to his surprise the gift is three books and a bottle of Crown Royal whiskey. The first book title is How to Retire and Be Happy, the second book is How to Drink and Not Get Drunk, and the third book title is How to Find a Good Woman When You Are Over Sixty. Trent laughs, as does everyone else, at the gifts Danny gave to his brother.

Trent smiles and says, "Looks like I have some important reading to do."

Trent thanks everyone for a terrific birthday party and says, "Now I don't know about anyone else, but I'm going change into some swim trunks, and go have some fun on that huge inflatable fun water slide."

All the grandchildren yell, "Yeah, Grampsy, let's go."

The next couple of hours everyone took their turn climbing up the stairs of the slide and sliding down to the pool of water at the bottom. Trent is the first to say after a few hours, "I'm getting tired of climbing forty feet up, believe I'll go change out of this swimsuit into my dry clothes."

Danny looks at Lisa and says, "Yeah, that sounds like a good idea."

Lisa and Danny change clothes, and after a few minutes, they are back on the patio sitting down watching the kids playing with their parents on the water slide and pool. Trent is busy making some coffee and asks Danny and Lisa if they would like a cup of coffee.

Danny says, "I'll take a cup."

Lisa smiles at Danny and says, "Trent, I'll take a cup with a teaspoon of sugar please."

When the coffee finish brewing, Trent pours three cups of coffee, and they all sit down and drink the coffee. Lisa smiles after taking a sip of coffee and says, "Boy, that hits the spot. I need some caffeine after all that climbing, but it was fun though."

Danny says, "Yeah, I believe we all will be sore tomorrow after that workout."

Trent laughs and says, "Well, my brother, that's what they make Aleve for."

Danny takes a sip of his coffee and says, "Man, that's some good coffee," then looks at Trent and says, "Jackie tells me they all got together and paid for a seven-day Caribbean cruise for your birthday."

Trent looks at Danny then smiles and says, "Yes, they did." Trent then puts down his cup of coffee and looks at Danny and says, "Yeah, but did they tell you it was a single-and-mingle cruise?"

Danny laughs and says, "Yes, they did and says it's time you get back on the horse and enjoy life with a good woman." Danny looks at Lisa and smiles.

He says, "I'm so happy I listened to my kids, Trent. I didn't want to find anyone else after Jennifer died in that car accident. I grieved for a year, and my kids told me I had to enjoy my life. They were right. Meeting Lisa was the best thing that could have happened to me."

Danny looks at Lisa, takes her hand, and smiles. "I miss my wife, but she has passed on like Rebecca. I tell you, Trent. I feel better now that I have a woman like Lisa in my life, and I know, Trent, if and when you have God bless you with a good woman, you will be feeling like I do, blessed by God."

Lisa looks at Danny and smiles. Then Lisa leans over to give Danny a kiss on the lips and says, "Trent, your brother is right. I lost my husband to cancer a few years ago. Since I met your brother, my whole outlook on life has changed for the better. I'm so happy."

Danny says smiling at Trent, "We are happy, brother, and you can be too."

Trent smiles at Lisa and Danny and says, "Well, anyone with two eyes can see that. I know this. My daughters have been trying to get me to go on these blind dates for over a year now, but I've been too busy with my electrical business to have time for that, but now I'm retired. I guess I can try to find time to date. I leave a week from today to get on that cruise ship in Galveston. I tell you, Danny. I am very nervous about meeting strangers. It's been a long time since I've talked to women in a romantic way."

Danny laughs and says, "Listen, Trent, sometimes we all get nervous, but just act like the woman you find attractive on that ship is a potential customer like in your electrical business, and act like it's a house call. Be nice, treat her with respect, and hopefully she will like you enough to trust you."

Lisa smiles at Danny and says, "Wow, is that how it works?"

Danny looks at Lisa and says with a look of joy in his eyes, "Sweetheart, I believe you respect me as much as I respect you, and that's how a relationship begins with a man and a woman."

Trent takes out his cell phone and says, "Let me take a picture of y'all because I think you two make a cute couple." Danny and Lisa pose for Trent as he captures the love in their eyes.

Trent thanks the lovebirds and says, "Now I'm going take some video of my kids and their kids on that big water slide."

An hour passed by quickly, and all the kids are tired just like their parents are. Everyone goes inside to change into dry clothes after everyone helps clean up all the decorations and get the patio back in order. Noah is thanking everyone for the help and saying goodbye to all the family. Trent picks up his presents and brings them to his car with Danny's and Lisa's help. Trent closes the trunk after putting the gifts gently in. Trent thanks Danny and Lisa for the help and gives each of them a hug.

CHAPTER NINETEEN

Danny looks at Trent and tells him in a relaxed tone, "Hey, brother, try to have fun on this cruise, and remember, love will find you."

Trent responds, "Yeah, that's what I'm scared of."

Lisa says, "Don't be scared. It's beautiful, very beautiful."

Trent says, "I remember what beautiful love used to feel like."

Danny smiles at Trent and says, "Hey, brother, don't fall overboard. There are plenty of hungry sharks in those waters."

Trent tells his brother, "I'll do my best to stay on the ship," and laughs then says, "I don't want to be any shark bait, that's for sure."

The grandchildren and their parents go outside to say their goodbyes to Trent. Trent hugs and kisses each and every one of his grandchildren and their parents.

Everyone wishes Trent a safe voyage and hopes he has a lot of fun. Trent tells his children, "I'll check in every morning with y'all at 7:00 a.m. to let y'all know what I have planned to do that day and let y'all know where I'm at."

Kelly smiles and says, "You be sure to do that, Dad. We want to make sure you are okay."

Noah speaks up loudly and says, "Yeah, Dad, let us know if you found a girlfriend on the love boat." That statement causes everyone to laugh.

Jackie says with a big grin on her face, "Oh, our dad will have to beat all them single women off of him with a golf club."

Leslie smiles and says, "Oh yes, Dad will have too many women after him."

Trent looks at his daughters, smiles, and says, "I'll be happy with just one woman with a good sense of humor and good-smelling breath." That makes everyone laugh.

Trent says goodbye as he gets in his car then drives away while waving his arm out of the car window. Everyone waves at Trent. Then everyone gives hugs to each other and thank Noah for the use of his home for the party.

Noah smiles at all of them and says, "I want to thank every single one of y'all for helping with the cleaning up of my patio. It looks great. Now y'all have a safe trip home."

The days pass by slowly for Trent as he is now retired from the company he created and established for thirty-five years. Trent knows that his sons and daughters along with their husbands will continue the electrical business without any problems because of the hard work and dedication they all have proven for many years. Trent could have stayed on as CEO but finds it is time to take it easy and enjoy what years he has left on planet Earth. Trent has been looking forward to retirement, but he always wishes it would be with his soul mate Rebecca. It's Friday morning, and Trent's cell phone rings.

It's Noah calling, and Noah says, "Hey, Dad, how are you doing this morning?"

Trent looks out of the kitchen window at his birdhouse he received from his good friend Willis and responds in a voice of slight anxiety, "I guess I'm doing all right, son. How are you today?"

Noah senses the nervousness in his dad's voice and tries to make him laugh by telling a joke, which does make his dad laugh. Noah asks his dad, "Are you all packed up for the cruise?"

Trent says with some excitement now in his voice, "Yeah, son, I finished packing last night, and I double-checked to make sure I have almost everything I need for the cruise."

Noah speaks with some excitement now, too, and says, "Well, this time tomorrow you'll be on a vacation of a lifetime. I've check the weather for the cruise, and for the most part, the weather should be smooth sailing."

Trent responds by saying, "Sounds like you are on top of things this morning, son."

Noah says, "Yeah, I just want you to have the best time you can, Dad. Dad I'm going to call you at 5:00 a.m. tomorrow morning, and be at your home at 6:00 a.m. to pick you up."

Trent says with anticipation in his voice, "I'll be up and ready to go. I already have a few clock alarms set so I get up on time for the trip to Galveston where the cruise ship is docked."

Noah says, "Okay then, I'll call you at 5:00 a.m., and Dad?"

Trent says, "Yeah, son."

"You're going to have fun. Just relax."

Trent says with some calmness in his voice, "I'll do my best."

Then they say goodbye. Trent puts down his cell phone for just a few seconds, and the phone rings again, but it's a different ringtone. Trent knows it by memory. It's his good friend Willis. Trent answers the call in a cheerful voice and says, "Hey, Willis, good morning, how are you?"

Willis answers back in an equally cheerful voice, "Hey, my friend, it's getting real close to party time on the love boat. You nervous?"

Trent says to Willis with a tone of apprehensiveness, "I'm a little nervous, buddy. I mean this is the first time I'm going anywhere without Rebecca."

Willis says with a reassuring voice to Trent, "Listen, old man, everyone on that ship is going to be nervous. After a few hours on board, and a few drinks of whiskey, you will start enjoying the cruise. You have to know whiskey makes us all frisky."

Trent tells Willis in a laughing voice, "Yeah, I know, that's right. Hey, Willis, that birdhouse you built for me already has some birds flying to it, and it seems they are right at home in it."

Willis says in a confident tone, "Well, Trent, I did put some bird-attracting paint on that birdhouse."

Trent says loudly, "What you talking about, Willis? There's no such paint that attracts birds. You must think I'm stupid."

Willis laughs over the phone. "You're right, Trent. There is no such paint. I guess the birds just like the birdhouse."

Trent says laughing back, "Yeah, you're right. Hey, thanks for calling, Willis. I'll call you from the ship a few times and let you know how things are going."

Willis says, "Yeah, you do that, and try to stay positive, and be safe, my friend."

Trent says, "I'll do my best," and says goodbye.

Trent puts the cell phone down and sits down on his easy chair, turns on the TV, and watches the weather channel to get information on the weather conditions for the upcoming cruise. It was just like Noah said earlier, smooth sailing for the most part of the trip. Trent is relieved that the weather will be favorable for this vacation on the water. He turns the channel on the TV and watches a few episodes of Judge Judy and relaxes, sitting on his easy chair.

The cell phone rings, and Trent answers the phone. The voice he hears is Leslie, who is asking questions like a detective in a robbery investigation. Leslie wants to know if he has his passport and other important ID documentation. Trent answers very politely that all his information is stored in a sealed pouch and will be easy to find when needed. Trent also tells Leslie that he is all packed and will be waiting for Noah to pick him up first thing in the morning to bring him to Galveston.

Leslie says, "That's great, Dad. I just want you to have a good time, not to overdo it, and relax."

Trent says to Leslie in a calm voice, "What do you mean not overdo it?"

Leslie says in a tender voice, "You know, Dad, you always go out of your way to help people you don't even know. Most of the time you get in over your head, and that's when the drama starts."

Trent tells Leslie in a loving, compassionate voice, "I'm sorry, sweetheart, but I've been like that my whole life. I will try to relax on this cruise, and have fun."

Leslie says in a more relaxed voice after hearing her dad say that, "I'm so happy to hear that. Just be safe. I love you so much, Dad. Dad, take a lot of pictures so we can kind of experience what kind of fun you will be having."

Trent says to Leslie with a voice of uncertainty, "Now, honey, you know your dad is not much on taking pictures, but I will take a few at the different places I travel to."

Leslie tells her dad with excitement in her voice now to have a great time. "Be sure to call every morning to let us know you are okay."

Trent tells Leslie, "I sure will, honey, like clockwork every morning at seven. I have already told that to your brother Noah since he gets up early every morning. Then you and your other sisters and brother can check in with Noah to see how my vacation is going."

Leslie says, "Okay, Dad, just try to call me sometimes while on your cruise. I'm anxious to hear how you are doing."

Trent laughs on the phone and says, "Yeah, Leslie, I know what you want to know. You want to know if I found a woman, and if she gets my motor running."

Leslie says in a voice of embarrassment, "Dad, you are being silly. Just call me please."

Trent tells his daughter in a reassuring tone, "Don't worry, I'll call you, and I love you too, my beautiful daughter. Now have a good day, and we will talk very soon."

Leslie says, "Okay, Dad, I love you, have a good night, goodbye."

After eating supper, Trent cleans up the kitchen and puts the dishes away. Trent goes into the bedroom and picks up a large suitcase, which he rolls to the living room. He puts the suitcase next to the front door. Trent has put a bright orange sticker near the handle of the suitcase that will make it very easy to identify when mixed with hundreds of other suitcases on board the ship.

Trent says out loud, "I should be able to find my suitcase very easily." Then he laughs. "Unless everyone puts a bright orange sticker like I did."

Trent then goes to bathroom and takes a shower. Trent has finished with his shower and has put on some shorts and a white T-shirt. Trent goes to check all the doors to make sure all the doors are locked like he always does every night before going to bed. Trent goes into his bedroom and kneels by his bed to say his prayers.

Trent begins to pray. "Dear Lord, my heavenly Father, watch over my family and all my friends so they may be safe while they sleep. Lord, I pray that you watch over Noah after he drops me off at the cruise ship tomorrow that he has a safe trip home." Trent looks at the picture of his wife on the nightstand next to his bed. "Lord, I pray, keep me safe on this trip I'm taking, and if it's your will I meet a woman, Lord, I pray she is as good of a woman as the first woman you blessed me with. I ask all these things in your son's holy name. Amen."

Trent kisses the picture of his wife Rebecca then says, "Good night, sweetheart."

Trent turns out the light and lays his head on the pillow and drifts off to sleep. While Trent was sleeping, he has a dream, and the dream was so real to Trent that he wakes up talking. Trent sits up in his bed and looks around his bedroom. He says out loud in a voice of disbelief, "Wow, now that's a crazy dream." Trent gets out of bed and walks to his bathroom to get a drink of water.

Trent returns to his bedroom, looks out his bedroom window, and says out loud to himself, "Man, I wish this trip was already over. I'm nervous. I hope that dream doesn't happen. We don't need a fire on a big boat."

CHAPTER TWENTY

The alarm clock goes off at 4:45 a.m. Trent rubs his eyes. He sits up in bed and looks around and says to himself, "Thank God I didn't have another nightmare after falling back to sleep." Trent's phone rings, and he knows it is Noah from the ringtone."

Trent says in a cheerful but sleepy voice, "Good morning, son, I'm up."

Noah says to his dad, "Glad to hear that, Dad. I'll be on my way in about fifteen minutes. I'll call you again ten minutes before I get in your driveway."

Trent says, "Okay, son, I'll be ready when you get here. Be safe."

Trent turns off the backup alarm he had set before it rings. He goes to the bathroom to shave then after washing his face looks in the mirror.

Trent says with a smile on his face, "Okay, we got this, dude. Be positive, and all will be well."

Trent gets dressed in some nice dress shorts and a comfortable shirt with the tennis shoes his grandson gave as a birthday gift. Trent receives his second call from Noah letting him know that he will arrive in ten minutes. Trent starts to go around the house, making preparations for the time he will be gone by setting the AC unit, turning off the water supply, and setting the house alarm. Noah rings the doorbell just as Trent is setting AC temperature on the thermostat. Trent opens the door, and there is Noah standing there dressed in long pants and a buttoned-up dress shirt.

Noah is smiling at his dad and says, "Good morning, sir. Your ride to the love boat is here. May I take your bags to the limousine?"

Trent smiles back at his son and says, "Good morning, son. Yes, you can. Be careful. The suitcase is heavy."

Noah says in a confident voice, "I can handle this, but are you sure you have everything you need?"

Trent says, "Yes, I have triple-checked, and I have all my documents, credit cards, and some cash. I'm good to go."

Noah puts his dad's suitcase in the trunk of his car. Trent sets his house alarm and walks to Noah's car and opens the door. Trent sits in the car, puts on his seatbelt, looks at Noah who is starting the car, and says, "Let's get this party started."

Noah smiles at his dad and says, "Now that's a good attitude, Dad."

Noah sets his GPS for the destination and tells his dad, "We will arrive at 9:00 a.m., right on time to start boarding the ship."

Trent says, "Well, that's good, son, I believe the ship doesn't depart till 10:30 a.m., so we will be just fine."

Noah has been driving about fifteen minutes with small talk between father and son when Trent tells Noah about the nightmare that woke him up during the night. Noah is all ears as his dad begins telling the dream he had last night about the cruise ship on fire in the middle of the ocean.

Trent continues talking as Noah is driving his car. Trent tells that he was sleeping in his room on the ship when he was awoken by alarms sounding very loudly outside his room. Trent tells his son, "I remember getting dressed as fast as I could, and I grab my passport, wallet, and cell phone. When I open the door to go into the hallway, it was full of smoke. I remember helping some people out to the main deck of the ship. There were hundreds of people in a state of panic. Crew members working on the ship were trying to calm down all the passengers while other crew members were fighting the fire. The sun was just rising over the blue sea, and the smoke was black. As the ship turned into the wind, it gave most of the people on board clean air to breathe."

Noah asks, "What happened next, Dad?"

Trent says, "I was doing my best to calm down a group of ladies when the captain's voice was heard over the loudspeakers on the ship. When everyone heard the captain's voice, everyone became very quiet to hear what he was saying."

Noah says, "Well, Dad what did he say?"

Trent says, "The captain said that the fire was in the kitchen area, but has been contained, and put out completely. The captain says to stay on the outside decks of the ship until he gives the announcement that it is safe to enter the interior parts of the ship. This will give time for the smoke to clear out, and everyone may return to their room, which he said would take up to an hour."

Noah says, "Wow, Dad, that was some dream."

Trent says with concern in his voice, "That's a nightmare, son. I woke up in my bedroom and was too nervous to go back to sleep, but I did after a few minutes."

Noah looks at his dad and says in a calm voice, "Dad, it was just a dream. I don't know why you had that dream, but it's going to be okay."

Trent says with a voice of conviction, "I know, son, but it was so real I woke up talking in my sleep. It was that real, son."

Noah says with concern in his voice, "Okay, Dad, I believe you, but it's over now. You will have a good time, and before you know it, I'll be picking you up this time next week with exciting stories to tell me."

Trent looks at his son, takes a deep breath, and says, "Yeah, I wish the trip goes by fast. I'm not ashamed to say I'm anxious about going on a ship full of strangers, and being out in the deep blue sea, it's not like you can call a taxi and get a ride home."

Noah smiles at his dad and with a voice of authority speaks firmly, "Listen, Dad, you are going to have a relaxing, fun time on this cruise, and that's an order."

Trent laughs at Noah's command and says with joy in his voice, "Roger that, Captain, I will enjoy myself even if it kills me."

Noah says to his dad, "Now wait a minute, you don't have to have that much fun. We all want you back here in a week safe and sound."

Trent says to Noah with a reassuring voice, "I'll do my best to have fun, and not get hurt."

Noah smiles and says, "That's what I want to hear."

The rest of the ride to Galveston was quiet in the car, except for the classic rock and roll music playing on the radio.

Noah speaks up, "We should be there in about five minutes."

Trent says, "I believe I can see the cruise ship."

Noah looks and says, "You are right, Dad, I see it too. We will be turning into the terminal in a few minutes."

Noah is slowing his car down as he enters the huge parking lot that is in front of the ship. The parking lot is full of vehicles, with many charter buses that brought hundreds of people. Noah stops his car near the gangplank where a short line of people are gathered waiting to go aboard the ship. Noah and Trent get out of the car, and both of them are amazed at how huge the ship is.

Trent says with excitement in his voice, "Well, son, this is it. This is where we say 'later 'gator.'"

Noah says, "After a while, crocodile," with a smile that gives his dad encouragement. Noah takes out the heavy suitcase out of his car. Noah extends the handle so his dad can roll it to where everyone else has stored their baggage for the crew of the ship to bring to the passenger's assigned rooms.

Trent gives his son a firm handshake then a big hug for a few seconds. Trent takes a step back, smiles at Noah, and says, "Okay, I guess this is where I go have a trip of a lifetime. Wish me good luck."

Noah says to his dad, "You got this. Now don't fall head over heels for the first lady that gives you the eye. Just be nice to all the ladies, and you'll find the one you can relate to."

Trent laughs and tells Noah, "That's excellent advice coming from a man that is still single and in his thirties."

Trent says, "I understand what you are trying to convey to me, son. I'll take my time and play the field."

Noah laughs and says, "That's right, Dad. You are the quarter-back now. A strong offense beats a good defense. You call the plays." Noah then notices a small group of single ladies looking at his dad. Noah says, "Hey, look over there, Dad, you have already have women checking you out. Dad didn't even get on board the ship yet."

Trent says to Noah very nervously, "What I'm going to say, what I'm going to do?"

Noah tells his dad, "Listen, Dad, remember these ladies are nervous too, so try to be confident. Women like confidence in a man. It makes them feel safe." Noah tells his dad in a calm voice, "Just be happy, and let everyone you meet feel comfortable. I know you can do that. Now go have fun in the sun. Call me every morning at 7:00 a.m. so I know you are all right. Maybe you will tell me you've met the woman of your dreams."

Trent says in a voice with slight enthusiasm, "I will, son, every morning at seven, because I know you'll be up waiting to hear any updates on my love life."

Noah pats his dad on his back and says, "Go get them tiger, looks like they are ready or you."

Trent walks away with his suitcase in tow and says, "Ready or not, son, here I go."

Noah watches his dad walk up to the man in a cruise ship crew member uniform and gives him some ID, along with his boarding pass. After a few minutes, the baggage is tagged, and Trent is given a ticket and his room key. Trent looks at Noah, smiles, and gives Noah a hand gesture of thumbs-up. Noah waves back, and he whispers a prayer, "Lord, today, please keep my dad safe from all these women on this ship, and bring him back in one piece. Thank you, Jesus."

Noah returns to his car and looks one more time before leaving the parking lot and sees his dad smiling. Trent's walking toward other passengers waiting to board the ship. Trent is getting close to the line of people, which is moving slowly. He notices that the line is 90 percent women. Trent is whispering to himself these words, "God, let there be more single men on this cruise. I won't be able to handle this many women without any escape." Trent gets close to the line now and can hear the women's voices. Some are looking at him, and Trent hears one lady say "Fresh meat." Another lady says, "Now that's a man."

Trent turns around to look and see if there are some men walking close to him, but he sees no one. Trent thinks to himself, Now Noah told me to be nice, respectful, and confident. Well, I'm confident that I'm out numbered. Trent walks up to the line carrying a small custom bag made for men to carry small items. Trent received it from one of his grandchildren as a gift for his birthday. Inside he has his passport, boarding pass, credit card, and a few pictures of his family. Trent looks at the line of people and can see that there are hundreds of men standing in line, but the women ratio to men looks to be 70 percent women and 30 percent men. Trent looks at the men and sees most all of them have big beer bellies. Trent is standing in line now and says "Good morning" to everyone that is within range of his voice. The group of ladies all responded with smiling faces and says "Good morning."

Trent looks again at the line of people and says, "It looks like we should be on the ship very soon. The line is moving quickly."

A lady who looks to be in her early fifties smiles at Trent and says, "Yes, honey, it won't take long. I was on this cruise last month."

Trent looks at the lady with curiosity and says in a kind voice, "Last month you must have had an awesome time to be going on another cruise so soon. By the way, my name is Trent from Orange, Texas, and what might your name be?"

The lady extends her hand for Trent to shake hands and says in a content voice, "I'm Judy, and this woman next to me is Trudy, my sister."

Trent looks at the two sisters and says politely, "Very nice to meet y'all, and where are y'all from?"

Judy speaks up and says, "From Baton Rouge. The last cruise we went on had to be cut short because of bad weather, so the cruise line gave us free tickets for this cruise."

Trent looks at the sisters, smiles and says, "Well, I looked at the forecast for this cruise. It should be smooth sailing."

Trudy, who is five feet nine inches tall, looks at her sister, who is only an inch shorter, and says loudly, "That's good news, because this Cajun lady is ready to get this party started."

Judy gives her sister a high-five and says, "Yeah, baby, we're going to rock this boat this time."

Trent is smiling at the two sisters, but in his mind he's thinking trouble is bound to be happening when these two get alcohol in their bodies, and Trent doesn't need that drama. Trent gets on board the ship and says goodbye to the two sisters, and they wave goodbye.

Judy says in a joyful voice, "We will see you soon."

Trent says to himself, "I hope not too soon." Trent looks for a person on the ship to ask directions to his room.

A young man in uniform looks at Trent's boarding pass and says, "Sir, you have a room on level C, a very nice room. I can take you there if you like, sir. It will only take a few minutes."

Trent says, "Sure, if it's not too much trouble."

CHAPTER TWENTY-ONE

The young crewman walks in front of Trent down the long hallway on Level C and says to Trent, "Sir, this is your room. Number 333. Is there anything else I can help you with?"

Trent smiles at the crewman and tries to give a five-dollar tip to him, but the crewman says very politely, "Sir, you don't have to tip me. I'm just doing my job."

Trent says to the crewman, "Yes, I know that, son, but please take this tip, because you deserve it for doing such an excellent job with a good attitude."

The young crewman takes the tip and says, "Sir, if you need anything at all, ask for Joshua, and thank you very much."

Trent enters his room and looks around after closing the door. Trent is pleasantly surprised at the size of the room and the bathroom. Trent walks over to the window. He opens the curtains and looks out to see an awesome view of the harbor. Trent hears a knock at the door and looks through the peephole and sees the bellhop with Trent's large suitcase.

Trent opens the door and says to the bellhop, "Come in, and you can put my suitcase by the bed."

The bellhop says, "Will that be all, sir?"

Trent gives the bellhop a tip and asks the bellhop, "Are all the rooms on the ship this big?"

The bellhop says with a smile, "No, sir. You have purchased one of the nicest rooms on board, sir, and thank you for the tip." The bellhop walks toward the door and says, "Lunch will begin at noontime, sir, on Level A. Have a wonderful time on your cruise."

Trent says with excitement in his voice, "Thank you. I plan on it."

Trent closes the door and dives onto the queen-size bed. Trent looks at the ceiling fan above the bed and says out loud, "Man, this bed is so comfortable I could take a nap now." Trent looks at the radio clock on the nightstand, which displays the time 10:45 a.m. Trent feels the ship move and gets out of bed, walks over to the huge window. Trent looks down toward the water and notices some harbor tugs pulling on the ship with heavy ropes. Trent looks as the crew of the harbor tugs untie the heavy ropes and then back away from the ship and blow their loud air horns as if to say "bon voyage."

Trent says out loud as he looks at the docks of Galveston harbor, "We are on our way now. God keep us safe."

Trent turns on the large flat-screen TV. He's looking at the channel that describes the ship and where all the locations of different venues can be easily walked to. Trent is amazed at the many bars, restaurants, swimming pools, and nightclubs on board. Trent starts to think how much electrical wire it must have taken to make this ship work properly. He laughs to himself and says out loud, "I need to stop thinking like an electrician now, because I'm officially retired, thank God." Trent turns off the TV and goes into the bathroom, looks at the mirror, turns on the water to wash his face, grabs a towel to dry his face, and notices how soft the towel was.

Trent looks in the mirror then smiles and says with a voice of contentment, "Man, my children sure gave me a fantastic vacation, I mean first-class all the way." Trent walks out of the bathroom and grabs his door key on the nightstand. Trent walks out of the room to take a long walk around the ship before going to the main dining room to eat some lunch. Trent is walking down the hall when he notices some members of the rock and roll band Loverboy coming out of their rooms. Trent doesn't say anything, but in his mind Trent thinks, Wow, the band is staying just down the hall from me. How awesome is that. Trent gets on the elevator with the band, and one of the band members says hello to Trent.

Trent looks at the one that says hello and says, smiling at him, "Hey, how's it going."

The band member says, "All right."

The singer of the band then says to the other band members, "Now remember, the gig starts at eight on the dot, so be on stage for 7:45 p.m. at the latest." Everyone on the elevator agrees, even Trent, and the band members start laughing.

One band member says to Trent, "Yeah, man, don't you be late."

Trent smiles back at him and says, "Don't worry, I'll be on time for sure."

The elevator door opens up. Trent goes in one direction, and the band Loverboy goes in another direction. Trent is walking around the inside of this huge cruise ship astonished by all the shops and different places you can walk in and buy almost anything you want.

Trent is noticing more men as he walks around, now many with women holding their hands, but from what Trent is seeing, the women still have the men outnumbered two to one. Trent continues to walk around the interior of the ship, amazed by the details and craftsmanship of the ship's decor.

Trent looks at his watch then rubs his flat stomach area and says to himself, "My watch and stomach tells me it's time to eat."

Trent stops a crew member and asks where might the dining area be. The crew member says politely, "Follow me, sir. I'll be happy to show you where the buffet is."

Trent walks alongside the young crew member for a few minutes. Then they enter a large room where the aroma of food is breathtaking. The crew member asks Trent, "Will there be anything else, sir?"

Trent says, "Where I pay for my food?"

The crew member says, "May I see your key card to your room, sir."

Trent gives the key card to the crew member. The crew member smiles and says with a voice of excitement, "Oh, sir, this key card allows you to go eat and drink, and do everything on this cruise. Sir, you are VIP, please enjoy, and, sir, the food here is delicious."

Trent thanks the crew member for the info and is ready to eat, but there is a long line just to wait for a plate. Trent is talking to a lady in line that looks to be in her late sixties.

She says the line is moving slow, and Trent smiles at her and says, "Well, I just found out I have a VIP key card."

The lady says, "Well, sir, you don't have to wait in this line. There is a place over there where you can get a plate without waiting."

Trent says to the lady with a voice of gratitude, "Oh really, I didn't know that."

The lady smiles at Trent and says, "By the way, just flash that card to any of the crew members on the ship, and they will help you ASAP. You paid extra for that, so you get the best the cruise has to offer."

Trent thanks the lady for all her help and says, "You have a good day." Trent walks past all the non-VIP passengers and is greeted by a young lady wearing the ship's uniform.

She looks at Trent's key card and says, "Sir, if there is anything I may do for you, please let me know."

Trent smiles at her and says, "Thank you very much. I just want to eat some of this great-smelling food."

The young lady gives an empty plate to Trent and says politely, "Enjoy your meal, sir. A waiter will bring you whatever drink you like at your table in the VIP section, which is right over there."

Trent looks where the young lady is pointing and says, "Wow, that's fancy-looking tables."

The young crew member smiles and says, "Yes, sir, only the best for our VIP."

Trent gets a plate of food and sits down at the table and begins to eat after saying grace. A waiter walks up to the table and asks Trent what he would like to drink.

Trent says, "A bottle of water."

The waiter says kindly, "Very good, sir."

The waiter returns quickly with a bottle of the most expensive bottle of water he has ever seen. Trent opens the bottle to drink the water, and the taste of the water is so pure that Trent is surprised that water can taste so good. Trent eats his food slowly, and after ten minutes, the waiter asks Trent if there is anything else he can do for him. Trent says no. "But where do I leave the tip?"

The waiter smiles at him and says in a whisper so only Trent can hear the waiter's voice, "Sir, for what you paid for this cruise with that VIP key card, all tips are included. There's no need to tip anyone on or off this entire cruise, sir."

Trent is surprised to hear that from the waiter and shakes the waiter's hand.

Trent says, "Okay, well, you have a good day." Trent leaves the dining room. Trent is walking back to his room feeling special and says to himself out loud, "Man, my kids must have spent a fortune on this cruise."

Trent says, "Hey, I'm worth it." Trent laughs out loud.

Trent walks back to his room and looks out the large window. The view is spectacular. The blue sea and the blue sky really look like a scene from a movie. Trent begins to change out of his clothes and opens up his suitcase. Trent pulls out a swimsuit one of his grandchildren gave to him as a birthday gift, along with a comfortable summer shirt. Trent looks in the mirror and says out loud, "Well, not too bad for an old man. Let me go see what is lying around the pool. Hopefully they will have some good-looking, in-shape women close to my age."

Trent arrives at the pool and is greeted by a young woman dressed in white shorts, white shirt, a ship's crew member uniform. The young woman asks Trent for his room key card, smiles, and says, "Welcome, sir, is there a special private cabana you would like to stay at?"

Trent looks around the large pool area. He notices a few women that seem to be having a good time and says, "Yes, this one over here would be nice." The young lady asks Trent to follow her, and she takes out some luxurious towels from a cabinet and places the towels on a very comfortable lounge chair. The young lady asks if there is anything else she can do for Trent.

Trent says, "I would like a cold drink."

The young lady says, "Right away, sir. I will send one of our VIP waitresses over to give any drink or food you would like."

Trent thanks the young lady and sits down on the lounge chair. Trent looks around the pool area to see hundreds of people in swimsuits. Trent notices some women have conservative swimsuits on while other have string bikinis that cover hardly any body parts. Trent is amazed at how some women like to show complete strangers all that skin. To each their own is what Trent always believes, as long as there are no young children around, and today there are no children around. Trent is asked by a beautiful young waitress a few minutes later for a food and drink request. Trent asks the waitress for a crown and seven.

"And can you bring some chips and dip?"

The waitress smiles at Trent and says, "Yes, sir, I'll be right back."

The waitress is back with Trent's order within five minutes and asks Trent, "Would there be anything else?"

Trent looks at the brunette lying on a lounge chair twenty feet away and says, "Yes, that beautiful woman right there"—and Trent points to the lady—"when she orders another drink, please put it on my tab, and say the drink is compliments from me."

The waitress says, "I'll go there right now, sir. It looks like she is almost finished with her drink." The waitress thanks Trent.

Trent responds to the waitress, "Thank you for being so nice."

The waitress asks the brunette for a drink order and tells the woman that Trent is buying the drink for her. The woman looks at Trent and smiles at him. When the waitress brings the drink to the brunette, she takes a sip of the drink, smiles as she is looking at Trent, and mouths with her lips "thank you."

Trent responds by raising his drink in the air and says, "You're welcome." Trent finishes his drink and takes off his shirt to reveal his chiseled chest and flat stomach. Trent decides to walk around the pool to get a closer look at the ladies. He notices that some women are in the pool while most are tanning on lounge chairs. Trent is feeling that women are staring at him, and some even give a whistle of approval as Trent passes near their chairs. Trent figures it must be the alcohol the women are consuming to have them act lively. Trent smiles and whispers to himself, "The whiskey is getting these women frisky." Trent walks back to his private cabana and sits down.

The waitress returns promptly and asks Trent, "Would you like another drink?"

Trent smiles and says, "Yes, please get me another crown and seven."

The waitress responds, "Very good, sir."

The waitress returns in a few minutes with Trent's drink. Trent notices the brunette that he paid a drink for get up, and she looks at Trent. The brunette walks over to Trent and thanks him for the drink.

Trent smiles at her and says, "By the way, my name is Trent, would you care to join me?"

The lady says, "Sure, my name is Mary Ann, and it's very nice to meet you."

Trent reaches out to shake her hand, but Mary Ann gives Trent a hug. Trent smells the perfume on Mary Ann's neck, and to his surprise it is the very same perfume that his dearly departed wife would wear. Trent compliments Mary Ann on the way she smells by stating, "Wow, Mary Ann, you smell so good."

Mary Ann smiles at Trent and says, "Thank you. I've been wearing this perfume for years. I tried other perfumes, but this one really makes me feel sexy."

Trent laughs and says, "Excuse me for saying this, but you have no need for a perfume to make you look sexy. You're beautiful and as sexy as can be wearing that blue turquoise bikini."

Mary Ann says with a look of contentment, "Well, thank you, sir, for noticing."

A few seconds later, Trent notices a parade of women in all different shapes and sizes coming toward his cabana. As they walk in front of Mary Ann and Trent, each one gives a smile and an eye wink to Trent. Trent smiles back because some of them look sexy in their swimsuits, while others look like they could exercise more and lose a few pounds.

Trent says, "Wow, what is going on."

Mary Ann says with a laugh, "Well, Trent, if you don't know, I'll tell you. When you did your walk around the pool earlier, every woman in eyesight of you was checking you out from top to bottom, including me. To be honest, you are the best-looking man around this pool."

Trent blushes and says, "Really, I wasn't trying to put on a show or anything."

Mary Ann smiles then laughs and says, "Well, baby, you did put on a show, a very hot and sexy display. You got all these women hot to trot." Mary Ann finishes her drink, and Trent asks her, "Would you like another?"

Mary Ann smiles and says, "Maybe just one more please. I'm feeling a little buzzed already. These drinks are strong."

Trent signals the waitress to bring two more drinks. Trent says to Mary Ann after the waitress leaves the drinks on the table, "What are your plans for the evening?"

Mary Ann says, "I am going to the Loverboy concert."

Trent smiles at her and says, "Me too. As a matter of fact, I was in the elevator with the band a few hours ago."

Mary Ann takes a sip of her drink and says with excitement in her voice, "Are you serious? Man, those guys are awesome."

Trent says, "I would like you to join me if you don't mind."

Mary Ann reaches over and gives Trent a quick kiss on the cheek and says, "It's a date."

Trent says to Mary Ann, "How would you like to meet the guys in the band?"

Mary Ann looks at Trent with disbelief and says, "Don't tease me, Trent, that's not funny."

Trent says, "I can't make any promises, but I'll try to get us backstage."

Mary Ann says, "That would be awesome."

Trent says, "Well, I'm going to head up to my room to take a shower, and relax before the show. What room are you staying in?"

Mary Ann says, "I'm on Level F room number 215."

Trent says, "I'll call you later so we can meet at the concert hall before the band starts."

Mary Ann smiles at Trent and says, "Great, I'll wait for your call."

Trent puts on his shirt, gives a short hug to Mary Ann, and tells her, "It was very nice meeting you. I will see you soon." Trent walks away smiling like a winner.

CHAPTER TWENTY-TWO

Trent walks out of the elevator on Level C and notices a man near his room having trouble getting into his room. Trent offers some assistance and gets the room key card to open the door. The man looks at Trent and smiles, and with a voice of relief, says, "Thanks so much. I was trying to get this door open for five minutes."

Trent says, "You're welcome."

The man looks at Trent and says, "Hey, was it you we met on the elevator earlier today?"

Trent says, "Yeah, it sure was," his voice sounding like an old friend.

The man reaches out his hand so Trent can shake it and says, "My name is Ronnie. I'm the manager for the band Loverboy." Trent shakes Ronnie's hand.

Ronnie says with kindness in his voice, "Are you going to the concert tonight?"

Trent says, "Yes, that's the plan."

Ronnie says, "Stay right here I'll be right back." Ronnie walks into his room while Trent is standing out in the hallway. Ronnie returns with two backstage passes and gives them to Trent.

Trent takes them in his hand and says, "Thanks, Ronnie."

Ronnie says, "These are two backstage passes so you and some-one else can meet the whole band after the concert."

Trent says, "Thanks so much, Ronnie. I met a gorgeous woman at the pool, and she really likes the band." Trent smiles and says with excitement in his voice, "She will be ecstatic when I tell her this good news."

Ronnie says with a smile, "Cool, man, see y'all later," and walks into his room with the door closing behind him.

Trent walks down the hall a few rooms and unlocks his door. Trent then takes off his sandals and lies down on the queen-size bed, sets his alarm for 6:00 p.m., and says to himself out loud, "I'll take a shower when I get up. Right now I'm taking me a nap. I have to rest up for tonight."

The alarm is ringing, and Trent turns off the alarm and gets out of bed. Trent walks into the large bathroom and removes his clothes to take a shower. Trent is finished with his shower then shaves and blow-dries his full head of salt-and-pepper hair. He looks at his watch and sees the time is 6:45 p.m. Trent picks up the phone in his room and dials Mary Ann's room. Mary Ann answers the phone after the third ring and says hello.

Trent says hello with a voice of confidence. "How are you doing, are you ready to have fun tonight?"

Mary Ann answers with enthusiasm in her voice, "Yes, Trent, I'm ready. Are you?"

Trent says, "That's good, because I know tonight will be a good night for us. I will meet you in front of the concert hall doors. It will take me a few minutes to get there."

Mary Ann says with excitement in her voice, "Awesome, I'll be looking for you, I should be there in ten minutes."

Trent says, "Okay I'll see you in a few minutes," and puts down the phone feeling like a kid in high school going on his first date.

Trent grabs his room key card, the backstage passes, and walks out of the room to meet Mary Ann at the concert hall. Trent arrives at the front doors of the concert hall within five minutes dressed in new blue jeans with a dark blue dress shirt and cowboy boots on. The concert hall is filling up with people quickly, as they have hundreds of people standing in front of the doors waiting in line to get inside.

Trent sees this beautiful brunette walking toward him dressed in a dark blue dress with her shoulders showing, and the length of the dress was just a few inches above her knees. Her cleavage was showing just enough to have any man want to see more. Her black hair was shining as she walks up to hug Trent. Trent can smell that perfume on her and says, smiling at her, "Boy oh boy, you sure look pretty in that dress, and smell so good I can hug you all night."

Mary Ann smiles at Trent and says, "Thank you, Trent, and you look very handsome this evening too."

Trent says, "There is a line of people, but I believe with this VIP key room card we can try to get in ahead of everyone else over here."

Mary Ann smiles and says, "That's good, because that's a long line."

Trent and Mary Ann walk over to the VIP line where there are only four people waiting.

When the usher looks at Trent's backstage passes, he says with a smile, "Would y'all follow me please?" The usher takes Trent and Mary Ann past everyone standing in line and takes them to the front row next to the stage.

Trent is given his backstage tickets back, and the usher asks, "Would y'all care for anything to drink before the concert starts?""

Trent says, "Yes, I'll have a crown and seven." Trent looks at Mary Ann.

She says to the usher, "I'll have a tequila sunrise with some cherries."

The usher says, "I'll be right back with your drinks."

Mary Ann is astonished with the front-row seats and gives Trent a kiss on the lips and says, "Man, you sure came through tonight with these seats."

The usher returns with two drinks each for Trent and Mary Ann and says, "These drinks should have you feeling okay in a few minutes."

Trent thanks the usher and realizes it is the crew member Joshua that showed him to his room that morning and says, "Thanks so much, Joshua."

Mary Ann tells Trent after taking a drink of her tequila sunrise, "I'm very impressed with the service you have been getting on this cruise."

Trent smiles at Mary Ann and says, "Yes, the service is very good, I must say."

Trent notices Ronnie cross the stage and waves at him. Ronnie stops and looks at Trent and yells, "How do you like the seats?"

Trent says back in a joyful voice, "They are awesome, Ronnie, thanks so much."

Ronnie smiles back at Trent, gives him two thumbs-up, and says, "Enjoy the show," and hurries off the stage.

Mary Ann asks Trent who that was.

Trent says, "That's the tour manager. He was having trouble with his key room card, he couldn't open the door, and I got the door open for him."

Mary Ann says, "Wow, and he gave you front-row tickets and backstage passes for that. That is very nice of him."

Trent smiles and says, "Yeah, right place at the right time. Ronnie is a nice guy."

The lights in the concert hall go down.

Ronnie comes out with a microphone and says loudly to the crowd, "Are y'all ready to rock and roll."

The crowd screams yes, and then the huge crowd of people chants "Loverboy" over and over. Ronnie then screams, "Please let's welcome to the stage the one the only Loverboy."

The band runs on stage and starts playing their song "Everybody Is Working for the Weekend." The crowd is rocking out with the band. Trent looks at Mary Ann, and she is singing along with the music and looks to be having a terrific time. The singer of the band looks at Trent and waves and continues to sing song after song. The concert is over after two hours of the band playing their greatest hit songs.

Ronnie is seen on stage making sure the roadies are taking care of the band equipment and notices Trent. Ronnie walks over to Trent and Mary Ann where they are standing near the stage in the front-row seating area.

Trent says to Ronnie, "Dude, that was a great concert."

Ronnie smiles and says, "Yeah, the band puts on a good show. Hey, Trent, is this the woman you told me about wanting to meet the band?"

Trent says with excitement in his voice, "Yes, this is Mary Ann, and, Mary Ann, this is Ronnie, the band's tour manager." Mary Ann smiles at Ronnie.

Ronnie says, "Nice to meet you. Are y'all ready to meet the band, if so follow me backstage."

Trent and Mary Ann follow Ronnie backstage to a large room where the band is relaxing, having some food and drinks. Mary Ann and Trent are introduced to the band members, and for ten minutes they take a few pictures with the band. They have small talk about music, being on the road touring. Then they say their goodbyes. Mary Ann receives a signed Loverboy shirt from all the band members. Mary Ann is so excited to have met the band and thanks Trent for the awesome night.

Trent says, "It's not over yet. Let's go sit down and have a meal and talk. I would like to get to know you a little."

Mary Ann smiles at Trent and says, "That sounds good. I'm a little hungry."

Trent and Mary Ann go eat and have a good conversation for an hour talking about the concert and some of the things they like to do to relax and have fun doing. Trent asks Mary Ann if she would like to take a walk on the outside deck of the ship.

Mary Ann says while looking into his eyes, "That sounds good. It will help burn off some of these calories I just consumed." They both laugh while walking out of the restaurant.

Trent walks alongside of Mary Ann while holding her hand, and when arriving outside, they both are surprised that the cruise ship has docked at the port of Cancun, Mexico.

Trent looks at all the lights of the city and says to Mary Ann, "I just have to tell you that I had a fantastic time with you tonight. To me you are the best-looking woman on this ship."

Mary Ann smiles and says, "Trent, that is so sweet of you to say that to me." Mary Ann looks into Trent's eyes and says, "I'd like to tell you that you made me feel special tonight. I know I'm with a very handsome man who I would like to kiss right now if you don't mind." With that before Trent can says yes to the kiss, Mary Ann gives Trent a long, passionate kiss on the lips.

A few women walk by while Mary Ann is kissing Trent, and one woman says out loud, "Girl, y'all need to get a room."

Mary Ann stops kissing Trent after recognizing the voice of the woman and smiles at her. The woman is Mary Ann's roommate and good friend Ginger. The other woman is a person Ginger met at the pool earlier today.

Ginger says to Mary Ann, "Are you all right? Is this man bothering you, because if so he can bother me too!" Then Ginger laughs and is reaching out her hand to shake Trent's hand, but Trent is hugged by Ginger before he can shake her hand.

Mary Ann says laughing, "Okay, girl, release him, give him some air to breathe." Mary Ann introduces Ginger to Trent.

Trent says hello to Ginger and her new friend Monica, and after a few seconds, Ginger says, "Y'all have fun. Mary Ann, I'll see you at our room later on." The two women walk away talking about Cancun and how pretty it looks. Mary Ann says with a compassionate voice, "I'm sorry about that. Now let's continue what we were doing."

Trent smiles and kisses Mary Ann with passion, using his hands to cup each side of her face gently. The kiss goes on for over a minute.

After the kiss, Mary Ann says with satisfaction in her voice, "Wow, Trent, I don't know when was the last time I was kissed like that."

Trent smiles at Mary Ann and says, "I'm glad you enjoyed it, because I sure did."

Trent looks at his watch and says, "I hate to have to say this, but I really have to get some sleep. I have an excursion early in the morning on shore."

Mary Ann smiles at Trent. "Well, we wouldn't want you falling asleep on that. Can you walk me to my room?"

Trent says, "Sure, I'll be happy to."

Trent walks Mary Ann to her room. Trent gives Mary Ann another passionate kiss and says, "I'll call you when I get back aboard."

Mary Ann says, "I'll be lying around the pool for most of the day if I don't answer the phone."

Trent says, "Okay, I'll remember that, and, Mary Ann, I had a good time tonight."

Mary Ann kisses Trent one more time and says, "I had an awesome time too. Good night, and have fun tomorrow."

Trent walks to his room and goes straight to bed after taking a shower and saying his prayers thanking God for Mary Ann, telling God, "She is exactly what I need." Trent wakes up early the next morning. At 7:00 a.m. he calls Noah and tells him that they are in Cancun.

Noah asks his dad, "How do you like the cruise so far? Are there any nice women on board?"

Trent says, "The cruise is great." He tells Noah, "I met a woman in her early fifties. I really like her, and her name is Mary Ann."

Trent says, "I'm going on a sightseeing trip in Cancun, and I have to get ready. Give everyone my love, and I'll call you tomorrow morning."

Noah says, "Be safe, and have fun, Dad."

Trent goes on the excursion with at least forty other people that are on the cruise. Trent goes sightseeing and rides horses on the beaches of Cancun. It is after lunch before everyone on the excursion return to the cruise ship. Trent returns to his room to shower and tries calling Mary Ann's room, but does not get an answer. Trent changes into some swim trunks and a shirt, and heads down to the pool hoping to find Mary Ann. Trent stands by the railing of the ship before going to the pool area and watches as the ship departs from the port of Cancun. Trent is amazed by the power of the tugboats that are pulling the huge ship from the dock.

Trent feels some person touching him on the back of his neck and turns around quickly and says, "Excuse me."

Ginger steps back and says, "Whoa, big boy, it's just me," with a nervous tone.

Trent says, "I'm sorry, Ginger," with a small grin. "I just don't like it when anyone sneaks up on me and touches me. I get very jumpy."

Ginger smiles at Trent and says with a voice of calmness, "I'm sorry too, I don't know you well enough to touch you like that. I'm just a little tipsy and playful with these strong drinks I've been having since noon."

Ginger says, "If you are looking for Mary Ann, you can find her by the pool. They had some guys trying to talk to her, but I told them to step off, because she's got a man."

Trent starts laughing at Ginger and says, "Wow, Ginger, I want to thank you for that, but I'm sure Mary Ann can take care of herself."

Ginger starts laughing now and says, "You know, that's what she told me after I ran the two guys off. You two sure think alike. Well, anyway, that's where she is at. I believe I will go in the water at the pool to cool off. It's hot today."

Trent says, "I'll walk with you to the pool if you're okay with that."

Ginger smiles at Trent and says, "Honey, you can walk with me anywhere. I'm lucky to be seen with a hot stud like you."

Trent smiles and says, "Thanks, Ginger, you better take it easy on the drinks for the rest of the day, and have plenty of bottled water."

Trent and Ginger enter the pool area to find hundreds of people enjoying the large pool. Ginger sees Mary Ann lying on her back right where she left her twenty minutes earlier.

Ginger tells Trent with a slight slur in her voice, "Look there, Trent, there's my hot little potato baking in the sun with that bright orange bikini on with all that sun tan oil all over her body."

Trent looks at Mary Ann and says out loud, "My lord, she is looking good in that bikini."

Ginger says, "Yeah, she got all the men checking her out. You better get over there."

CHAPTER TWENTY-THREE

Mary Ann notices Trent and Ginger walking up to her lounge chair.

Ginger says loudly, "Hey, girl, look who I found. You want him? If not, I'll take him."

Mary Ann looks at Trent then looks at Ginger and says, "Ginger, no more drinks for you, lady, you are three sheets into the wind." Mary Ann says to Trent, "I'm sorry for my friend being so tipsy."

Trent sits down next to Mary Ann and smiles while looking at her glistening skin in the evening sunshine.

Trent says, "That's all right, Mary Ann, Ginger is just having fun. She told me she's going to stop drinking alcohol, and only drink bottled water."

Ginger says, "Yes, I am, but now I'm going cool off in that pool." Ginger slowly walks to the pool and jumps in.

Trent says, "You are looking fine."

Mary Ann smiles at Trent and asks, "Can you put some oil on my back and legs please?"

Trent says, "I sure will, but would you like to go to the VIP cabana for more privacy? We could order some food and drinks."

Mary Ann gets up off the lounge chair and says to Trent, "That sounds good. I could eat a burger and fries."

Trent helps Mary Ann gather her things and walk to the VIP cabana. They spend the rest of the afternoon talking about Trent's excursion on Cancun, having food and drinks. Ginger and Monica join them for drinks, and Trent gets to know the women more as the hours passed by.

A crew member named Joshua walks up to the cabana and asks Trent if he doesn't have any plans for supper, if he would like to have supper at the captain's table tonight. Trent looks surprised to hear the request and asks Joshua, "Why me?"

Joshua tells Trent that all VIP passengers will get an invitation to do that if they desire to. Trent asks, "May I bring a guest to the table?"

He says, "Yes, you are allowed to bring one guest of your choosing."

Trent asks, "What time would this be, and how do we dress?"

Joshua says the time will be 7:00 p.m. and to dress formal.

Trent says, "Yes, we will be there."

Joshua says with a smile, "Very good, sir, I'll let the captain know, have a good day," and walks away.

Trent looks at the women and says, "Well, I need a date for supper."

Mary Ann smiles at Ginger and Monica and waits for a few seconds. Trent kneels down before Mary Ann, takes hold of her right hand, and asks, "Will you do me the honor of joining me at the captain's table this evening?"

Mary Ann says, smiling at Trent, "I would love to."

Trent says, "Cool. I'll be by your room at six-thirty to escort you down for a memorable evening."

Ginger and Monica look at Mary Ann, and they both give her a high-five. Trent returns to his lounge chair and smiles like a man enjoying life on his vacation. Trent orders some food and drinks for the ladies, and after an hour or so, Trent says, "I will have to say goodbye for now, ladies. I have a big date to get ready for." The ladies smile at him.

Mary Ann says, "Now you go get all cleaned up. I'll call you at 6:15 p.m. to let you know I'm ready."

Trent says, "Sounds good, Mary Ann," and walks away.

Ginger looks at Mary Ann and says with a giggle, "Girl, you must be living right to find a man like that."

Mary Ann smiles and says, "I have been praying for God to send me a good man, and Lord today he has answered my prayers."

Monica says with a laugh, "Amen, sister. I need to start praying for that too."

Ginger laughs and says, "Yeah, we all need to pray more."

Mary Ann stands up and says, "Well, I'm going back to our room. Are you coming with me, Ginger?"

Ginger says, "No, girl, I'm going to stay around the pool with Monica a little while longer. I'll see you later on tonight. Now go get all beautiful for your man."

Mary Ann smiles and says, "I'll do my best," then walks away.

Trent is looking sharp dressed in a gray suit with a white shirt and red tie he got as a birthday present. You can say he looked like a lawyer or politician—they're both the same, some good, some bad. Mary Ann hears the knock at the door. Looking in the mirror, Mary Ann is smiling. She thinks to herself, That man is on time. Mary Ann opens the door to see Trent standing there looking very handsome. Trent smiles as he sees Mary Ann wearing a beautiful sundress with the length just covering her knees, with white high heels that makes her legs look sexy. The color of the dress is yellow like the sun.

Trent tells Mary Ann, "Wow, you look beautiful."

Mary Ann responds with a smile and says, "Thank you, sir, and may I say you look debonair in that suit."

Trent tells Mary Ann, "I have only worn this suit one time. I just like to dress casual most of the time."

Mary Ann asks Trent when he wore the suit.

Trent's expression shows grief and sorrow and says, "It was at my dear wife's funeral."

Mary Ann's compassion shows in her eyes, and she gives Trent a hug. Mary Ann says, "I'm so sorry I asked. I didn't know. I wouldn't have asked if I only knew."

Trent says, "It's okay. We all have times that are sad to remember, but, Mary Ann, tonight is going to be a good night. You and I will make happy memories for this suit tonight, I promise."

Mary Ann closes the door to her room as they walk holding hands down the hall toward the elevator. Trent and Mary Ann arrive at the dining area where the ship's captain will be seated.

The hostess says to Trent, "Would you mind sitting next to the captain?"

Trent looks at Mary Ann as to get her approval, and she nods yes. Trent says yes to the hostess.

The hostess says to Trent and Mary Ann, "The captain will be here in a few minutes, and your waiter will be here to take your drink order."

Mary Ann thanks the hostess as Trent pulls out a chair for Mary Ann to sit down. Another couple arrives at the captain's table a few minutes later. Trent introduces Mary Ann and himself to the couple, whose names are Ryan and Kerri. It's a couple who met on the ship like Trent and Mary Ann. The two couples have small talk for a few minutes when the captain of the cruise ship arrives dressed in his white uniform wearing his hat.

The captain smiles at the two couples saying, "Good evening, everyone. I'm Captain Bobby Boatman, and it's a pleasure to meet everyone."

Trent, who is seated next to the captain, introduces himself, and then everyone else introduces themselves to the captain. The captain asks Trent how he likes the cruise so far.

Trent, with a look of joy, tells the captain that the ship has everything to enjoy life on the water and that all the crew has been so nice and helpful.

The captain says to Trent, "That's good to hear. We try to make it a vacation to remember."

Mary Ann says to the captain, "I love this cruise because I have met this handsome gentleman right here."

The captain smiles at Mary Ann and says, "Well, some may say that our singles cruise is called the love boat," and everyone at the table laughs.

The rest of the dinner the captain talks about his life on the sea and has everyone at the table in full attention. An hour has passed, and the meal and drinks are excellent.

The captain tells his guests at the table that he really enjoyed the meal and company but has to get back on the bridge of the ship. They will be docking at Grand Cayman Island in about two hours. Trent asks the captain if it's possible to a take a picture with him and his friend Mary Ann.

The captain smiles and says, "I thought you would never ask." The captain calls for one of the ship's photographers to take a few pictures and says, "I'll have those pictures sent to your room tomorrow."

Trent shakes the captain's hand and says, "We thank you so much." Everyone tells the captain that they also had a good time as the captain waves goodbye and walks away. Trent tells the other couple that they are going to the nightclub to have a few drinks if Ryan and Kerri would like to join them later on.

Ryan says, "We may just to that."

Trent stands up and pulls the chair out for Mary Ann like a gentleman should do, and they walk out of the dining room. Trent and Mary Ann walk into the nightclub, and the manager asks Trent after seeing his VIP room key card if they would like to be seated at the VIP table.

Trent smiles at Mary Ann, and Mary Ann says to Trent, "Why not."

Trent says, "Yes, that would be fine."

The manager leads the couple to a very nice booth with food snacks and drinks set up on the table and says, "Your waitress will be here in a few minutes. Please let me know if there is anything you need, and I'll try to accommodate that for you."

Trent thanks the manager and turns his eyes to Mary Ann and says, "I just want to say that I'm so glad I met you and hope to see more of you."

Mary Ann is taken back from the remarks that Trent just conveyed and says with love in her voice, "Trent, I have to say this must be destiny. I am having an awesome time on this cruise, and 90 percent of the pleasure is because I met a man who shows respect to me and shows it in every way toward me."

Trent gives a kiss to Mary Ann that lets her know that he truly cares for her. A song is played by the DJ that has everyone dancing, and Mary Ann asks Trent to dance.

Trent smiles at Mary Ann and says, "Sure, let's go have some fun."

Trent and Mary Ann stay on the dance floor for at least twenty minutes before returning to the VIP area. On the way back, they meet Ryan and Kerri and asks the couple to join them. The two couples exchange stories of their life, family, and how they met each other on the ship. An hour passes by, and Mary Ann asks Trent if they could go walk on the deck to get some fresh sea air.

Trent smiles at Mary Ann and says to Ryan and Kerri, "We had a good time with y'all tonight. Maybe we can meet up with you two tomorrow."

Ryan says to Trent, "We had a good time too, and yes, we will try to get together."

Trent and Mary Ann dance themselves out of the nightclub, feeling good with each having a few alcoholic beverages in their bodies. Trent follows Mary Ann to the stern of the large cruise ship where they are all alone with no other passengers around. Trent watches her twirl around and dance with a sense of contentment.

Trent says, "You are so graceful when you dance like that." Mary Ann takes off her high heels and does a cartwheel and then a split to the floor of the deck that shows Trent her flexibility.

Trent claps his hands in approval and says with astonishment, "Wow, woman where did you learn to do that?"

Mary Ann walks over to Trent to give him a kiss and says, "When I was in college at LSU, I was one of the best gymnasts on the school's gymnastics squad."

Trent asks Mary Ann, "What was your specialty?"

Mary Ann looks at Trent with boldness in her voice and says, "Well, sir, I was good at the floor exercise and the vault. My best skills were on the balance beam where I scored many times close to perfection. I always took first place in that division, but, Trent, that was over twenty-five years ago."

Trent gives her a hug and says, "Well, honey, you still have it."

Mary Ann smiles at Trent and says, "Really, let me show you something," and before Trent could react, Mary Ann climbed on the banister that surrounded the ship's stern. Mary Ann was walking with perfect balance and twirling when Trent begs Mary Ann, "Please come down before you fall."

Mary Ann says to Trent with a voice of confidence, "I got this, baby, don't worry."

Mary Ann does another 360 turn and starts to lose her balance, because the cruise ship encounters a rogue wave that causes the ship to lean sharply to one side.

Trent does his best to reach Mary Ann, but before he can grab her, she falls off the stern of the ship. Mary Ann screams "Help!" as she falls thirty feet down into the ocean. Trent leans over the banister to see Mary Ann hit the water feet first. Trent runs to the closest life rings and grabs two life rings. Trent notices a man smoking a cigarette looking intoxicated.

Trent yells at the man, "Please go get help. My girlfriend has fallen overboard, and I am jumping in to save her."

CHAPTER TWENTY-FOUR

Trent yells at the man, "Please hurry, go get help to stop the ship," and runs away.

The man, who is clearly very confused by the yelling, watches as Trent runs toward the stern of the ship and throws the two life rings overboard. The man watches as Trent removes his socks and shoes; then he climbs on the banister and jumps feet first into the ocean.

Trent is praying to God as he hits the water hard, going underwater at least fifteen feet. Trent swims to the surface. Trent finds the life rings and holds on to both of them, frantically searching for Mary Ann.

The drunkard man walks into the interior of the ship only to find a pretty woman who is having a hard time walking. The pretty woman stumbles and falls into the arms of the man Trent told to go get help.

The woman says, "Hey, baby, thanks for catching me. My name is Susan. Would you please help me to my room, and if you do, I promise to be very nice and give you some good kisses and hugs."

The drunkard man is holding the woman as best he can and says, "My name is Charlie, and yes, I will help you," completely forgetting about getting help to stop the ship. Susan and Charlie walk down the hall wobbling and laughing, walking past a ship's crew member. The crew member whose name is Joshua looks at the stumbling couple and says, "Have a good night."

Joshua looks at his watch, says to himself aloud, "Two thirty a.m.," time for them two to go to bed.

Trent is screaming for Mary Ann but does not hear her voice because of the noise of the ship's engine.

Mary Ann can see the cruise ship's lights get dimmer by the minute and starts to pray to God, "Please send help for me." Mary Ann is doing her best to tread water but is getting tired quickly.

Trent remembers the keychain with the powerful flashlight that was given to him as a birthday present by his grandchild Billy. Trent takes the flashlight out and starts to point in the opposite direction of where the ship is going. The ship's engine noise now is gone with the ship being miles from Trent, and as he shines the light, Mary Ann sees it clearly.

Mary Ann screams at the top of her lungs, and Trent barely hears her over the noise of the waves. Mary Ann uses all of her strength to swim to the light. Trent does his best to swim to the voice of Mary Ann who is now screaming "Help, please help me."

Trent is only fifty feet from Mary Ann when he sees her go underwater. Trent panics and lets go of the two life rings and rushes to the point where Mary Ann goes underwater. Trent dives down into the dark water, reaching for Mary Ann, and by the grace of God, he feels her arm. Trent swims with such force that the two exhausted swimmers reach the surface quickly.

The two life rings are only ten feet away, and Trent grabs both of them with one arm while he holds on tightly to Mary Ann. Trent calls out to Mary Ann, but she is unresponsive. Trent starts giving Mary Ann mouth-to-mouth resuscitation, and very quickly Mary Ann regains consciousness.

Trent is looking at Mary Ann, and she is smiling at Trent and says, a little short of breath, "Hey, baby, looks like you joined me for a midnight swim." They both start laughing, and Trent asks, "Are you hurt?"

Mary Ann says, "No, the water broke my fall."

Trent smiles and says, "You're full of jokes this morning." Trent says, "I told a man on the ship to go get help before I jumped overboard, so someone will be coming to rescue us very soon."

Mary Ann gave Trent a big kiss and says, "You are my hero. I thought I could swim to you, but I was so tired I couldn't swim anymore. I saw the light and did my best to reach it, then went underwater."

Trent tries to calm her down by saying, "It's going to be okay, honey, I got you. I saw you go under, and somehow in the darkness I grabbed your arm and pulled you up to the surface. I gave you mouth to mouth, and you came back to life."

Mary Ann says to Trent, "I can't believe you jumped off that ship to save my life. Thank you so much."

Trent takes off his red tie and uses the tie to secure the two life rings together so they will not separate in the moderate seas. Trent is looking at the purple sky with millions of stars twinkling when Mary Ann says to Trent with a weak voice, "Trent, what would you have done if you had not been able to grab me when I went down. Tell me, what would you have done if I had drowned a few minutes ago?"

Trent looks at Mary Ann with waves lightly washing their faces with warm sea water and says very compassionately, "Well, I know there would be a rise in the ocean's depth, because of all the tears I would be crying." Trent gives Mary Ann a hug as best he can in the rolling seas while looking over the horizon for the ship's return, but sees nothing.

Mary Ann begins to look around also for any lights on the seas and says with great concern, "Trent, where is the ship? Honey, how long does it take to stop a ship? Something's wrong."

Trent does his best to console Mary Ann by telling her, "They must be sending a small boat to rescue us. It should be here shortly. Please don't worry."

Trent keeps looking as the minutes turn into hours. Trent has given up hope on a rescue by the ship.

Mary Ann says, "Why, why, why did I get up on that banister to show off my moves? How stupid can I be."

Trent smiles at Mary Ann and says with a laugh, "You were awesome. I was going to give you a score of ten till that wave caused the ship to lean and throw you off balance to fall off the ship."

Mary Ann laughs, too, and says jokingly, "Yeah, buddy, I was going for an awesome dismount, and the whole ship moved too quick for me to react. The next thing I know I'm in the water watching the ship get smaller and smaller."

Mary Ann looks deep into Trent's eyes and says with a tear rolling down her face, "I just knew I was going to die. Really, Trent, I was going to die, but I prayed to God please save me, and that's when out of the darkness with the ship cruising away, I saw a light."

Trent looks back at Mary Ann and gives her a kiss on the lips and says, "I am so glad my grandson gave me that light for my birthday."

Mary Ann says, "One day I will give a big hug to your grandson, because that light saved my life."

Trent smiles at Mary Ann and says, "That's the attitude that will keep us alive, honey." Trent looks at his watch.

Trent tells Mary Ann that the sun will be rising up soon. "If we see a ship or boat, we will use that bright yellow dress you are wearing to signal for our rescue."

Mary Ann smiles at Trent and says, "Sounds like a plan to me. The time is 7:30 a.m. now."

Trent is looking at his watch over and over when Mary Ann tells Trent in a very exhausted voice, "Why are you looking at your watch like that?"

Trent says, "Well, I promised to call my son at seven every morning, and by now he's very concerned why I haven't called him yet."

Trent smiles at Mary Ann and says, "I bet he has already called his sisters and brother to let them know that he will be calling the cruise ship to find out where I'm at."

Mary Ann is starting to cry with joy and yells, "Thank God for children that care about their parents. We will be rescued soon."

Trent is correct about Noah. He did call his sisters and brother. Noah did call the ship, which is docked at Grand Cayman. The ship's communications officer was notified, and he gave orders for a crew member to go to Trent's room to look for Trent, only to find that Trent is not there. The captain of the ship is then made aware of Trent not being seen anywhere on the ship after a thorough search on board. The captain orders a picture of Trent to be shown on every TV on the ship and asks anyone that's has any information on Trent's disappearance to come forward ASAP.

Charlie and Susan are just waking up in Susan's room when on the TV the picture of Trent is being shown with the announcement that this passenger is missing.

Charlie is looking at Susan and says with regret, "That's the man that jumped overboard to go save his girlfriend."

CHAPTER TWENTY-FIVE

Susan is looking at Charlie with confusion and says, "What are you talking about?"

Charlie rushes to the phone and says, "Who do I call? I know what happened to this man."

Susan screams, "Call 911. Tell me, Charlie, what the hell is going on?"

Charlie tells Susan with excitement in his voice, "Just before I met up with you in the hallway early this morning, that man whose picture is on the TV screen who they are saying is missing on the ship ran up to me. The man was yelling something like my girlfriend fell overboard."

Susan is looking at Charlie in disbelief now and says, "Oh my god, Charlie, what happened after that?"

Charlie is rubbing his full head of black hair now and says with clear recollection, "I remember the man grabbing two life rings and running to the stern of the ship, taking off his socks and shoes." Charlie looks at Susan who now is standing next to Charlie, looking into his nervous eyes.

Charlie says in a voice of panic, "The man threw the life rings off the ship, climbs on the banister, and without any hesitation jumps off the ship into the water."

Susan is yelling, "What happened next, Charlie?"

Charlie looks at Susan and says, "That's when I met you in the hallway and helped you to your room."

Susan screams at Charlie, "Why didn't you tell someone, anyone about the man jumping overboard!"

Charlie says with sadness in his voice, "Well, you looked so beautiful, you told me you needed help, and promised me hugs and kisses if I helped you back to your room. I completely forgot about going get help for that man."

Susan tells Charlie, "We have to notify the captain, let him know what happened."

Charlie says to Susan, looking worried, "Do you think I'm in trouble for not reporting this right away?"

Susan looks at Charlie and says, "Charlie, we can't be concerned about that now. We have to inform the captain. Hey, you remember that crew member we met in the hallway when you were holding me up?"

Charlie says with a confused look on his face, "No, Susan, I only had eyes for you, why do you ask?"

Susan rubs her eyes and says, "I believe his name tag read Joshua. He was really good-looking." Susan smiles for a second, and with a serious expression that covers her face, she says, "Yes, that's it. His name is Joshua."

Susan says to Charlie, "Now call someone so we can talk to the captain."

Charlie calls the number on the TV screen and talks to the dispatcher. The dispatcher connects Charlie with the first mate on the bridge of the ship where the captain is standing looking worried.

The first mate calls the captain, saying with a voice of urgency, "Sir, I have a passenger on the phone saying he has information about the man that is missing. He says the man jumped overboard."

The captain orders the first mate to put the call on speaker phone so everyone on the bridge of the ship can hear the conversation.

The captain says, "Who am I'm speaking with?"

Charlie clears his throat and says loudly, "I'm Charlie."

The captain says with a voice of authority, "This is the captain speaking, what information about this missing man can you tell me?"

Charlie tells the captain how early this morning the man whose picture is being shown on the ship's TV is the same man that jumped overboard the stern of the ship. The captain now has an expression on his face of extreme concern and asks the man, "What else can you tell me?"

Charlie tells the captain, "I was standing on deck when this man runs up to me yelling that his girlfriend fell overboard and for me to go tell someone to stop the ship. The man then runs toward the stern of the ship and grabs two life rings." Charlie takes a deep breath. "The man takes off his shoes and socks. The man throws the two life rings overboard then climbs on the banister and jumps overboard."

Charlie tells the captain excitedly, "I couldn't believe what I was seeing, so I went inside looking for someone to tell what just happened." Charlie pauses, and the captain yells over the phone, "Charlie, are you still there, what happened next?"

Charlie says, "That's when I saw this beautiful woman having trouble walking. As I got closer to her, she fell and I caught her before she fell to the floor." Charlie then tells the captain, "We introduced ourselves to each other, and she, I mean her name is Susan, promises me if I help her to her room, she would give me hugs and kisses."

Charlie then says to the captain, "So we are making our way back to her cabin. We meet one of your crew members, and he asks if we needed any help. Susan tells him that she already had a good man to help her."

The captain asks Charlie, "Do you remember who the crew member was?"

Charlie tells the captain, "I don't, but Susan remembers his nameplate, because he was so good looking."

Susan speaks up on the phone loudly, "His name is Joshua."

The captain tells Charlie and Susan with a stern voice, "Thank you for calling in this information. You might have just saved the lives of these people."

Charlie and Susan look at each other.

Charlie says "Man, I hope so" and hugs Susan.

The captain orders the first mate to have a crew member go to the stern of ship to check if there are any shoes on the deck. Then the captain orders the first mate to call the ship's photographer to get any pictures he took with any passengers last night up to the ship's bridge ASAP. The first mate receives a call from the stern of the ship from a crew member stating that he has found a pair of men's dress shoes with gray socks and a lady's pair of white high-heel shoes.

The captain's expression has turned into a face of deep concern now. He orders the first mate to get any crew member on the ship named Joshua to report to the ship's bridge ASAP. The minutes pass by slowly as three crew members with their first name being Joshua walk on to the ship's bridge where the captain is eagerly waiting.

The captain says while looking at the three crew members, "It was reported that one of you three met with a couple that was intoxicated this morning trying to walk back to their room."

Two of the crew members look confused, but one of the crew members speaks up and says, "Sir, I met up with a couple early this morning. I asked them if they needed any assistance getting back to their room, because they were both stumbling trying to walk, when the man spoke up loudly, 'I got this buddy, you just go on your merry way,' so that is what I did."

The captain says to Joshua, "Do you remember what time it was when this happened?"

Joshua smiles at the captain and says, "Yes, sir, it was 2:30 a.m. I remember because I looked at my watch saying to myself it was past their bedtime."

The captain thanks the crew members and dismisses them. The captain orders the first mate to find the ship's position at 2:30 a.m. and to call the UK Coast Guard Air Rescue. The captain pauses for a second then with a voice of hope tell them, "We have a man and woman floating on life rings in that general area."

The captain then orders the ship's air rescue helicopter to start a search of the area where the two passengers were said to have fallen into the water. A crew member from the ship's communication room enters the ship's bridge and asks the captain if he can talk to the missing male passenger's son.

The captain tells the crew member, "Yes, I can."

The captain is on the phone with Noah, who is very worried about his dad, and asks the captain if they found his dad. The captain informs Noah of all the information that he has on his dad and says,

"We are now sending the ship's helicopter to the last known position of your dad and the woman that fell overboard."

Noah is beside himself with confusion and concern and yells, "What do you mean overboard, and a woman?"

The captain tries to reassure Noah that the waters are warm where his dad and this woman are. "Your dad threw two life rings overboard before jumping off the ship to save this woman's life."

Noah is freaking out now and says to the captain, "You mean to tell me my dad jumped overboard to save this woman?"

The captain says, "Yes, that is the report I am receiving. Now, sir, we have the UK Coast Guard of Grand Cayman flying an air search rescue along with our helicopter from the ship, and, sir, soon as we find them we will contact you ASAP."

Noah thanks the captain and says, "Please find my dad," and disconnects the phone. Noah calls his sisters to give them the news he has found out from the captain. The captain asks the first mate to get the chart of where Trent and the woman went overboard. A crew member brings pictures that were taken with the captain last night. The captain remembers Trent and Mary Ann.

The captain looks over the chart and tells the first mate that the currents would have set them adrift eleven miles in seven hours.

"Please radio our air rescue team of the new area to search, and be on the lookout for a man in a gray suit and a woman in a bright yellow dress."

The first mate says to the captain, "Roger that, Captain" and relays the message to the cruise ship's air rescue helicopter.

Trent and Mary Ann are now looking at each other with the bright sun shining on the blue sea.

Mary Ann says with a dry voice, "Trent, I'm so thirsty."

Trent says to Mary Ann with a reassuring tone, "I know, Mary Ann, I'm thirsty too, but we can't drink this salt water, and besides, it won't be long, we will be rescued."

Mary Ann laughs and says, "You know, Trent, I love your faith, but you said that six hours ago, and still we are in this water."

Trent tells Mary Ann, "Yes, I know, but something happened with that man that was supposed to have let someone know we went overboard. But I know my son, Noah, called someone on the ship to let them know I didn't make my morning check-in call."

Trent looks around to see if he can see any boats or any aircraft that may be searching for them, but instead of seeing any of that, Trent see the tips of two sharks sixty feet away. Trent does his best not to show the danger and asks Mary Ann very calmly, "Hey, honey, let's get you lying as flat as you can on these two life rings so as to show the bright yellow dress."

Mary Ann looks at Trent like he's the smartest man in the world and agrees to the request. Trent is relieved that Mary Ann is not arguing with him because he really just wants her legs out of the water so the sharks will not bite them. A minute in time passes by when Trent hears the faint sounds of a helicopter coming toward them.

Trent's hopes escalate to the point that he kisses Mary Ann on her lips and says loudly to her, "Do you hear that? I hear a helicopter, and it's getting closer."

Mary Ann is so excited that she nearly falls off the two life rings, and Trent does his best to keep her steady on the life rings. Trent yells at Mary Ann, "Please be still. We have to make sure they see your yellow dress. It's our only chance."

Mary Ann calms down and tries her best to spread her dress wide over the blue sea so it will be more visible.

The ship's air rescue helicopter passes a few thousand feet away from Trent and Mary Ann when the rescue swimmer yells at the pilot that he sees the yellow dress. The helicopter pilot turns the helicopter quickly and hovers sixty feet over Trent and Mary Ann.

The rescue swimmer notices the two large sharks close to Trent and Mary Ann and tells the pilot, "I'm going in now. They have two sharks too close for comfort."

The pilot hovers the helicopter as steady as he can while the rescue swimmer drops into the water from forty feet above. The rescue helicopter lowers the rescue cable with the life ring. The rescue swimmer swims to Mary Ann and Trent, and before he can say anything, Trent yells at him, "Hurry, put the life ring on her quickly and get her out of the water."

The rescue swimmer realizes that Mary Ann has no clue that there are two sharks swimming very close to them because Mary Ann is being so calm. The rescue swimmer and Mary Ann are lifted up to the helicopter safely. Mary Ann is saying thank you to everyone on board. The rescue swimmer jumps back into the sea. Mary Ann looks down, and she sees the two large sharks getting even closer to Trent and the rescue swimmer.

Mary Ann screams, "Oh my god, they have sharks in the water."

The rescue cable with life rings jams while going down, and the other helicopter pilot gets out of his seat to try to fix the problem. The sharks begin their attack on Trent and the rescue swimmer when out of nowhere a dolphin pod of at least ten bottlenose dolphins start attacking the two large sharks, giving Trent and the rescue swimmer precious time. The winch cable for the lifeline has been fixed and is being lowered to the surface of the sea. The rescue swimmer and Trent are raised to the helicopter and are safely inside.

Mary Ann holds Trent with such force that Trent begs for her to loosen her grip. Mary Ann yells, "Y'all, we're almost shark bait, did you see what happened?"

Trent yells back over the noise of the helicopter engine, "Yes, those dolphins attacked the two sharks and saved our lives. What a miracle."

Mary Ann asks Trent, "How long did you know they had sharks all around us?"

Trent yells back, "I knew when I put you lying flat on the life rings. I wasn't going to let those sharks bite those beautiful legs."

Mary Ann smiles at Trent and says, "You are my hero. You kept me calm. You know I would have freaked out if I saw those sharks."

The rescue swimmer and Trent looked at each other and smiled.

Trent said, "Yeah, honey, that was my plan to keep you calm. Sharks love frisky bait."

The helicopter pilot radios the cruise ship's communication room to acknowledge the news of the successful rescue of the missing passengers. The captain is informed, and his reaction on the bridge of the ship is ecstatically happy. The captain asks the first mate to get Trent's son on the phone so he can personally tell him the news.

Monica is watching the news on the ship's TV when she sees Trent's picture being shown as a passenger that is missing. Monica runs out of her room to Ginger and Mary Ann's room, which is two rooms down. Monica begins banging on the door screaming, "Ginger, Ginger, wake up, open the door."

Ginger is awakened by the banging on her room's door and gets out of bed to open the door.

Monica says in an excited voice, "Ginger, it's on the ship's TV news bulletin that Trent is missing."

Ginger is rubbing her eyes and is confused by the news that Monica is saying. Ginger looks at the bed next to hers and sees that Mary Ann's bed has not been slept in.

Ginger looks at Monica and says in a worried voice, "Monica, where is Mary Ann? She did not sleep in her bed."

Ginger grabs the phone. "I have to call someone. I thought she stayed the night with Trent. Oh my god, what has happened to my friend?"

Monica turns on the TV only to see another bulletin come on the ship's new channel, and in disbelief Ginger and Monica watch the ship's air rescue helicopter land on the ship's helicopter landing pad. They then watch the rescue swimmer help Mary Ann and Trent out of the helicopter still dressed in a very wet yellow dress and Trent wearing a very wet gray suit, both of them barefoot. Members of the ship's crew run to them and wrap blankets around them to keep Mary Ann and Trent warm.

Ginger puts down the phone and says in a voice of astonishment, "Well, I guess they are not missing anymore."

Monica is relieved by the news, and happy but curious of what has happened to both of them, to be rescued by a helicopter.

CHAPTER TWENTY-SIX

The doctor on the cruise ship does a routine checkup on Mary Ann and Trent. He finds that they are in good physical condition, except for needing some water and food. The ship's chef prepares a big breakfast for the both of them. Trent and Mary Ann is allowed to take a warm shower to rinse off the salt water and then given some clothes to wear before returning to their room to put on their own personal clothes. The captain sends a crew member to investigate what happened to cause them to go overboard.

Trent and Mary Ann discussed a story while floating on the life rings that would not cause Mary Ann to get in trouble when they were rescued. The story line is that Mary Ann was leaning a little too far over the banister when a rogue wave caused the ship to pitch and list to one side, which caused Mary Ann to fall overboard. Mary Ann knew she should have never climbed on that banister, but she was tipsy with a few alcoholic drinks in her, which gave her the courage to do something dangerous. Trent told that story to the ship's investigator, and after reporting back to the captain with his report, the captain was satisfied with Trent's version of events. The captain was so relieved that Trent and Mary Ann was successfully rescued from the sea that he wanted to show his appreciation to Trent by having a news conference on the ship's TV station and giving him a Medal of Honor for showing courage and bravery for jumping overboard and saving the life of a fellow passenger.

Trent calls his daughters and sons as soon as possible to let them hear his story of his and Mary Ann's ordeal at sea. They are so happy to hear their dad's voice and want him to relax and enjoy the rest of his cruise. Trent promises them that he would do his best to finish the cruise without jumping off the ship again. The rest of the cruise

Trent is treated as a hero. Everywhere he goes passengers and crew members want to shake his hand, give him a hug, and pat him on the back for his bravery. Trent is grateful for all the people that says thank you, but after hearing it a few thousand times, Trent is ready to be just another passenger on the ship and enjoy the relaxing times he thought he would have on this cruise.

The captain makes a big deal about Trent risking his life to save another passenger at a huge gathering in the ship's largest room. Trent is nervous to receive a standing ovation that lasted at least five minutes. The captain pinned the Medal of Honor from the cruise ship's company on his shirt in front of all those people. Trent feels proud, and Mary Ann starts to cry, as do many other people in attendance. The captain gives a salute to Trent then shakes his hand, and says in a loud and proud voice, "Sir, you have my utmost respect and gratitude."

Trent smiles at the captain and says, "I only did what anyone on the ship would do, try to save a life."

The captain responds to Trent with a serious voice, "Believe me when I tell you, not very many people would have done what you have done, sir, you are a very brave man."

Trent thanks the captain and walks off the stage with Mary Ann who is wiping her tears away with a tissue, smiling at Trent and whispering, "You are my hero."

The ship departs from Grand Cayman heading for Nassau in the Bahamas where Mary Ann and Trent go onshore for a few hours. They are treated like rock stars with everyone wanting to shake their hands and say "God bless." The cable news stations around the world are televising the rescue and show Trent as a brave hero. The ship cruises on to Jamaica after departing from Nassau, and the Jamaicans give a parade in honor of Trent's bravery.

Trent is beginning to be overwhelmed with all the attention he is receiving, but Mary Ann tells Trent that he deserves every minute of the limelight. The last night of the cruise before the ship's arrival back in Galveston, Trent is looking forward to hearing and seeing the rock and roll band REO Speedwagon.

Trent is given four backstage passes. He invites Ginger and Monica to join him and Mary Ann. The band is excited to meet Trent because of the news they have been hearing of his heroic courage. The band REO Speedwagon gives Trent and his guest signed T-shirts and CDs of their greatest hits. The band also gives them front-row tickets for the concert. During the concert, the lead singer Kevin asks everyone in the crowd to applaud a real live hero.

Trent goes on stage after some coaxing from the band, and even sing with the band one of their hit songs. Trent is very excited to have the opportunity to sing on stage.

The concert is over. Ginger and Monica thank Trent and Mary Ann with hugs and kisses. Ginger tells Monica with a laugh, "Okay, girl, we have to give Trent and Mary Ann some alone time, because it's the last night of the cruise. Lord knows with all the attention Trent has been receiving, this poor couple has had none, I mean no time to be alone."

Mary Ann laughs and says, "Yeah, you're right, girlfriend, we had more time alone on those life rings than the last four days." Ginger and Monica say their goodbyes for the night.

Trent says with a smile on his face, "Thank y'all, ladies, for a good time." Trent asks Mary Ann if she would like to go to his room to have a cold drink.

Mary Ann smiles and says, "I thought you would never ask."

Trent opens the door to his room and ushers Mary Ann into his room. Mary Ann sits down in a chair next to a lamp that is sitting on a table and takes off her red high-heel shoes.

Mary Ann rubs her feet and says loud enough so Trent can hear her clearly, "Man, it's good to take off these shoes."

Trent looks at Mary Ann, who is dressed in a red dress that fits her curves tightly. Trent walks over, kneels down, and takes her foot to rub it gently.

Trent looks at Mary Ann and sees her smile with delight and says, "You know, to me you were the most beautiful woman at that concert tonight."

Mary Ann looks at Trent and says almost in a whisper to Trent, "Well, thank you, sir, and may I say you were looking very handsome tonight when the captain pinned that Medal of Honor on your chest. I was so proud of you."

Trent takes his hands off Mary Ann's foot and gets closer to Mary Ann's to give her a kiss on the lips that makes Mary Ann respond with a moan of satisfaction.

Mary Ann gently pushes Trent back and says in a tone of determination, "Please excuse me while I go to the bathroom."

Trent is feeling the pressure in his heart on what may happen in the next few minutes. Trent's mind is twisting and turning like an alligator on a hook about to be raised out of the water by some gator-killing swamp people from Louisiana. Trent sees Mary Ann come out of the bathroom wearing only a white T-shirt and shorts. Mary Ann sashays toward Trent, who is standing near the queen-sized bed with a big smile on his face.

Trent's blood pressure is rising as Mary Ann holds her perfectly proportioned body against Trent. Mary Ann smiles at Trent as she slowly unbuttons his shirt. Trent is looking into Mary Ann's eyes as she takes his shirt off and it falls to the floor. Mary Ann slowly caresses Trent's chest with her soft hands and then runs her hands across Trent's broad shoulders. Mary Ann starts to run her fingers through Trent's salt-and-pepper hair while bringing her full lips close to Trent.

Trent is about to lose his mind, and then Mary Ann says in a whisper, "I could kiss you all night, baby."

Mary Ann slowly and softly kisses Trent's neck a few times. She reaches down to grab Trent's hands and slowly pulls him toward the bed where she falls back. Trent falls softly on top of her so as not to put his entire weight on her as they both lay on the bed. Trent still has on his pants, and his mind is racing as what he should do. Mary Ann is kissing his cheek, looking into his blue eyes, wondering, Why does Trent still have his pants on?

Trent is holding each side of Mary Ann's beautiful face gently, and he kisses her on her lips long and soft. Trent is thinking that this is the first time in his thirty-seven years that he has ever kissed a woman with such passion other than his wife Rebecca. Trent is thinking of the many memories that he and Rebecca shared while being passionate, and in a moment that seem to be forever, he was lost in confusion at what should he do. On one hand he thought, I have a woman whose life I saved from certain death wanting to reward me with a night that would change our relationship forever. Mary Ann is a beautiful and kind woman that needs to show her gratitude in a way that would let Trent know she only has eyes for him.

Trent knows that having sex outside of marriage is wrong, but the woman has his motor running, and he isn't sure he can fight the feeling that is raising more than just his heartbeat and temperature. Mary Ann is sensing a lack of willingness from Trent and with compassion for his feelings stops her seductive kissing, and asks Trent, "Are you not ready to take our friendship to another level?"

Trent smiles at Mary Ann and says with a tender voice, "Oh, God knows I do, but, Mary Ann, is it the right thing to do, or is it the devil trying to give temptation to both of us to commit sins we will regret in the morning?"

Mary Ann looks at Trent and says, "I am ready to love you, honey, to show what you really mean to me, but if you feel that you are not ready to cross a line that will change our relationship forever, I understand and respect you for that."

Trent is both delighted and relieved that Mary Ann is being compassionate of Trent's hesitation to give in to the temptation to do the right thing.

Trent smiles at Mary Ann, kisses her on her lips, and says, "Can we just hold each other, and kiss each other, but not go all the way."

Mary Ann laughs then kisses Trent all over his face and says, "Darling, whatever you want I am happy just to be holding you. Anyway we have plenty of time to have good times in the near future."

Trent holds Mary Ann tight and says, "I am so happy you said that because I really want our friendship to grow slowly, steady, and to be very special."

Mary Ann laughs and says, "Oh, baby, it's going to be special. You can take that to the bank. I'm going to be your best friend."

Trent says, "Would you mind sleeping in this bed with me tonight? I would really like to wake up next to you in the morning."

Mary Ann says with a twinkle in her eye, "Under one condition."

Trent says to Mary Ann with an expression on his face, wondering what she wanted, "What would that be, baby?"

Mary Ann says, "You have to take off these pants you are wearing. They are causing me to itch."

Trent laughs and says, "You have a deal, sweetheart."

The next morning Trent wakes up at 6:50 a.m. and watches Mary Ann sleeping. Trent then calls Noah at exactly 7:00 a.m. and tells him that the ship will be arriving in Galveston on time and that all is well and will meet him at the dock at 10:00 a.m.

Noah says to his dad he will be waiting for him when he gets off of the ship and will be happy to have his dad back home.

Trent smiles as he is looking at Mary Ann sleeping and says, "Yeah, son, it will be good to be back home."

Trent orders a big breakfast while Mary Ann is sleeping, and there is a knock at the door. Trent opens the door to see Joshua, the crew member, delivering the meal.

Trent thanks Joshua for his service during the cruise, and Joshua tells Trent it has been a pleasure meeting him. Joshua tells Trent that he is the bravest man he has ever known and wishes him a safe journey home.

Trent gives Joshua a twenty-dollar tip and says with a smile, "Thank you very much." Trent walks into the bedroom with the tray of food, and the aroma of the coffee fills the room.

Trent softly lies next to Mary Ann and whispers in her ear, "Good morning, sleepyhead." Mary Ann moans in delight to hear Trent's sexy voice then smiles while opening her eyes.

Mary Ann says, "Good morning, baby. What smells so good?"

Trent brushes back Mary Ann's soft black hair from her face and says, "I ordered us a big breakfast before we get off the ship this morning."

Mary Ann smiles at Trent, gives him a big hug, and says, "You are so thoughtful, sweetheart."

Trent gives Mary Ann a kiss on the cheek, and says, "Honey, just sit up and I'll bring you your coffee, and a plate of food."

Mary Ann sits up in the bed and asks Trent, "Why are you so nice to me?"

Trent returns with the tray of food and places it in front of Mary Ann. Trent then gets his tray of food and sits next to Mary Ann and says, "Darling, the reason I'm so nice to you is you deserve a man that treats you with kindness."

Mary Ann takes a drink of her coffee and says to Trent, "This coffee is as good as you are, my love."

Trent says, "What do you mean by that?"

Mary Ann smiles at Trent and says, "Well, the short version is this, it's strong, gives me energy to face the morning, and tastes delicious."

Trent laughs and says, "Well, I see what you saying. I feel the same way about you."

Trent says, "We have a few hours before we have to get off the ship, so if you'd like to take a shower..." Then Trent stops talking.

Mary Ann says, "What is wrong, Trent?"

Trent smiles. Then he looks at Mary Ann and says, "You have your own room. You can take a shower there."

Mary Ann laughs and tells Trent, "Yeah, dude, I do have a bathroom in my room."

Trent and Mary Ann finish eating their breakfast, and after getting dressed, Mary Ann walks to the door with Trent and says, "I hope to see you at the dock in a little while."

Trent says, "I'll be looking for you. I would like for you to meet my son, Noah."

Mary Ann says, smiling, "I would like that too." Mary Ann gives Trent a big kiss on the lips and says, "Later, 'gator."

CHAPTER TWENTY-SEVEN

Trent has his suitcase in tow and is making his way toward the gangplank to exit the ship when his cell phone rings. Trent answers the phone to hear Noah's voice saying, "Hey, Dad, I'm waiting near the ship where everyone is getting off the ship. What are you wearing this morning?" Trent tells Noah that he's wearing a green shirt with blue jeans and will be getting off the ship in about five minutes.

Noah tells his dad, "There are thousands of people getting on the dock, but I'll find you."

Trent gets on the dock to find Mary Ann and Ginger waiting to say goodbye to Trent.

Noah is looking for his dad in the crowd and sees his dad, but Trent has not seen Noah yet. Trent hugs Ginger and then gives a long kiss to Mary Ann. Noah stops walking about thirty feet from his dad and sees him give that kiss to this beautiful woman.

Noah is smiling and says to himself, "That's my dad. He's still got the charm." Noah walks up to his dad and gives him a big hug while Ginger and Mary Ann watch the father and son reunite.

Trent smiles at Noah after hugging him and says, "Noah, this is Mary Ann and her good friend Ginger. Ladies, this is my son, Noah." Mary Ann and Ginger smile at Noah, and each one gives Noah a hug.

Noah says to the ladies, "It's a pleasure to meet y'all. My dad has told me that y'all have been very nice to him on this cruise, and I just want to thank y'all for that."

Mary Ann laughs and looks at Ginger and says, "Noah, your dad, this sweet handsome, brave, generous man is the one that's been so kind to us."

Trent says to Noah after looking at Ginger checking out Noah up and down, "Well, I guess it's time to get on the road."

Mary Ann gives Trent a kiss and a hug and says, "I'll call you when I get back home in Lafayette."

Trent smiles at Mary Ann and says, "Please do and drive safely, because the traffic will be heavy this morning."

Noah looks at Ginger who is smiling at Noah like he is the catch of the day.

Noah says, "It's a pleasure meeting you again," and then tells Mary Ann, "Have a safe trip home."

Trent and Noah walk away and are heading toward Noah's truck that is parked a few hundred feet away. Noah pats his dad on the back.

Trent looks at Noah with an expression of confusion and says, "What's up, son?"

Noah laughs and says, "You old dog, you still got it, I mean come on, Dad, that Mary Ann is beautiful."

Trent smiles at his son and says, "Yeah, I guess you're correct on that statement, son. Mary Ann is awesome."

Noah opens up the truck door and puts his dad's suitcase in the back seat and says, "Well, I don't know her like you do, but from the five minutes I spent with her, Dad, she looks like a keeper."

Trent gets into Noah's truck and closes the door. He looks at Noah as he gets into his truck and says, "Son, I risk everything for that woman. I truly believe God has brought us together for happiness and companionship."

Noah starts his truck and is driving away from the ship, saying to his dad, "I'm so happy for you, Dad. You deserve a woman like Mary Ann to feel joy again."

Trent says to Noah, "Yeah, I hope to get to know her more in the near future, that's for sure."

Noah asks his dad many questions during the trip back home to Orange Texas, which took longer than usual because of the heavy traffic on the interstate, but within a few hours they were pulling up to Trent's home where he noticed some familiar vehicles parked in the driveway.

Trent looks at Noah and says, "What's going on, son, why are all these cars at my house?"

Noah looks at his dad with a smile and says, "I don't know, Dad, it could be a welcome home party for you."

Trent grabs his suitcase out of the truck and walks up to the front door. Noah is only a few steps behind his dad when Trent walks into his home, and all the grandchildren and Trent's children are yelling "Surprise, welcome home, our hero!" Trent is very surprised by the greeting, and even his best friend, Willis.

Willis shakes hands with his dear friend and says, "Trent, you old light bulb, it's great to see you again."

Trent smiles at Willis and says, "What are you talking about, Willis? I have only been gone for a week."

Willis says, smiling at Trent, "It seems longer than that, but anyway, we have a lot of time to talk about your cruise. Right now enjoy this time with your beautiful family."

Everyone is excited to talk to Trent about his cruise while Noah's sisters are asking Noah about the woman that their dad jumped overboard to save.

Noah smiles at his sisters and says, "I've met her briefly, and from what I can tell, Dad has hit the jackpot with this lady. She is beautiful and very sweet."

Noah then looks at his dad who is talking to his grandchildren and back at his sisters, saying, "I know one thing. Dad is not the same man that we knew a week ago. Dad is now happier than I have seen him in years. I truly believe that God has brought this woman named Mary Ann into our dad's life to let him feel the joy of being with a good woman."

Leslie is looking at her dad and sees the smile on his face as he tells the story of riding on horseback on the beaches of Cancun, Mexico, and how he went scuba diving in the waters of Grand Cayman Islands. The grandchildren are listening to every word their grandfather speaks, waiting for the story of how he saved the life of this woman who fell overboard. Willis has a couple cups of coffee and walks over to Trent to offer a cup to him. Trent reaches for the cup.

Willis says, "I'll give you this delicious cup of coffee if you tell us the story of how you jumped overboard in the middle of the night to save a woman you barely knew."

Trent says to Willis, "Okay, now everyone gather around because I'm only going to tell this story once."

Noah tells his sisters and brother, Micah, "Let's go listen to this."

Trent is standing there with his cup of coffee in his hand with everyone looking at him as he begins his ordeal on the ship.

Trent says as he looks at everyone watching and listening very intently at every word, "The pretty lady fell over the railing of the ship, and I jumped in the water with two life rings after telling some man to go for help. The man was drunk and didn't go for help till seven hours later. There were sharks about to attack us when the coast guard rescued us. About ten dolphins fought with sharks while we were rescued." Trent smiles at everyone. "That's about it, a short story and not too exciting."

Willis looks at Trent and says, "Give me that cup of coffee back."

Trent says, smiling, "What you talking about, Willis, I told you the story, what else you want to know?"

Noah and Micah look at each other.

Micah says, "Well, for one thing, how did this pretty lady fall overboard?"

Noah says, "And why didn't that man go for help?"

Leslie speaks up and says, "How did you meet this woman?"

Jackie asks her dad, "What did y'all talk about in the water for seven hours?"

Kelly asks her dad, "Did you kiss this pretty woman?"

Willis asks, "If you did kiss her, did she slap your face?"

Trent is scratching his head and says loudly, "Wait a minute, all these questions, do I need a lawyer before I say another word?"

Everyone laughs.

Kelly speaks up and says, "Well, I don't know about a lawyer, Dad, but the local TV station has been calling at work asking if you would give them a short interview about the way all this happened, so you might need a lawyer before talking to anybody."

Trent looks at Kelly and, with a serious look on his face, says, "Well, I told the story enough times on the ship. I was given a Medal of Honor for my bravery by the ship's captain."

Trent pulls the medal out of his pocket and shows it to everyone then lets everyone hold it. Trent tells everyone, "When the ship was docked at a scheduled destination and I would go on an excursion, the leader of that country would make a big deal of my heroism, and one place even had a parade in my honor."

Micah stands up and stands by his dad and says proudly, "Well, Dad, we are not going to give you a parade, but we are extremely grateful for God's grace in saving you and that woman. By the way, when are we going to get to meet her?"

Trent smiles and says, "I didn't know y'all would want to meet her."

Jackie stands up and says with a voice of determination, "You better believe we all want to meet this woman who you were willing to die for, Dad."

Trent looks around at his family and then looks at Willis and says with a smile, "How about I call her up and ask her to join us for have a family BBQ this weekend? I am not sure she will come, but I'll ask her."

Willis says to Trent, "You old dog, you know that she will come."

Noah smiles at his dad and says, "That's great, Dad, and we can have it at my house." Noah then says, "And, Dad, you can invite Ginger, too, so Mary Ann won't feel uncomfortable being with all these people and not knowing anyone."

Trent says with a grateful tone in his voice, "Thanks, son, that's a great idea."

Leslie laughs and says, "Mary Ann and Ginger, where's Gilligan, is he coming too?"

Everyone laughs, and the welcome home party goes on for a few hours, and then slowly everyone kisses and hugs Trent goodbye. Trent is closing the front door when his cell phone starts to ring. It is Mary Ann calling him. Trent answers the phone, and Mary Ann lets him know that she and Ginger have made it home safely. Trent is relieved to hear the news and asks Mary Ann if she has no plans for this weekend would she and Ginger like to come by for a Texas BBQ at Noah's home.

Mary Ann speaks without any hesitation, "Yes, I would love to go, and I will ask Ginger if she would like to join me."

Trent says, "That's awesome. I will text you Noah's address later."

Mary Ann asks Trent, "How does it feel for you to be back home?"

Trent laughs and says, "Well, my family had a surprise welcome home party for me." Trent tells Mary Ann about the party and how everyone can't wait to meet her. Mary Ann laughs and tells Trent that she also had a welcome home party and everyone wants to meet the man that saved her life.

Mary Ann tells Trent, "It sounds like our families are interested in each of us."

Trent says with a voice of agreement, "Yes, sweetheart, that is exactly what it sounds like."

Trent and Mary Ann talk on the phone for almost an hour before saying goodbye. Trent goes into his bedroom and begins to unpack his suitcase when he looks at the picture of his wife, Rebecca.

Trent holds the picture close to his face and says, "I wonder, my love, did you and God have anything to do with this connection between me and Mary Ann?" Trent smiles at the picture and puts it down. Trent then gets on his knees and begins to pray, "Heavenly Father, thank you for protecting me during this cruise, and my family, and, Lord, thank you for bringing Mary Ann into my life. I give you all the praise and glory in your son's name Jesus Christ. Amen." The next morning after a good night of sleep, Trent receives a call from Mary Ann telling him that she and Ginger will be able to join Trent and his family at the BBQ.

Trent is happy to hear the news and tells Mary Ann to bring a swimsuit just in case she would like to go swimming.

Mary Ann laughs and says, "Are there any sharks in the water?"

Trent says, laughing, "No, I promise there are no sharks."

Mary Ann says with a voice of relief, "Well, in that case I'll bring a swimsuit and ask Ginger to bring one also."

Trent speaks with excitement in his voice, "That's great. I know y'all will have a great time because we will have good food, good music, and most of all good people."

Mary Ann is smiling and says, "Well, honey, you be sure to tell everyone I am looking forward to meeting them, and can't wait to eat some Texas BBQ."

Trent tells Mary Ann as soon as he ends the call with her that he'll send her a text with the time and address of Noah's home. Mary Ann and Trent continue talking on the phone for another ten minutes. They are talking about each other's welcome home party. They say their goodbyes. Trent calls Noah to let him know that Mary Ann and Ginger will be able to make it to the BBQ this weekend.

Noah is happy to hear the news and tells his dad, "I have everything under control for the BBQ."

Trent says with curiosity in his voice, "Son, if you have any surprises planned, let me know now."

Noah laughs and says, "Dad, there are no surprises for the BBQ."

CHAPTER TWENTY-EIGHT

It's Saturday morning and the sun is shining bright with only a few clouds in the sky to play peek-a-boo with the bright sunshine. Noah is busy at his home in the backyard preparing for the BBQ. Noah receives a call from his sister Kelly's husband, Kenny that he and the other brothers-in-law will be at his house in thirty minutes to help with the barbecue.

Noah says with gratitude in his voice, "Awesome, man, I could use some help."

Kenny arrives at Noah's house and is helping with the tables and chairs, when Micah and his sisters' husbands start to help.

Noah is delighted with all the help and tells everyone, "They have cold drinks in the refrigerator when y'all get thirsty." Kenny yells "Break time," and everyone goes to the refrigerator to grab a cold drink.

Noah says, "Come on, guys, we still have a lot of work to do before everyone starts showing up hungry." The men finish their drinks quickly and get back to work, making the patio look like a Texas BBQ with all the bells and whistles. Noah rolls out a karaoke machine from the back door of his house, and Micah asks Noah, "What is that thing?"

Noah smiles and says, "It's a state-of-the-art karaoke machine I just got yesterday." All the guys gather around as Noah turns on the machine, and everyone is amazed at the awesome sound of the speakers.

Kenny is laughing and says, "Now we are going to have some fun."

Noah laughs and says, "Yes, sir, that is why I got it, to laugh at each other when we try to sing our favorite songs."

Noah says to the guys while music is playing, "Let's finish setting up, and I'll get the grill ready to put the meat cooking."

Trent gets a call from Mary Ann saying she and Ginger will be in town in ten minutes. Trent asks Mary Ann if she wants to park her car at his house and they could ride together to Noah's home.

Mary Ann says in an excited voice, "Sure, honey, give me your address and we will be there shortly."

Trent opens the front door of his home to see Mary Ann looking beautiful dressed in a blue shirt with white shorts, which made her look terrific with her tanned legs. Ginger is smiling at Trent as he welcomes the women into his home, Ginger is wearing a sundress that is the color of mint green, and Trent compliments both women on how pretty they both are looking. Mary Ann gave a big hug to Trent and then a kiss on his lips.

Ginger is looking at Trent and Mary Ann kiss and says with a laugh, "Y'all need to get a room."

Mary Ann gently wipes some lipstick off Trent's lips and says, smiling at Trent, "Sorry, sweetheart, I put some lipstick on those soft lips of yours."

Trent smiles at Mary Ann and says, "That's okay, sweetie, I enjoyed the kiss."

Ginger tells Trent, "You have a very nice home."

Trent says, "Thank you, if y'all need to use the restroom to freshen up, it's right through this door."

Ginger laughs and says, "Yeah, we both need to use the restroom."

Mary Ann and Ginger come out of the bathroom together, and Trent asks the women if they were ready to go.

Ginger speaks up with enthusiasm in her voice and says, "Yeah, let's get this party started."

Trent looks at Mary Ann and says with a smile on his face, "Well, okay, ladies, let's go, we should be at Noah's home in just a little while."

Willis and his wife Wanda are at Noah's house with everyone else waiting on Trent to arrive, and Willis asks Noah, "Where is your dad at? He's running late."

Noah smiles at Willis and says, "I just talked to him on the phone. He should be arriving any minute."

A few minutes pass as everyone is getting the food ready to serve, and there are a lot of food to eat from potato salad, vegetables, burgers, hot dogs, rib eye steaks, and many different desserts.

Trent, Mary Ann, and Ginger get out of Trent's truck and begin to walk toward Noah's front door.

Ginger looks at the house, smiling, and tells Trent, "Wow, your son has a beautiful home."

Trent says, "Yeah, Noah really likes the best of the best, and since he has no wife, no children, he works hard to have money for the nicer things in life."

Ginger says in a voice of agreement, "He sure does, Trent."

The front door is unlocked as Trent leads the way to the back-yard patio through the house as Mary Ann and Ginger gaze at the beauty of Noah's home.

Trent is the first to enter the backyard patio when he is met by Willis, who says, "Hey, my friend, y'all running a little late."

Trent smiles at Willis and says, "Just a little late, but we are here now." Trent asks everyone for their attention, and Noah turns down the music so everyone can hear Trent.

Trent says, "I'd like to introduce Mary Ann and her best friend, Ginger."

The sisters are the first people to give hugs and smiles to Mary Ann and Ginger, thanking them for coming to the BBQ. Noah walks over to Ginger, and he is surprised when Ginger gives him a hug and a kiss on his cheek.

Noah says in a shocked voice, "Well, thank you for that, Ginger, may I ask how you like your steak cooked?"

Ginger smiles and says, "I like my steak medium rare."

Noah smiles and says, "Okay, medium rare coming right up."

Everyone is sitting at the tables ready to eat, and Trent is asked by his daughter Jackie to say grace.

Trent bows his head and begins to pray.

"Heavenly Father, we ask you to bless this food and everyone here. We pray that everyone returns home safely after this gathering in Jesus's name. Amen."

Everyone says Amen. The food is delicious, and after the desserts are eaten, Noah says he bought a karaoke machine, and if anyone had the courage to sing their favorite song to step up to the microphone. The grandchildren are excited to try this karaoke machine, and most of the grandchildren are decent singers. The adults are having some adult beverages, such as wine, beer, and whiskey, and are far from being intoxicated since none are heavy drinkers. Ginger is talking to Trent's daughters having a good time when she says to them, "We have to get Mary Ann to sing."

Kelly asks Ginger, "Is Mary Ann a good singer?"

Ginger smiles at Kelly and says, "Well, I have to say she is very good, but that's my opinion."

Kelly smiles and looks at her sisters and says, "Well, I for one would love to hear her sing."

Trent and Mary Ann are sitting talking to Willis and his wife Wanda when Kelly interrupts their conversation and says, "I'm sorry for interrupting, but I have a request for Mary Ann."

Trent looks at Kelly and says with a tone in his voice of concern, "What do you need, Kelly?"

Kelly says, "We heard from Ginger that Mary Ann can sing very well, and if she doesn't mind, would she sing a song for us?"

Mary Ann looks at Trent and says with a grin on her face, "Sure, I'll give it a try."

Mary Ann walks over to the karaoke machine and asks Noah to get the song "Jesus Take the Wheel" by Carrie Underwood ready. The song starts to play as Mary Ann holds the microphone close to her mouth, and with a strong, confident voice, she starts singing the song. Mary Ann sings so well that everyone is amazed by her talent. The song is finished, and everyone is asking for Mary Ann to please sing another song. Mary Ann asks Noah to play the song "I Want to Know What Love Is" by the band Foreigner. As Mary Ann sings the song, everyone is feeling the compassion that Mary Ann is feeling through the song. Some of the sisters are wiping tears from their face knowing that their dad wants to know what love is again. The song is over, and everyone is clapping their hands in appreciation for Mary Ann.

Trent walks over to Mary Ann with astonishment showing on his face and says to Mary Ann, "I am truly impressed with your talent of singing."

Mary Ann smiles at Trent and gives him a hug and says, "Well, what can I say, honey, I can sing a little." Kelly and Jackie walk up to Mary Ann smiling.

Kelly tells Mary Ann that her voice is amazing. Jackie tells Mary Ann that she should enter some singing contest because she would do very well.

Mary Ann thanks the two sisters for their kind words and says, "She has won a few contests in the past, but doesn't know if she is really that good."

Noah walks up to Mary Ann with Ginger by his side and says, "Mary Ann, you definitely won the best singer here today."

Ginger smiles at Mary Ann and says to Noah, "I believe she took first place, but I am being partial because she is my best friend."

Noah laughs and says, "Well, Ginger, the fact is Mary Ann can sing better than anyone here, so she is the best." Kelly and Jackie nod their heads in agreement.

Kelly says, "I'm going to put on my swimsuit. That big swimming pool is calling my name."

Ginger speaks up with excitement, "I would love to get in that water too. It's so hot today."

Noah says, "Sounds like a great idea, Kelly," and yells, "Hey, everybody, we are all going swimming."

Trent tells Mary Ann and Ginger, "Follow me, and I'll show you where you can change clothes in Noah's house."

The grandchildren are the first to get in the pool, and then their dads and moms join them. Mary Ann, Ginger, and Trent come out of the house, and Trent dives into the pool. Mary Ann removes her cover-up while Willis and Wanda are sitting on the lounge chair. Willis spills his drink when he sees Mary Ann's sexy body in a pink bikini. Wanda slaps Willis in a facetious manner to let him know it's not polite to stare. All the adults in the pool, both men and women, are surprised to see Mary Ann in such great shape in her fifties. Mary Ann walks to the far end of the pool where steps lead her in to the cool clear water.

Trent swims over to her and says, smiling, "Hey, pretty woman, there are no sharks in these waters."

Mary Ann laughs and says, "I sure hope not, we don't need that for sure."

Ginger dives into the deep end of the pool where she is met by Noah, and they enjoy the cool water together. Ginger tells Noah that he has a beautiful home.

Noah says, "Thank you. I did my best to make it like I always wanted my home to look like, very relaxing after a hard day at work."

Everyone is having a fun time in the pool. After a few hours, most of the guests say goodbye to Mary Ann and Ginger and how nice it was to meet them and hope to see them again. Mary Ann and Ginger give hugs to everyone and say they hope to see them soon also. Trent and Noah are the only men left by the pool along with Mary Ann and Ginger. Trent asks Mary Ann to join him in the shaded area of the patio for some cool drinks while Ginger and Noah are sitting in the hot tub area of the pool relaxing.

Trent tells Mary Ann that his daughters have expressed their feelings of her being with him, and Mary Ann looks at Trent with anticipation, wanting to know if she passed their test of approval.

Trent says, "They all love you and are very happy for me."

Mary Ann smiles in delight.

CHAPTER TWENTY-NINE

Trent looks at his watch and knows it's getting late. Mary Ann has a two-hour drive back to Lafayette. He asks Mary Ann if they are ready to go so they won't be traveling on the road at night.

Mary Ann smiles at Trent and says, "You are so sweet, always being concerned with my safety."

Trent laughs and says, "Well, I'm just being me, and besides, it's always better to travel in daylight."

Mary Ann smiles and gives a kiss on Trent's lips and says, "Thank you for this BBQ. I really enjoyed meeting your family and friends. Soon you can meet my family and friends."

Trent gives her a big hug then looks into her eyes and says, "I would love to do that, sweetheart."

Mary Ann looks at Ginger and says, "Hey, woman, it's time to go. I want to get home before dark."

Ginger smiles and says, "Okay, I'm coming."

Noah helps her out of the hot tub. Ginger gives Noah a hug and a short kiss and tells him that she had a great time. "You should call me sometime."

Noah smiles at Ginger and says that he has had a fun time too and sure he will call her soon. After everyone has changed into some dry clothes, Noah follows Trent, Mary Ann, and Ginger to Trent's truck in Noah's driveway.

Noah thanks them for coming, and Trent hugs Noah and tells him that the BBQ was perfect and tells him, "I love you."

Noah says with a smile, "I love you too, Dad."

Noah then hugs Mary Ann and Ginger, who both are impressed how a father and son can express openly their love for one another.

Noah says, "I pray y'all have a safe trip home."

Mary Ann says, "Thank you for an awesome day." They get in the truck and wave goodbye as Noah waves from his driveway. Trent arrives at his house and opens the truck doors for Mary Ann and Ginger.

Mary Ann smiles at Trent and tells him, "You are a gentleman."

Ginger says to Trent, "Yes, sir, you are, because you don't see men opening doors too much anymore for women."

Trent laughs and says, "I guess that's the way I was raised."

Mary Ann gives Trent a kiss and says, "Well, your parents did an excellent job."

Trent says, "Thank you," as he walks them to Mary Ann's car. Trent asks Mary Ann to call him when they get back home.

Mary Ann kisses Trent again and says, "I sure will, honey."

Mary Ann and Ginger drive away as Trent is waving goodbye from his driveway. Trent goes inside his home and calls Jackie and asks her what she thinks of Mary Ann.

Jackie tells her dad that Mary Ann is a wonderful person. "I can tell by the way she looks at you, Dad, that she really cares about you."

Trent is smiling as he tells Jackie, "I'm happy to hear you say that, because I have strong feelings for her, but I don't want to move too fast."

Jackie is laughing on the phone and says, "Dad, you are not moving too fast. If anything, you are moving too slow."

Trent says with confusion in his voice, "What do you mean too slow?"

Jackie speaks with a calming voice and says, "What I mean is, Dad, you have to let her know in no uncertain terms that you really care for her."

Trent calms down and tells Jackie, "Okay, I understand now what you are saying, you want her to know from me that I want to be her one and only."

Jackie says, with approval in her voice, "Yes, Dad, that's what I mean, let Mary Ann know you found what you need in her and you are happy."

Trent laughs and says, "Well, she does make me happy, and I'll be sure to convey that to her every time I talk to her."

Jackie says to her dad, "That's all you have to do, Dad, and y'all both will be happy. I love you, Dad, and have a good night."

Trent tells his oldest child, Jackie, that he loves her. "And you have a good night too."

Mary Ann calls Trent to let him know that she dropped off Ginger at her home and that she has made it home. Trent tells Mary Ann that he is glad that they made it home safely and that he is so happy being with her. Mary Ann is pleased to hear that and asks Trent what are his plans for tomorrow.

Trent says that he is officially retired and should get his first social security benefits check tomorrow, which he will promptly deposit tomorrow afternoon at his local bank.

Mary Ann laughs and says, "You are too young to retire, but I know you have earned it for sure."

Trent tells Mary Ann that Kelly has been getting calls from the local TV station asking her for me to give a short interview regarding the cruise rescue.

"I guess I'll do that in the morning, and I hope that will be the end of the limelight of this hero recognition."

Mary Ann laughs and tells Trent to enjoy the spotlight because people forget quickly the good things people do. "But I'll never forget or stop showing you gratitude for saving my life."

Trent tells Mary Ann that he will let her know when the interview will be shown on TV.

Mary Ann tells Trent to please do that and says, "Have a good night." The next morning Trent calls Kelly at work and asks her to contact the TV news reporter to let her know that he is ready to give an interview about the rescue at sea.

Kelly is excited to hear that news and tells him, "Dad, I will call you ASAP after talking to the news reporter."

Kelly calls the reporter. Her name is Paula Richards. She tells Kelly that they will be happy to interview her dad live on the noon news show today. Kelly agrees to that after talking to her dad who will be at the news station for noon to be interviewed. Trent lets his friends and family know about the interview, and lets Mary Ann know also. Trent arrives at the news station early, wearing a yellow shirt and blue jeans. After talking to the reporter, Paula, for a few minutes about the questions she would be asking Trent during the live interview, Trent takes a seat next to her.

The interview starts with Paula saying that she is sitting here with a real live hero. Trent is asked about what happened before, during, and after the heroic rescue. The interview lasts less than five minutes, but whoever is watching the interview learns that Trent risked his life to save another human being and has no regrets for doing so.

Paula thanks Trent for his time. Trent says to Paula with a sense of relief, "It went by quickly and was not as evasive as I thought it would be."

Trent goes back home after the interview and gets a call from his friend Willis. Willis tells Trent that he watched the interview and liked it, and he was glad to be his friend. Trent thanks Willis for his kind words and tells him he is waiting on his first check from Social Security. Willis tells Trent to cash that check as soon as possible.

Trent laughs and tells Willis, "Not to worry, my friend. I'll be going to the bank as soon as the mailman drops it in the mail slot through my front door."

Willis tells Trent he will call him later and to have a good day. The mailman puts the mail through the mail slot around 2:00 p.m. Trent opens up the letter from Social Security, and there it is, Trent's first retirement check.

Trent is smiling looking at the check and says, "Wow, it took a long time to earn this." Trent grabs his truck keys with his check in hand and goes to his local bank to deposit his check. Trent is talking to a lady who works at the bank who is helping deposit his check. Trent tells the lady that this is his first retirement check.

The lady smiles at Trent and says congratulations for receiving his first retirement check. Trent is saying "You're welcome" when a man in a mask rushes through the front doors of the bank holding a pistol and a small home-made bomb with a cell phone and some wires attached to it. The bank robber is yelling for everyone to put their hands up.

Trent and about ten other people put their hands up in the air. The bank robber yells for everyone to get against the wall and to throw their cell phones on the floor away from them. The bank robber orders everyone to face the wall and to keep their mouths shut.

He says he will shoot anyone that screams. Then the bank robber yells for the bank manager to retrieve all the money he can and put the money into a backpack that the bank robber gives him. The bank manager fills the backpack with money and hands the bag to the bank robber.

The bank robber tells the bank manager if he put a blue dye explosive in the backpack he would set off the bomb. The bank manager tells him he did not put that in his backpack.

The bank robber tells everyone in the bank that if anyone moves or calls the police he will set off a bomb in the bank. The bank robber tells everyone he can make the plastic explosives explode by cell phone if he needs to, so everyone better listen to his demands. The bank robber has been in the bank less than five minutes and is ready to leave when a pregnant woman walks into the bank, and when she sees the bank robber, she begins to scream. Trent turns around to see the bank robber pointing his gun at the lady, and without hesitation, Trent runs toward the lady. The bank robber shoots his gun, and the bullet strikes Trent in his chest. Trent falls to the floor moaning in pain with his blood spilling onto the bank floor. All the women in the bank are crying at the sight of all the blood. The bank robber yells at everyone to be quiet and reminds everyone of the bomb.

The bank robber looks at Trent as he walks by and says, "You had to be a hero. Now look where that got you." The bank robber runs out of the bank. Everyone rushes to Trent who is lying on the floor bleeding from his chest. The bank manager runs to the phone and calls 911. One of the bank clerks runs to the bathroom for some paper towels and returns to put direct pressure on Trent's chest to try to stop the bleeding.

The bank manager tells everyone to run outside just in case the bank robber decides to detonate the bomb. Everyone in the bank runs out the front doors of the bank, while the bank manager drags Trent outside. Trent's yellow shirt is soaked with blood as the clerk continues to apply direct pressure to stop the bleeding. The ambulance arrives at the bank within five minutes, and paramedics immediately start an IV in Trent's arm. Trent's chest wound is serious. He is put on a gurney and loaded into the ambulance quickly.

Trent is in a lot of pain but tells the bank manager to call his family at Electrical Experts Company and let them know what is going on. The bank manager promises Trent he will do that. The police arrives at the bank with sirens blaring from their police car and are asking questions about the bank robbery as the ambulance speeds away to the hospital. A bomb squad is sent into the bank to retrieve the bomb the bank robber left, which later on is found to be a fake bomb. Trent's family is notified that Trent has been shot, and they arrive at the hospital within twenty minutes.

Jackie is very nervous, and asks the nurse on duty where is her dad. The nurse's name is Nancy, and she tells Jackie in a calm voice that her dad is in the ER and the doctors are removing the bullet from her dad's chest. Nurse Nancy tells Jackie that as soon as she finds out any more information she will let her know.

Jackie is looking at the nurse and says, "Thank you," and Jackie hugs Kelly, who is standing next to her. Micah and Noah arrive at the hospital together and asks Jackie what's going on. Jackie hugs Noah and cries, "Dad has been shot in the chest."

Noah says "What the hell" in a loud voice. "Is he okay, where is he at?"

Kelly cries to Noah, "He is in the ER now, and the nurse will let us know anything as soon as she hears any news."

Leslie arrives at the hospital and enters the ER waiting room and is hugged by her sisters and brothers. Leslie asks, "Is there any news on Dad's condition."

Kelly tells Leslie with tears in her eyes, "All we know is the doctors are operating on Dad now."

Noah asks everyone to hold hands as he prays out loud, "Heavenly Father, we pray to you now that your supernatural power will heal our dad and give our dad the strength to recover from this injury. In Jesus's name we pray," and everyone said "Amen."

A police detective from Orange Police Department named Detective Watson arrives at the hospital with information about the robbery at the bank. Detective Watson introduces himself to Trent's children and begins to tell what happened at the bank to cause Trent to get shot.

Detective Watson begins his story by saying, "This is what I have gathered by asking questions to the workers and customers at the bank during the robbery."

Trent's children are listening to every word that the detective is saying explaining how their dad saw the bank robber pointing his revolver at a pregnant woman who walked into the bank as the bank robber was on his way out of the bank. The detective continues his statement by saying that the pregnant woman was surprised to see a man wearing a mask with a large pistol and began screaming.

"The witnesses told me when the woman began screaming, the bank robber got very upset and pointed his gun at the pregnant woman. I found out her name is Diane Brown. Well, what happened next is truly astounding." Detective Watson looks at Trent's children. He observes Trent's daughters holding each other's hands with tears streaming down their faces.

The detective says, "The people at the bank saw your dad turn and run from the wall of the bank and stand in front of Mrs. Brown just as the bank robber shoots his pistol, which was pointed at the very pregnant Mrs. Brown. The bank robber ran out of the bank, leaving everyone in the bank hysterical. The bank manager then dragged your dad out of the bank onto the sidewalk because the bank robber placed a bomb in the bank. The bomb squad was sent in the bank and found that the bomb was a fake bomb."

Jackie is holding her sisters' hands, Leslie and Kelly who are saying, "My god, what kind of person does this kind of stuff?"

The detective shakes his head slowly from side to side and says, "I've been doing this job for nineteen years. I thought I had seen it all, but this bank robber was crazy."

Nurse Nancy walks into the waiting room and asks Trent's children if they knew their blood type because their dad needed AB negative blood now. The sisters all had that blood type. Noah and

Micah's blood type was B negative. Nurse Nancy asks the sisters to follow her so they could donate blood for their dad, who desperately needs that blood type. Noah asks Nurse Nancy in a serious voice, "Could you please tell us the condition of our dad?"

Nurse Nancy looks at all of Trent's children and says with a voice of compassion, "All I can say is your dad is in critical condition, but we have the best doctors at this hospital trying to save his life."

Nurse Nancy tells the sisters, "We must hurry because your dad needs your lifesaving blood."

The sisters follow Nurse Nancy out of the waiting room to go to a room where volunteers donate blood. The detective asks Noah and Micah if they have any questions that he might be able to answer.

Noah is very upset and asks Detective Watson if they arrested the bank robber yet.

Detective Watson looks at the floor then suddenly looks at Noah and says with regret in his voice, "No, I'm sorry to say that the lowlife SOB has not been located, but we have our entire police force working hard to catch the bank robber."

CHAPTER THIRTY

It has been two hours since Trent has been in the operating room with the doctors and nurses trying to keep him alive. The waiting room at the emergency room is full of Trent's family and friends trying to console each other. The nurses on duty have been giving updates to Trent's children but can only say that Trent's condition is very critical. A news crew from the news station that did the interview with Trent earlier in the day at noon arrives outside the waiting room hoping to talk to Trent's family. The news reporter, Paula Richards, walks into the waiting room without her cameraman. Paula asks Kelly if she would like to say a few words on camera for the TV audience.

Kelly looks at Micah and says, "What would you like me to say?"

Paula tells Kelly, "I will ask you a few questions about your dad's current condition and how you feel about your dad risking his life to save a pregnant woman from being shot."

Noah steps up to address the news reporter's request and says, "As long as we see what you will show on air before it is shown on live TV, it will be okay."

Paula agrees to do that for Trent's family. The cameraman sets up his camera, and room is made in the waiting room as family and friends watch Kelly have an interview with Paula Richards. The lights come on the camera, and the interview starts with Paula saying, "We are coming live from the hospital where family and friends wait for news from doctors on a man being operated for a gunshot wound. I interviewed this same man just a few hours ago live at our TV station for his heroic act on a cruise ship less than a week ago. It's been said by eyewitnesses at the bank that was held up by a lone bank robber that this same man ran into the line of fire to protect a pregnant woman entering the bank at the time of the robbery. Witnesses have stated to police that the bank robber was leaving the bank with stolen money when the pregnant woman named Diane Brown walked through the front doors of the bank and saw the bank robber wearing a mask. The woman started screaming, and the bank robber was very upset and pointed his pistol at the woman. The hero on the cruise ship I interviewed is the same man that jumped in front of the pregnant woman and was shot by the bank robber. The bank robber ran out of the bank and is still at large with police using all their resources to capture this criminal."

Paula turns to Kelly and says to Kelly, "What is your name?"

Kelly clears her throat and says, "I'm the daughter of the man who has risked his life to save the life of a complete stranger. My name is Kelly, and my dad's name is Trent. My family and I are asking for prayers for my dad." Kelly starts to cry. "This is very difficult for us because we thought we lost our dad on this cruise he was on a few days ago, and now this happens."

The reporter Paula tries to console Kelly by holding her hand and asks Kelly if there is any news about her dad.

Kelly looks at Paula and says, "All we know is what the nurse has told us."

Paula asks Kelly with a sincere voice, "What has the nurse told you?"

Kelly says as she wipes a tear from her eye, "She has told us that my dad is in critical condition."

Paula looks at Kelly and says with a compassionate voice, "Kelly, we have a lot of viewers watching, and we will all be praying for your dad and your family." Paula then says in a professional voice, looking at the camera, "This is Paula Richards live at the hospital where a hometown hero is fighting for his life."

The cameraman shuts off his lights for his camera, and Paula shows the recorded video to Kelly and her siblings. Noah and Micah agree that the interview is acceptable to show on the news while Leslie and Jackie hug Kelly and told her she did a great job with the interview.

Meanwhile in the operating room, the doctors are doing their best to make sure Trent survives his gunshot wound, but they have major concerns for his prognosis. Dr. Roger Manson, the chief surgeon, looks at the assisting surgeon, Dr. Leon Chandelle, and both doctors are looking at the open chest cavity of Trent. Dr. Manson says that the bullet had to be a hollow point that he was shot with because of all the damage it has caused once it penetrated the skin.

Dr. Chandelle says with confidence, "I have to concur with that analysis, Dr. Manson. It sure looks like the bullet did extensive damage while going through the body."

Dr. Manson tells Dr. Chandelle that it doesn't look good. "This hero lost so much blood before getting to the hospital that major damage has happened to his vital organs that we cannot repair." Dr. Manson, using his expert skills, retrieves the bullet from Trent's chest and drops it in a metal tray.

Dr. Manson checks the vitals on the monitors and tells Dr. Chandelle, "Let's close up this surgery. We will put this patient in an induced coma so he will not feel the pain of recovery for a few days."

Dr. Chandelle agrees with Dr. Manson as they start to sew up Trent's chest. The doctors inform Nurse Nancy that she can tell the family the surgery is done and they will be out in twenty minutes to talk to the family. Nurse Nancy walks out of the operating room and arrives at the waiting room where Trent's family is eager to hear any news on their dad's condition. Nurse Nancy tells the family that the doctors will be out in twenty minutes to let them know how their dad is doing.

"Your dad has survived the surgery."

Jackie asks Nurse Nancy, "When can we see our dad?"

Nurse Nancy tells Jackie, "I can't answer that, but I'm sure the doctors will let you know." Nurse Nancy tells everyone that Trent is being moved to Critical Care Unit for his recovery.

Noah thanks Nurse Nancy for her help and says with relief in his voice, "Thank God for saving his dad's life."

Noah says with panic in his voice, "I completely forgot about calling Ginger so she can let Mary Ann know what has happened to Dad." Noah takes his phone out and calls Ginger to explain what happened to his dad. Ginger is shocked to hear the news that Noah is telling her and says she will call Mary Ann immediately and do their best to get to the hospital as soon as possible.

Noah thanks Ginger and tells her to please be safe traveling on the road. Ginger promises Noah that they will. Ginger calls Mary Ann and starts to cry on the phone, telling Mary Ann that Trent was shot during a bank robbery. Mary Ann is very upset to hear the bad news and asks Ginger if she will ride with her to the hospital to see Trent. Ginger responds quickly to say, "I'll be waiting on you when you get to my house."

Mary Ann calls Trent's cell phone, which is in Noah's pocket; the detective gave the phone to Noah when he visited the hospital. Noah tells Mary Ann that they are waiting for the doctors to let them know the results of the emergency surgery to remove the bullet.

Noah sounds nervous on the phone and says, "We have not yet been able to see Dad, but the nurse says that Dad is recovering in the Critical Care Unit."

Mary Ann thanks Noah for the call. With a voice of comfort, she tells Noah that his dad is strong and will be okay. Noah thanks Mary Ann for her kind words and asks her to be safe traveling here to the hospital.

Mary Ann tells Noah that she and Ginger will be leaving Lafayette very soon and says goodbye to Noah.

Noah tells his family that Mary Ann and Ginger are on their way to the hospital. Mary Ann gets some overnight clothes together before leaving her home to pick up Ginger at her home. Dr. Manson and Dr. Chandelle are walking toward the waiting room where Trent's family and friends of are waiting for the doctors to explain his condition.

Willis sees the doctors walking toward the waiting room and walks into the waiting room and announces to everyone that he sees some doctors coming this way. Everyone in the room looks at Willis and pays close attention to the doorway of the waiting room. Dr. Chandelle is in his early fifties, standing five feet ten inches tall with salt-and-pepper hair, weighing 170 pounds. Dr. Manson is in his early sixties, standing six feet two inches with mostly gray hair weighing 190 pounds.

Dr. Chandelle speaks loud and clear, "We would like to talk to Trent's immediate family."

Micah speaks up with a voice of authority to the doctors, "You can speak freely to all of us, because we all care deeply about Trent."

Dr. Chandelle looks at Micah and says, "Very well, I'm Dr. Chandelle. I was assisting in the operation of removing the bullet, and this is our chief surgeon at the hospital, Dr. Manson."

Everyone eagerly listens to Dr. Manson speak.

Dr. Manson says loudly that Trent was brought into the hospital in rough shape, his blood pressure was eighty over forty, and he had a significant loss of blood.

"We immediately gave blood to get his vital signs up to normal."

Dr. Manson could see the women in the waiting room were beginning to cry while their husbands did their best to console their wives with hugs. Dr. Manson continues speaking and says that after giving Trent an MRI, they found that the bullet was in a difficult area of the chest to remove it safely.

Dr. Manson puts his arms to his side and speaks with confidence, "I decided that in order to save this man's life the bullet had to be removed. Dr. Chandelle assisted me in the operation, and we found that the bullet caused extensive damage to some major organs in Trent's body."

Noah interrupts Dr. Manson and asks with deep concern in his voice, "Doctor, what are the chances of our dad surviving?"

Dr. Manson looks around the room at all the faces and then looks at Noah with compassion and says, "I'll give your dad a fifty-fifty chance of survival, because he is in good shape for his age."

Dr. Manson pauses for a few seconds and says with a voice of concern, "We had to put Trent into a medically induced coma to ensure that his recovery is not disturbed by the pain his body is going through now. We have Trent in a Critical Care Unit where all his vital signs are being closely monitored by our nurses."

Jackie wipes away her tears and says to Dr. Manson, "When will we be allowed see our dad?"

Dr. Manson looks at Jackie and tells Jackie in a calm voice that everyone may go a few at a time for five minutes to hold Trent's hand.

"Trent needs our prayers to survive this ordeal, because we have done all we can do."

Kelly tells the doctors, "Thanks so much for all you've done, but it was always in God's hands to keep our dad alive."

Kelly's husband gives her a big hug and says with a tender voice, "That's right, sweetheart, it's in God's hands."

Dr. Manson asks if it was okay if we all said a prayer together, and Micah says loudly, "Of course it is."

Dr. Manson asks everyone to hold hands, and he bows his head and says, "Heavenly Father, we give you praise and glory for all your love and mercy, and, Lord, we believe you are all-powerful. We pray to you here and now that you heal Trent's body and fully restore his wounds as only God can, and, Lord, we ask that you give peace and strength to Trent's family and friends that they may have the comfort in knowing that God Almighty is in control of this situation. Whatever circumstances evolve we know it is your will. We ask all this in Jesus's name. Amen."

Dr. Manson asks if anyone had any more questions, and no one speaks up. Dr. Manson looks at Noah and says, "If you will please coordinate the line of family and friends to visit with your dad."

Noah smiles at Dr. Manson and says, "Thank you, Doctor, I will do my best."

The doctors exit the room after many family members say thank you to them. Noah tells Jackie that since she is the oldest, she and her family will be able to go visit her dad first.

Jackie gives Noah a hug and says, "We will be back in five minutes, because I know everyone wants to see Dad." Jackie, her husband, and their children walk down the hall where they are met by Nurse Nancy.

Nurse Nancy gives a smile to Jackie and says, "Please don't be alarmed by the tubes connected to your dad, because the machines are doing all the work for your dad so he can recover quickly." Jackie smiles back at Nurse Nancy.

She says, "Can I hold his hand?"

Nurse Nancy smiles and says, "Of course you can, you can talk to him too, because I believe he can hear you talking. He just can't talk back right now with the tubes helping your dad breathe."

Jackie thanks Nurse Nancy again and enters Trent's room to see her dad lying in the hospital bed with all kinds of tubes attached to his body, and she begins to cry as she walks closer to her dad. Jackie's children also begin to cry softly while they stand close to their mom.

Jackie's husband takes a deep breath and says to Jackie, "He's going to be okay, sweetheart, we have to believe God will heal him."

Jackie wipes away her tears and says with hope in her voice, "I know, but I have never seen my dad in this condition before."

Jackie takes hold of her dad's right hand, holds it gently, and fighting back the tears, she says, "Dad, it's me Jackie. We are all here. We love you, and we need you to get better real soon, so you listen to me. You have to fight to get well."

Jackie's youngest son, who is thirteen years old, looks at his mom, and with tears in his eyes says, "Mom, will Grampsy die? He looks like a man on his deathbed."

Jackie forces herself to smile and says, "Come give me a hug, son, now listen to me." Jackie looks at her son and says with a voice of compassion, "We all one day will die, and only God in heaven knows the moment in time that will happen." Jackie tells her son that Grampsy is strong. "I believe that God will let him live and have many more years with his family, so we have to believe that this is God's will to let us have more time with your grandfather."

Jackie, her husband, and their three sons hold hands and pray as Jackie says with tears falling from her eyes onto the bed where her dad is lying, "Dear God, please heal my dad, and give him strength to be with us. We need our dad and want him to live. We pray, God, that you answer our prayers in Jesus's name. Amen."

Jackie and her family give Trent a kiss on the side of his face, and each one says out loud, "We love you, and get well soon," then walk out of the room holding hands, fighting back tears of emotion. Kelly's family goes in next to see Trent, then Leslie's family, and then Micah's family. All are shocked by the sight of Trent in his hospital bed holding on to life by a thread. Noah is the last to visit his dad and is joined by Trent's best friend, Willis, and his wife Wanda. Willis looks at Trent and can't help but cry.

He tells his best friend, "Man, look at you, why did this happen to you?"

Wanda does her best to console her husband and hugs him close and says, "Now, Willis, you know Trent will be okay, let us pray."

Noah cries, "Please, God, save my dad."

CHAPTER THIRTY-ONE

Nurse Nancy walks into the room and checks the monitors with Trent's vital signs.

Noah asks, "How is my dad really doing?"

Nurse Nancy looks at Noah and says with sincerity, "Your dad has a big fight ahead of him to make it out of here, but with prayer all things are possible."

Noah smiles at Nurse Nancy and says, "Thank you for being honest, and not giving us false hope. His family needs to know the truth."

Nurse Nancy smiles and says, "The truth is that your dad is strong, but the bullet really did a lot of damage to your dad's insides, and it's a miracle that he made it to the hospital alive."

Willis says with a grin on his face, "Yeah, my best friend is one tough son of a gun. He will make it through this. He just has to."

Noah leaves the room followed by Willis and Wanda, and return to the waiting room where the rest of Trent's family are seen waiting. A man and pregnant woman arrive at the waiting room and see all the people that are there for each other's support for Trent's well-being.

Leslie looks at Jackie and says in a whisper, "Hey, sis, that woman looks like she could have that baby at any time."

Jackie says, "Yeah, I guess that's why she's here, to have that baby."

The man with the pregnant woman speaks up with a voice of uncertainty and says, "Excuse me, but we are here on behalf of the man that saved my wife's life today."

Everyone turns to look at the man with the pregnant woman.

The man is looking at Micah, who is the closest to him, and says, "This is my wife, Diane, and I'm Jack. We just wanted to visit with his family." Jack continues by saying, "We have been praying for him constantly and are hoping he will be okay."

Diane is fighting back the tears, but she is overwhelmed with compassion for Trent's family. She says, "I'm so sorry this has happened, and it should have been me that got shot, but I was saved by a hero that I didn't even know. He is the bravest man I've ever seen. I just want to thank him."

Jackie, Kelly, and Leslie look at each other, and walk over to console Diane.

Kelly says, "Our dad has been our hero forever, and we all hope he gets to meet you so you can thank him personally."

Diane asks Kelly with tears coming down her face, "Will your dad be okay?"

Kelly looks at Diane with a serious expression and says, "We have hope of Dad recovering from this. The doctors give him a 50 percent chance of surviving."

Diane is seen getting weak, and the sisters help her to a chair in the waiting room.

Jack rushes toward his wife and kneels down in front of her and with love in his voice says, "Are you okay, honey?"

Diane looks at her husband and says in a whisper, "I just got weak suddenly. Can you get me some water to drink please? I'm thirsty."

Noah sees what is happening and gives an unopened bottle of water to Jack. Jack thanks Noah and gives the water to Diane, everyone looking at Diane drink the water.

Jackie asks, "Diane, do you want me to find a doctor?"

Diane says, "Thank you for your concern, but I believe I'll be okay. It's just been a day of too much stress, and this little boy inside of me is moving around like he is ready to be born."

Kelly asks Diane, "When are you due to have your baby?"

Diane says smiling at Kelly, "We have one more week, and I'm ready to get this big boy out."

Jack smiles at Jackie and says with exhaustion in his voice, "Yeah, the fun will begin with three o'clock feedings and smelly diapers."

Jackie smiles at Jack and Diane and says, "Yeah, the sacrifices are many, but the joy of having a child to love is worth every minute."

Danny and Lisa arrive at the hospital holding each other's hand to see so many people at the waiting room.

Lisa speaks with nervousness in her voice and says, "Danny, all of your brother's family seems to be here."

Danny lightly squeezes Lisa's hand and says, "God, I hope Trent is going to be okay."

Micah is the first person to say hello to Danny and Lisa with a hug, and Danny asks Micah with a compassionate voice, "How is Trent doing?"

Micah takes a deep breath and says with hope in his voice, "The doctors have told us that Dad is a strong man, but the bullet tore up his insides."

Then Micah gets emotional, and his voice cracks as he says, "The doctors give Dad a 50 percent chance of survival."

Danny looks at Micah and immediately gives him a hug then says to him, looking directly in his face, "Don't worry, Micah, your dad is tough, and with all of our prayers, he will make it. He just has to."

Micah says, "Would you and Lisa like to see him?"

Danny smiles and says, "We sure do. Can we see him now?"

Micah says, "Right now they are letting everyone see him for five minutes, but I must warn you, the doctors put him into a coma so he wouldn't feel all the pain his body is going through, and he has a lot of tubes and wires connected to him."

Danny tells Micah concern in his voice, "Thank you for telling us that."

Danny and Lisa hug everyone in the waiting room before going to see Trent. Danny and Lisa slowly walk into the room where Trent is recovering from surgery. Danny is shocked by all the wires and breathing machine attached to his brother. Lisa feels Danny's hand squeeze her hand tightly as Danny's emotions go from bad to worse, and Danny cannot hold back the tears as he and Lisa walk next to the bed Trent is lying in. Lisa does her best to console Danny by giving him a hug and saying softly to him, "Your brother is strong, honey. He will pull through this. Just give him some time."

Danny wipes away his tears with his hand and looks at Trent with a face of disbelief and says to Lisa, "You are right, sweetheart. My brother will be all right. He's in a lot better shape than me."

Danny lets go of Lisa's hand and takes hold of Trent's hand and says in a hopeful voice, "Hey, my brother, it's Danny."

Danny looks at all the monitors that are keeping track of Trent's vital signs. The noise of the breathing machine is very distracting, but Danny continues his one-sided conversation with his brother. Danny tries to smile and sound upbeat as he tells Trent that he and Lisa are here to make sure everything is being done so he can get back on his feet as soon as possible. Danny looks at Lisa with an expression that tells Lisa that hope is slipping away.

Lisa speaks after clearing her throat and says, "Hey, Trent, it's Lisa. We are all praying for Jesus to heal you quickly, and to make you as good as new, so you get all the rest you need, and listen to those nurses that are here to help you." Lisa begins to cry as she sees Danny looking at his brother. Then Danny looks to the ceiling of the room, looking up to heaven.

Danny says out loud, "Dear heavenly Father, please give my brother strength. He is a good man, and his family needs him on Earth."

Lisa hugs Danny as he continues his prayer by saying, "Lord, give his family the peace of knowing that everything will be okay, and in your Son's holy name Jesus we believe this will be done."

Danny looks at his brother and says to Trent, "We will talk to you soon."

Lisa says to Trent, "You get some rest. We will be back. We love you."

Danny squeezes his brother's hand gently. He lets go of his hand and turns to walk out of the room with Lisa by his side. Danny and Lisa are walking back to the waiting room, and he whispers to Lisa, "I have a bad feeling about this, honey." Lisa stops walking and looks at Danny with an expression of confusion on her face.

Lisa asks Danny, "What do you mean?"

Danny looks at Lisa's pretty face and says with compassion, "I hope I'm wrong, but, I have this feeling that my brother is not going to make it out of this hospital alive."

Lisa is surprised by what Danny just said, and with confidence in her voice, she tells Danny that Trent will be just fine and to never doubt the power of God Almighty's healing hands. Danny smiles and kisses Lisa softly on her lips and says, "I'm sorry, honey, you are right. Trent will be out of here in just a few days."

Noah meets Danny and Lisa outside the waiting room in the hallway and gives his uncle Danny a hug. Noah whispers to Danny, "Don't worry, my dad is going to make it. He just has to make it."

Danny looks at Noah after the embrace and says with a smile, "You are right about that, Noah. Your dad will make it."

Noah gives Lisa a hug and thanks her for being here.

Lisa says with a smile, "This is where the family needs to be at times like this, giving loving support to keep each other strong."

Noah's cell phone rings, and he answers the phone. On the phone is Ginger, and she is telling Noah that they have just arrived at the hospital. Noah tells her that he will walk toward the entrance of the hospital to meet her and Mary Ann then says goodbye to her on the phone.

Noah tells Danny and Lisa that Trent's friends that he met on the cruise are here to see Trent. "I'm going to meet them at front doors of the hospital."

Danny and Lisa say goodbye to Noah and walk into the waiting room where Jackie walks close to Danny. Jackie can tell that her uncle Danny is upset and tells him in a voice of comfort, "Uncle Danny, please relax. My dad is going to be okay. He just needs a few weeks to recover from his wounds."

Danny looks at Lisa then looks at Jackie and smiles and says, "I know, Jackie. I just don't know why this happened. It's just crazy something like this could happen to your dad."

Jackie smiles at Danny and says, "Well, my dad was being a hero again, and saw this pregnant lady about to be shot by this deranged bank robber and took the bullet, saving the life of the woman and her baby."

Lisa speaks up, "I saw the news report. Your dad is definitely a hero. How is the pregnant lady doing, does anybody know?"

Jackie smiles at Lisa and Danny and says, "See for yourself. She is sitting over there with her husband."

Danny looks at the pregnant woman and whispers to Jackie, "Oh my god, it looks like she could have that baby any day now."

Jackie laughs just a little and says, "Yes, you are right. She will be having a little boy very soon, and she told me a few minutes ago that she and her husband decided to name the baby Trent."

Lisa smiles at Danny and says, "Well, what this world needs is another Trent for sure."

Noah is at the entrance of the hospital when he sees Ginger and Mary Ann walking toward him.

Ginger hugs Noah and gives a quick kiss on his lips and says, "We are so sorry this has happened to your dad."

Noah says, "Thank you."

Mary Ann hugs Noah and asks Noah, "What is Trent's condition."

Noah tells Mary Ann that his dad is doing okay but is not out of the woods. "The doctors give him a 50 percent chance of survival."

Mary Ann's facial expression shows deep concern when she hears Noah say those words and says, "Can I please see your dad?"

Noah says with compassion in his voice, "Of course you can. We can go see him right now, but I must let you know the doctors have him hooked up on a breathing machine and wires all over to monitor his vitals, so don't be shocked when you see him, because it does look terrible to see him like that."

Mary Ann tells Noah, "Thank you for letting me know what to expect when I walk into your dad's hospital room."

Noah holds hands with Ginger as they walk down the halls of the hospital with Mary Ann following closely. Noah is the first to walk into the room with Ginger behind Noah and Mary Ann a few steps behind Ginger. Mary Ann walks close to the hospital bed and begins to cry as she takes Trent's hand and holds it firmly.

Ginger tries to hold back her tears as she watches her best friend suffer with the pressure of seeing her boyfriend on life support. Noah holds Ginger as he feels her lose her balance from getting weak from emotions of sorrow. Mary Ann begins to talk to Trent with the hope that he can somehow hear her comforting words. Mary Ann speaks with loving tones in her voice telling Trent that she is here beside him.

Mary Ann wipes away her tears and says, "Now, sweetheart, the doctors are doing everything they can for you, but you have to fight with all your strength to live."

Mary Ann clears her throat as her voice begins to crack and says, "I know you can do this, you are my hero, and I need you, baby, to be with me, so you listen to me. I believe you will be out of this hospital very soon. God will heal you sweetheart, I just know he will."

Noah looks at Mary Ann as she is telling him those words of encouragement and says to Mary Ann, "Thank you for being here, the nurses say that there is a good chance that Dad can hear us talking to him even though he is in a coma."

Ginger asks Noah why he is in a coma. Noah says to Ginger, "The doctors feel that the pain is too great for Dad to bear because of the extensive damage to his internal organs."

Noah then says with hope in his voice, "The doctors want him to heal quickly without any more complications that might hinder his recovery."

Mary Ann gently kisses Trent on the side of his face and says out loud, "I love you, Trent, and you rest, my love, and get strong so we can be together soon outside this hospital."

Ginger holds Mary Ann's hand that is holding Trent's hand and says with a loving tone in her voice, "Hey, Trent, it's Ginger. I just want you to know that we are praying for you to get well. We need you to be strong. We love you."

Noah speaks up while standing next to Ginger, "Dad, it's Noah. We are going to let you rest, but your family is here for you, so don't you worry. We are very close to you if you need us."

CHAPTER THIRTY-TWO

Noah leads the way out of the hospital room down the hall toward the waiting room where Trent's family is gathered. Leslie and her husband are standing outside the doorway of the waiting room.

Leslie sees Noah, Ginger, and Mary Ann walking toward her. She tells her husband with a voice of excitement, "Look, honey, it's Mary Ann."

Leslie greets Mary Ann with a big hug and thanks her for being here in this time of crisis. Mary Ann asks Leslie how she is doing, and Leslie responds in a voice of hope saying, "I'm doing my best to be strong for my family, but the truth is I'm so worried about my dad I can't think straight." Mary Ann begins to have tears run down her face, which makes Leslie start to cry.

Noah says with compassion in his voice, "Now listen, you two. Dad is going to be all right, so please stop crying."

Ginger looks at Mary Ann and with a reassuring voice tells Mary Ann that Trent will get through this. "We have to believe."

Mary Ann and Leslie both wipe their tears away, and Mary Ann tries to smile and says, "You're right. I don't know why I'm so emotional."

Leslie tells Mary Ann with a voice of nervousness, "We are just all on edge, not knowing what will happen next."

Mary Ann walks into the waiting room and begins hugging everyone and doing her best to show a brave face. All of Trent's family welcome Mary Ann and Ginger with open arms and thank them for coming to the hospital. A few hours pass, and most of the family have left the hospital, with only Noah, Ginger, Mary Ann, and Kelly left in the waiting room.

Kelly says that she will stay at the hospital till the morning. Just in case there is any change with her dad, she will call everyone to let them know.

Mary Ann tells Kelly, "They will be back in the morning," and gives Kelly a hug and a kiss on the cheek. Noah is walking out of the hospital with Ginger and Mary Ann. Mary Ann asks Noah if there is a good hotel he can recommend to stay at.

Noah smiles at Mary Ann and says, "Well, the best one I can recommend is at my house."

Ginger tells Noah with gratitude showing in her voice, "That's so nice of you, Noah."

Mary Ann smiles at Noah and says, "Yes, thank you, Noah."

After arriving at Noah's home, Mary Ann and Ginger change into their pajamas. Noah asks the girls if they would like a glass of wine to help them sleep.

Ginger says with a smile on her face, "It sure would do me good to have one, because I'm still wound up tight."

Mary Ann agrees with Ginger, and after drinking a glass of wine, and Noah tells some stories about Trent. They all decided to call it a night and try to get some sleep. The next morning Noah has breakfast cooked and is getting the coffee brewing. Mary Ann is the first to smell the aroma of the coffee and wakes up Ginger who is sleeping next to her in the big king-size bed.

Ginger stretches and says, "Good Lord, that coffee smells good."

They both walk to the kitchen to find a delicious breakfast prepared. Mary Ann and Ginger both smile and thank Noah for the breakfast. After breakfast, everyone gets dressed and return to the hospital.

Dr. Chandelle is seen coming out of Trent's room talking to Kelly. Noah who is standing there asks if there is any improvement in Dad's condition.

The doctor looks at Noah with hope and tells Noah, "Your dad is getting stronger, and I will take him out of the medically induced coma after lunch today so he may be able communicate with his family."

Noah smiles at the doctor and says, "Thank you so much."

Dr. Chandelle tells Noah that his dad is still in critical condition and has a long recovery to endure. Mary Ann thanks the doctor for all his help.

Dr. Chandelle says, "You're welcome," and walks away, leaving some hope in the minds of Trent's loved ones.

Noah immediately calls his sisters, who in turn call other family members about the good news. Noah is followed in the hospital room by Kelly, Ginger and Mary Ann, and they see the supervising nurse checking all of Trent's vital signs, looking at all the monitors that are attached to Trent by wires. Mary Ann asks Nurse Georgia how Trent is doing today.

Nurse Georgia turns to look at Mary Ann and smiles and says he is doing well today. She writes down on a clipboard some of the readings from the monitors and tells Noah, "Everyone has heard what your dad did to protect that pregnant lady in the bank, and we at the hospital are praying for your dad to recover as soon as possible."

Noah smiles and says, "I am very proud of my dad, and please thank all the people at this hospital for the prayers."

Nurse Georgia says with a smile, "I sure will," and walks out of the room. Mary Ann walks over to Trent's hospital bed and takes hold of his hand and begins to sing a song by Brooks and Dunn called "You Are My Angel." Noah comments to Ginger in a whisper, "That is a beautiful song, and Mary Ann sings it with such compassion."

Mary Ann finishes singing the song, and she notices Trent squeezing her hand softly. She tells Noah, "Your dad just squeezed my hand." Noah, Kelly and Ginger are surprised to hear what Mary Ann just said, and Noah asks Mary Ann, "Are you sure?"

Mary Ann tells Trent, "Hey, sweetheart, it's Mary Ann. If you can hear me, please squeeze my hand."

Trent squeezes Mary Ann's hand gently. Noah rushes out of the room to find a nurse to tell that his dad is conscious and to come see for themselves. A few minutes later, Nurse Georgia and Noah return, and Mary Ann asks Trent to squeeze her hand again. Without hesitation, Trent squeezes her hand for the third time. Nurse Georgia is astonished and, after checking Trent's vital signs, tells Noah that she will inform Dr. Chandelle right away.

Ten minutes passed quickly while waiting for Dr. Chandelle to arrive at Trent's hospital room. All the while, Noah and Mary Ann carry on a conversation with Trent by asking questions, and Trent squeezing Mary Ann's hand once for yes and twice for no. Dr. Chandelle enters the room and asks Trent if he is in any pain, and he squeezes Mary Ann's hand once for yes. Dr. Chandelle gives Trent a small dose of morphine, and after a minute, Dr. Chandelle asks Trent if the pain has gone away. Trent squeezes Mary Ann's hand once for yes.

Dr. Chandelle then asks Nurse Georgia to assist in removing the breathing machine from Trent. Dr. Chandelle gives Trent a few minutes to breathe on his own, and slowly Trent opens his eyes. Dr. Chandelle asks Trent, "Would you like a drink of water?" Trent nods his head yes and is given a straw from a cup to enjoy some refreshing water. Trent clears his throat and speaks in a scratchy tone of voice, "Thank you, Doctor."

Everyone in the room is amazed that Trent is awake. Mary Ann smiles at Trent and tells him with tears in her eyes, "I love you."

Trent smiles at Mary Ann and says, "I love you too."

Trent tells Mary Ann that her singing made him feel strong, and he started to move his hand with ease.

Trent tells Noah, "I could hear everyone talking when they came to visit, but I couldn't talk back to them."

Dr. Chandelle looks at all the monitors and tells Trent that his health is improving but needs to get his rest to get stronger. Dr. Chandelle asks Nurse Georgia to check on Trent's condition every twenty minutes for the next six hours. "Let me know if there are any changes in his vitals."

Dr. Chandelle tells Mary Ann, Noah, Kelly and Ginger that they can visit with Trent a few more minutes but will have to let Trent get some much-needed rest. Noah thanks Dr. Chandelle. The doctor smiles and leaves the room with Nurse Georgia.

Trent asks Mary Ann what day it is. Mary Ann looks at Trent, wipes a tear from her eye, and says with a tender voice, "It's Tuesday."

Trent says in a confused voice, "How many days has it been since I got shot?"

Noah looks at his dad and says, "Only two days, Dad."

Trent asks for another drink of water, and Mary Ann puts the straw to Trent's mouth and watches Trent drink.

Trent says in a content voice, "That is some good water." Trent asks if Noah could ask all of his family to come see him.

Noah says, "I will call them, Dad, but you heard what Dr. Chandelle said. You have to get your rest to get stronger."

Trent smiles at Noah and says, "Yes, son, I will get my rest, but I need to see my loved ones as soon as I can."

Mary Ann looks at Noah, and she tells Trent with a loving voice, "We will have everyone here this afternoon, and you can give all your loved ones hugs and kisses."

Trent smiles at Mary Ann and says, "Honey, you are the best girlfriend any man could hope for."

Trent looks at Ginger and Kelly, says, "Hey, ladies, how are you all doing?"

Ginger and Kelly smiles at Trent, and they tell Trent, "We are doing great now that you are talking to us."

Trent smiles at Ginger and says, "Please take care of Mary Ann while I'm trying to get better. She needs you now more than ever."

Ginger smiles at Trent and wipes away a tear that was running down her face and says sincerely, "Don't you worry, Trent. We lean on each other through times like this."

Nurse Georgia enters the room and checks on Trent. Nurse Georgia tells Trent in a firm but nice voice, "I'm glad to see you doing so well, but it's time to say goodbye for now to your loved ones, because the doctor gave me strict orders for you to get some rest."

Trent smiles at the nurse and asks Mary Ann and Kelly for a kiss before they leave. Mary Ann leans over and gives Trent a long, soft kiss on his lips. Kelly kisses her dad's cheek.

Trent smiles and says, "That's the best medicine I had all day."

Noah holds his dad's hand and says, "We will be back this afternoon, Dad, with all the family. Now you get some rest."

Trent smiles at Noah and says with a tear in his eye, "I love you, son."

Noah looks at his dad and says, "Now, Dad, please don't cry, because you are going to make me cry. Everything is going to be fine. We love you and will see you soon."

Nurse Georgia tells Trent that she is going to give Trent some medicine to help him sleep but he will be able to visit with his family this afternoon.

Trent smiles at Georgia and says, "Okay, I'm ready to take a nap," and with that Nurse Georgia puts a sleeping aid in Trent's IV.

Noah, Kelly, Mary Ann, and Ginger are walking down the hall from Trent's room.

Mary Ann tells Noah, "It's a miracle that Trent is up, alert, and talking so well."

Noah looks at Mary Ann and says with excitement in his voice, "Yes, our prayers have been answered, thank God for his love and grace."

Noah calls his sisters and tells them, "Dad is awake and doing well." He also tells his sisters, "Dad wants to see everyone this afternoon." Noah takes Mary Ann, Ginger, and Kelly to a restaurant for lunch near the hospital, and they talk about the power of prayer.

CHAPTER THIRTY-THREE

It's now four thirty in the afternoon, and Noah, Ginger, and Mary Ann have been at the waiting room in the hospital for an hour waiting for visiting hours to begin. Dr. Manson and Nurse Nancy are at Trent's hospital room, and Dr. Manson is looking at Trent with a clipboard of data for Trent's latest vitals. Dr. Manson begins to tell Trent he has some news on his condition.

Trent interrupts the doctor by saying with a smile, "Well, Dr. Manson, may I tell you my news before you tell me yours?"

Dr. Manson puts down his clipboard and sits on the bed next to Trent and says in a curious voice, "Sure, I'm listening."

Trent begins talking as Nurse Nancy stops looking at the monitors and gives her undivided attention to Trent. Trent clears his throat and says, "I have something to tell you that you may not believe because while I was in a coma I had a visit from a very important person in my life."

Dr. Manson smiles at Trent and says, "Yes, I heard you had many visitors, Trent. I even heard that you told them you could hear them talking. That's amazing."

Trent looks at the doctor and the nurse and says, "Yes, that is true, but that's not the visitor I'm talking about. The visitor I had was Jesus Christ, and he told me that I have only a short time left on this earth, and then he and his angels would come to take me to my eternal home in heaven." Trent smiles. "Jesus told me that he could heal me if he wanted to, but Jesus said it was time for me to go to paradise with him."

Dr. Manson and Nurse Nancy are astonished by the words that Trent is saying. Dr. Manson looks at Trent and says in a voice of compassion, "Trent, I believe in Jesus Christ, and if you tell me you had a visit from the Son of God, well, I have to take your word for that. The news I was about to tell you on your physical condition is you are getting worse. I have to be honest and not sugarcoat the news."

Dr. Manson holds Trent's hand and says, "You are correct in telling us your time on this Earth is almost over. Most of your vital organs, such as the liver, kidneys, and pancreas, have been damaged to the point of critical shutdown. All we can do for you now is give you painkillers to relieve the pain you are going through."

Nurse Nancy wipes a tear from her eye and says with sympathy in her voice, "Trent, please take hold of this cable," and Nurse Nancy gives Trent a cable with a small red button at the end of it.

Nurse Nancy says with a smile, "If the pain gets too great for you to deal with, and I know it will, you may press this little red button, and it will give you a small dose of morphine to take away the pain."

Trent says, "Can I try it now?" with a smile.

Dr. Manson tells Trent, "Sure, give it a try, Trent."

Trent pushes the little red button, and within a few seconds Trent is looking at Nurse Nancy with a sense of ecstasy and says, "Wow, it really works fast."

Dr. Manson smiles at Trent and says, "Is there anything else we can do for you?"

Trent, who is feeling no pain now, smiles. "Yes, sir, could I have some time with my family?"

Dr. Manson says, "Of course."

Trent looks at Dr. Manson with a serious face and says, "Would it be all right if I tell my family that I'm going to die soon?"

Dr. Manson looks confused and says, "Trent, you are the bravest man I know, and if that is what you want, I will let you do that, but if your family has any questions, I will explain the best I can why you will die."

Trent smiles at Dr. Manson and says, "Thank you. I believe it will be better hearing the news from me, even though news like that is never good or acceptable."

Dr. Manson asks Nurse Nancy to inform Trent's family that they are allowed to visit Trent as long as they want too.

Nurse Nancy looks at Dr. Manson and says, "Yes, I will go right now to let them know." Nurse Nancy walks into the waiting room and sees Noah looking out of the window.

Nurse Nancy says to Noah in a voice of assurance, "I have just left your dad's room, and you may visit him now."

Noah looks at Nurse Nancy and asks with a voice of concern and hopefulness, "How is my dad doing?"

Nurse Nancy smiles and says, "Your dad told me he really wants to be with his family."

Mary Ann and Ginger look at each other, and Mary Ann laughs and says, "That sounds like Trent. Let's go see our hero."

Nurse Nancy does her best to hide her true emotions of sadness and walks out of the waiting room. Noah is the first one to walk into the room to see Trent looking at the door. Noah walks to the bed and gives his dad a kiss on the cheek.

Noah says with enthusiasm in his voice, "Hey, you are looking like you're not in any pain today."

Trent smiles and says to Noah, "Yeah, I feeling like I'm walking on sunshine with this morphine running through my veins."

Mary Ann walks next to the bed, leans over, and gives a soft kiss on Trent's lips and says, "It's great to see you, sweetheart."

Trent smiles at Mary Ann and says, "Your kiss is just what I needed."

Mary Ann smiles and says, "Well, honey, I have plenty more when you need them," and they both laugh.

Trent looks at Ginger and says, "Hey, pretty lady, did you sleep well last night?"

Ginger walks next to the bed and says in a caring voice, "Well, Trent, it was tough falling asleep, because we are all worried about you."

Trent smiles at Ginger and says with a reassuring voice, "I'm going to be okay, please don't worry." Trent asks Noah if he could call his sister Kelly to bring her fancy camera when she visits this evening.

Noah looks at his dad and says, "Do you want her to take some pictures of you, Dad?"

Trent tries to hide his true emotions and says, "I think it would be nice to have some pictures of my loved ones visiting me at the hospital." Trent asks Mary Ann, "You think I could get my face shaved and my hair combed, so I look good in the pictures?"

Mary Ann smiles at Trent and says in a joyful voice, "Honey, we will have you looking very handsome, and if it's okay with you, I'll go buy you a purple shirt. You look so nice in purple."

Trent smiles at Mary Ann and says, "It's like you can read my mind. Thank you so much, darling."

Mary Ann kisses Trent again and says, "Ginger and I will be right back, you don't go anywhere."

Trent says, "Be safe, honey, I'll be waiting right here for you."

Noah looks at his dad and says, "Dad, you look like you are doing better. I'm glad to see you in such good spirits this afternoon."

Trent smiles at Noah and says in a loving voice, "Son, I just want you to know that I am so proud of you, and I love you, and yes, I do feel better."

Noah takes hold of his dad's hand and with compassion in his voice says, "Thank you for saying that, Dad. I love you too, and all of your children are proud of you. You're the best dad in the world."

Trent looks at Noah, and a tear slowly runs down his face.

Noah says to his dad, "Hey, what's up with the waterworks, old man?"

Trent smiles as he wipes the tear off his face and says in a voice of contentment, "I guess it's the drugs. I'm sorry."

Noah smiles at Trent and says, "Dad, please don't ever be sorry for showing your feelings. It's only human nature. I'm going to call Kelly now and do my best to get everyone here to visit with you and take some pictures."

Trent says with gratitude in his voice, "Thank you, son, and could you call my best friend, Willis, and my brother Danny to stop by too?"

Noah looks at his dad with a hint of concern on his face and says, "Sure, Dad, I'll get them here as soon as possible. Twenty minutes pass by quickly, and Mary Ann and Ginger return to the room with a beautiful purple shirt and shaving supplies. Mary Ann shaves

Trent's face with gentleness and helps Trent put on the new purple shirt. Then she combs his hair.

Ginger looks at Mary Ann and Trent and says, "Wow, Trent, you look very handsome."

Mary Ann laughs and says, "Yes, he looks awesome."

Trent smiles and says, "Well, I appreciate that compliment, ladies. I feel lucky to be in the presence of two pretty women."

Kelly walks into the hospital room with her husband and children and notices how nice her dad looks. Kelly walks over to her dad and says, "Dad, you look amazing," and gives her dad a kiss on the cheek.

Trent smiles at his daughter and says, "Why thank you, dear, you look beautiful too."

Trent tells Kelly that he's in a good mood and would enjoy taking photographs with everyone today if she wouldn't mind taking most of the pictures. Kelly is smiling at her dad, but she is feeling a sense of uneasiness on the urgency of taking all these pictures today. Trent asks if he could take individual pictures with his grandchildren.

Kelly says, "Sure, Dad."

Kelly begins taking pictures of everyone in the room with Trent, and Mary Ann is smiling but is starting to realize that something just doesn't feel right about this picture-taking situation.

Jackie and her family are arriving at the hospital when she notices Jack and Diane entering the hospital.

Jack tells Jackie in a frantic voice that Diane's water has broken and she is going into labor. Jackie is excited but nervous, hoping the birth goes without complications. Diane is seen in pain as the contractions are only five minutes apart.

Jackie tells Diane, "Our prayers are with you and that baby boy."

A nurse at the hospital brings a wheelchair for Diane, and she is pushed to the birthing room in the hospital. Ten minutes later, Diane gives birth to a healthy nine-pound baby boy. Jack and Diane are so happy and thank God for the precious gift from God.

The rest of Trent's family with Danny and Lisa arrive at the hospital to visit Trent and to take photographs with Trent. An hour has passed and Willis and Wanda arrives. Trent asks if they wouldn't mind taking a picture with him.

Willis looks at Trent and says to Trent in a joking voice, "You know I don't take good photographs."

Trent smiles at his best friend and says, "What you talking about, Willis, you are a handsome old man."

Willis laughs and says, "Yeah, I guess you are right," and then takes a photograph with his old friend of forty years. Trent is seen pushing the red button on the cable.

Willis says to Trent, "Are you trying to call the nurse?"

Trent laughs at Willis and says, "No, I'm giving myself a small dose of morphine to ease my pain."

Willis shows a look of discomfort on his face because he hates to see his friend in pain. Trent asks if the grandchildren could wait outside his room because he would like to speak to the adults. All of Trent's grandchildren give their Grampsy a hug before leaving the room and tell Trent how much they love him and to get well soon. Trent sees all the faces of his children—Jackie, Kelly, Leslie, Micah, and Noah. Trent then notices Willis and Wanda leaving the room.

Trent says to Willis, "Could you and Wanda please stay? I would like for y'all to hear what I'm going to say."

Willis smiles at Trent and says, "Okay, my friend, we will stay tell us. What's on your mind?"

Danny holds Lisa's hand while Trent takes a drink of water and clears his throat and begins to speak while looking at the faces of all his loved ones.

"I'd like to say a prayer first if we could all bow our heads." Trent begins his prayer. "Heavenly Father, I thank you for all your blessings you have given me. I ask for wisdom and courage for the words to show my true feelings to my loved ones in Jesus's name. Amen."

Everyone looks at Trent, waiting for an explanation for that prayer. Trent starts talking, and as he speaks, he scans the room at all the faces looking at him.

Trent tells everyone how he loves everyone so much and how proud he is of all his family and friends. Then he tells the story of how Jesus visited him while he was in a coma. The faces of everyone listening turns to joy, and Trent then tells the story of how Jesus is going to come back for him with a few angels to take him to paradise.

Trent smiles, and he sees his daughters crying and says, "I know it's hard to believe this. Believe me when I say I was skeptical of this vision myself." Trent continues as he sees Mary Ann wiping tears from her eyes. "The doctor was going to tell y'all today that all of my vital organs are shutting down and was shocked when I told him what I just told y'all. Dr. Manson is a good doctor, but he knows I'm going to die soon." Trent sees Wanda hug Willis tight as he sees Willis begin to cry.

Trent takes a deep breath and says, "I asked Jesus to please let me stay on Earth a few more years because I just retired." Trent laughs. "Jesus says he needs me in heaven."

Trent says with a smile on his face, "When Jesus calls, you just can't say no."

Micah takes hold of his dad's hand and says, "Dad, we all love you and are so proud of you. Is there anything we can do for you?" Trent looks at Micah and says, "Yes, tell my grandchildren to grow up with Jesus in their heart, and I'll be waiting in heaven for all my loved ones."

The husbands and wives in the room are hugging, trying their best to console each other when there is a knock at the door. The door opens, and Diane is in a wheelchair holding her newborn child with Jack slowly pushing her close to the bed where Trent is lying.

Trent smiles and says, "Hello, it's good to see you again," in a voice of excitement. Everyone wipes their tears away as Jack speaks with confusion in his voice, "Did we enter this room at a bad time?"

Trent says, "No, of course not, how y'all doing?"

Diane says, "I just want to introduce our new gift from God to the man that saved our lives."

Trent looks at the baby boy and says in a sincere voice, "Wow, that is a fine-looking baby boy."

Diane smiles at Trent and says, "We want you to know that Jack and I named him Trent Charles Brown."

Trent is smiling and says, "That's a good name, and his initials are TCB."

Trent laughs and says, "Just like Elvis's mantra."

Jack tells Trent, "We never thought of that, but you are right."

Trent asks Kelly if she could take a picture of Jack and Diane with Trent holding the little baby, and Kelly says, "Sure, Dad, whatever you want. After taking the picture, Trent kisses the little baby and gently gives the baby back to Diane.

Jack smiles at everyone and says, "Nice to see everyone, but I have to get mother and son back to their room for some much-needed rest."

Trent thanks Jack for bringing his family to see him and says, "God bless y'all."

Trent is seen by everyone wincing in pain as he pushes the red button repeatedly to give more morphine to ease the increasing pain his body is going through. All his loved ones now surround his bed.

Trent is now going through pain that the morphine can't control and tells Mary Ann with tears falling down on his smiling face, "I just want you to know that you have brought joy into my life the short time I have known you, and I love you."

Mary Ann smiles at Trent and wipes away his tears and says with a compassionate voice, "I love you too, my sweetheart. You have made me so happy, words can't express."

Trent is now in extreme pain as Noah runs out of the door yelling for a doctor. Nurse Nancy hears Noah yelling and runs into the room. Nurse Nancy tries her best to relieve the pain by giving more morphine to Trent, but the pain is too great. Trent starts to cry and say out loud, "I believe I'm knocking on heaven's door. Dear Jesus, please have mercy on my soul."

Trent's monitors begin to sound alarms, and at seven o clock in the evening, Trent takes his last breath on planet Earth, and all the monitors show flat line. Trent dies. Every person in the room begins to sob intensely, and Nurse Nancy calls Dr. Manson to let him know that Trent has died. The news of Trent's passing travels through the halls of the hospital quickly. Many condolences are being given at the waiting room where Trent's family is grieving by hospital staff only ten minutes past 7:00 p.m.

Jackie is talking to Kelly asking, "What is protocol now?"

Kelly wipes tears from her eyes and says, "The nurse should be coming by soon to let us know something."

Noah walks close to Jackie and says, "I will be back in a few minutes."

Mary Ann is seen drinking a bottle of water, and her hands are shaking, trying to grasp the bottle, and Ginger tries to reassure Mary Ann by saying, "It's going to be okay."

Mary Ann puts down the bottle of water and says with an angry voice, "It's not okay, a good man has just died, my heart is broken. I feel so upset I want to break something."

Willis hears Mary Ann's outburst and walks over to Mary Ann and says in a compassionate voice, "Listen to me, dear, we are all heartbroken now, but we have the peace in knowing that Trent is in heaven."

Mary Ann smiles at Willis and says, "I know, but I miss Trent so much," and starts to cry and says, "Why couldn't God let him be with us longer?"

Willis takes hold of Mary Ann's hand and says with a tender voice, "I miss my best friend so much right now it hurts for me to breathe."

Willis releases Mary Ann's hand and says with a smile on his face, "To have joy in my life, I will remember all the good times I had with Trent, and that's how I will deal with him not being in my life anymore."

Mary Ann wipes away a tear from her face, smiles at Willis, and says, "I only knew Trent for a very short time, but the man risked everything to save my life, and I will always be grateful for that." Mary Ann pauses for a few seconds then says, "But I will follow Trent's last request to keep Christ in our lives."

Mary Ann hugs Willis and thanks him for talking to her. Noah returns to the waiting room to announce that the hospital has called the funeral home and the funeral director will take care of all the necessary arrangements.

Noah smiles and says, "Dad took care all of his burial plans a few months after Mom was buried a few years ago."

Leslie laughs out loud and says, "That's our dad, always taking care of business, to be proactive just in case things don't work out like we planned."

Micah speaks up with anger in his voice and says, "Well, things surely didn't work out with this situation."

Micah looks up at the ceiling as though he was looking up to heaven and with a voice contempt says, "First, you take our mother, and now you take our father. Why, God, tell me why you need them more than we need them." Micah drops to his knees and starts to cry. Kelly and Jackie kneel down beside their brother.

Jackie tells Micah, "God does things to good people to test our faith, and this test is going to be tough on all of us."

Kelly hugs her brother and says, "We have to be strong, my brother, because the devil wants to destroy our belief in God Almighty. That is how the devil wins, but he will not win."

Micah looks at his sisters and hugs both of them and says with tears in his eyes, "I love you. Thank you for giving me compassion. I will not let the devil take hold of me. With God all things are possible, and by the grace of God, I will, we all will, get through the loss of our dad, and be better Christians for it."

Kelly and Jackie help Micah stand up.

Jackie says, "We have to lean on each other now and in the future when we are feeling depressed. We need to call on one another so we can pray together to sustain our faith in God."

Everyone in the waiting room witnessed this scene, and all said Amen to give praise to God. Noah said to everyone, "If anyone would like to pass by my house and have some food, please call me so I know how much pizza to pick up."

Noah asks Mary Ann and Ginger to please stay for a few hours before returning to Louisiana. Mary Ann tells Noah that she and Ginger would love to stay because they need time to recover from this tragedy. Everyone in the waiting room is seen giving hugs to one another before leaving and said they would call Noah soon to let him know if they would gather at his home.

An hour has passed since leaving the hospital, and Trent's family is at Noah's home, where Trent's children are eating pizza on the backyard patio. The big screen TV is on, but the volume is turned down.

Leslie says while pointing at the TV, "Look, everyone, it's that news reporter that was at the hospital."

Noah quickly turns up the volume on the TV so everyone can hear what is being reported. The news reporter is talking about how the man who saved the life of a pregnant woman during a bank robbery has died and that the pregnant woman has given birth to a baby boy, who she has named after the hero that saved her and her newborn baby. The news reporter also says that this hero was the same man who jumped off a cruise ship two weeks ago to save a woman that fell off that same cruise ship some twenty-five miles from Grand Cayman Islands in the Caribbean Sea. The news reporter says they will give information on the funeral services for this local hero as soon as arrangements are made.

"We should all pay tribute to this man who paid the ultimate price in saving three human beings."

Everyone is surprised that the news of Trent's death was being reported so soon.

Noah turns down the volume on the TV and raises his glass of soda and says to everyone, "I'd like to make a toast to the hero in all of our lives, and may he rest in peace, our dad."

Everyone is touching glasses and bottles of water and says, "We love you. Rest in peace." After a few minutes, Noah gets a phone call from Trent's neighbor and says that strangers have been putting flowers, balloons, and thank-you cards in front of Trent's front door. The neighbor says that she went out to talk to some of the people and they said that they didn't know Trent but wish they could have.

Noah tells the lady, "Thank you for calling," and that he would be stopping by his dad's home soon.

Noah is smiling as he puts down his cell phone and tells everyone the news he just received from their dad's next-door neighbor.

Kelly smiles and says, "The world is not all bad. There are plenty good, caring people on this planet."

Micah looks at Kelly and says with a smile on his face, "And our dad was one of the best. We were very lucky to have him as a dad."

After ten minutes, everyone helps Noah clean up. Noah says that he is going pass by Dad's house to check things out, and everyone agrees to follow Noah to see what is going on. The scene at Trent's house is amazing, and as Trent's family gets out of their vehicles, they are surprised to see all the thank-you cards and flowers that are stacked up near the front door. Mary Ann is crying as she reads some of the notes on the flowers, which read "Gone too soon," "The world needs more heroes like this man," "He will not be forgotten," "Rest in peace."

Ginger hugs Mary Ann and says with a tear in her eye, "It's going to be okay, darling. I know how much it hurts, but this makes me feel good."

Mary Ann says, wiping her tears away, "It makes me feel good too, but I miss him."

Ginger says in a compassionate voice, "It's going to hurt for a long time, but it will get better in time. You know this is true."

CHAPTER THIRTY-FOUR

The funeral director has called Trent's family, and they all agreed to meet at the funeral home at nine o'clock in the morning. The three sisters and two brothers are having a meeting with the funeral director. His name is Mr. Clay.

Mr. Clay reads in detail what kind of funeral service Trent wanted. Trent asks in this handwritten letter that he wanted a slide-show of photographs both recent and not so recent. Trent wanted only happy videos to be played, because he wanted his life to be celebrated, not mourned. Trent also picked out some upbeat music to be played while his body is being viewing, and during the final hour of the service, he would like this list of songs that praised Jesus Christ. Mr. Clay reads the songs out loud while his children are smiling at the songs their dad has selected, which are all songs that are recent and not old-fashioned. Mr. Clay reads that Trent would like to be cremated and his ashes spread over the Gulf of Mexico one year after his death to celebrate a year in heaven.

Kelly speaks up and says with a smile on her face, "Our dad had a plan, and we didn't know one thing about it."

Noah smiles and says, "Yes, I thought I knew everything. Dad never told me a word about this letter."

Micah stands up at the table and says, "Well, we all know that Dad liked to have a plan for everything in his life, and now we know he had a plan even after death."

Jackie smiles and says, "That's our dad. He always said be ready for the future."

Leslie wipes a tear from her eye and says, "Well, I'm so sad that this future has happen so damn early. I miss my dad and wish he was still here to talk to and hug."

All of Trent's children gather around Leslie."

Noah says, "We have each other to hold now, and don't ever forget that." And with that the tears start falling from all the children's eyes as they grieve the death of their dad.

Mr. Clay stands up and says quietly, "I will give y'all time to mourn," and leaves the room. A few minutes pass, and everyone wipes the tears from their face.

Noah says, "Wow, it just hit me that this is not a dream. Our dad is really gone."

Micah hugs his brother and says, "Yeah, Dad is gone, but we have great memories."

Jackie clears her throat and says, "Well, let's get out of here. We have a memorial service to plan."

Leslie laughs and says, "Well, Dad pretty much did all the planning. We just have to set a date."

Kelly smiles and says, "Yeah, that's one thing only God knows, the date of your death. We can't plan that unless you take your own life."

Noah says, "Well, I'm sure God knows that too."

Everyone walks out of the room and leaves the funeral home. The memorial service arrangements for the date and time are given to the local newspaper to be printed to inform anyone that would like to attend the service. The local news on TV are also reporting on the death of Trent, how he was a hero who gave his life to save another life, and they talk about the memorial service date and time.

The day of the memorial service, Jackie was having a difficult time accepting the death of her dad. She being the oldest child, she knew she had to be strong. Larry, her husband, gives Jackie a big hug and says with compassion in his voice, "Sweetheart, I miss your dad too, but we will get through this."

Jackie looks at her husband and says with a smile on her face, "I know we will. It will just take time and a lot of tissues."

Larry smiles and says, "I will go to WalMart. I'll buy a truckload of tissues for you, honey."

Jackie says, laughing, "Well, thank you so much for that, my love."

Larry says, "It's time to go to the funeral home, and, darling, you look beautiful."

Jackie says to Larry, "Thank you, honey."

Jackie, Larry, and their children arrive at the funeral home. Jackie's brothers and sisters have arrived with their families also. Mary Ann, Ginger, and Noah are walking in the parking lot.

Noah tells Ginger, "This reminds me of my mom's funeral two years ago. That feeling of loss and wishing you could just say I love you one more time."

Ginger smiles at Noah and says, "Yes, we all want a few more minutes with our loved ones when they die."

Mary Ann is quiet while walking then says, "I wanted many more years with Trent," and begins to cry and says, "God needed him more than us."

Everyone walks into the funeral home, and they see the arrangement of flowers that are amazing. Mr. Clay meets them in the large room where the memorial service will be conducted.

He says, "We have never had so many flowers at a funeral, and I've been here thirty years."

Mr. Clay says with a smile on his face that flowers were sent from all over the United States. "We had to put some of them on the outside rooms because we didn't have any room in the large room."

Kelly looks at the flower arrangements and notices the addresses from some of the flowers that are from different parts of the United States, from complete strangers, and has comments on the card that Jackie begins to read out loud.

"Your dad was our hero too. God bless and give you peace."

Everyone started reading the many different cards that were attached to the flowers and are amazed at the outpouring of sympathy for Trent and his family. Danny and Lisa walk through the front doors of the funeral home, and both are astonished by the display of flowers. Danny hugs his brother's family, and Noah tells Danny that these flowers are from all over the country. Danny and Lisa read some of the cards, and Danny begins to cry.

Lisa asks, "What is making you cry?"

Danny asks Lisa to read the card, and Lisa begins to cry, and the card has in print: "I lost my brother too, and it was tragic, but this brave man that these flowers are for, and that my fellow workers got together to send, is a true American hero. He had so much to live for and without hesitation sacrificed all that for a complete stranger, and if that's not love, well, there is no sun in the sky. May God bless his family and give them serenity."

Lisa hugs Danny and says, "I see why that made you cry. It's sweet how other people that don't know Trent can feel compassion for his family."

Danny says while wiping a tear from his eye, "Well, I see it made you cry too, and you are right. Trent showed so many people what it means to be courageous."

People are starting to come into the funeral home, and Noah notices a line of people that are waiting to enter the large room. Noah decides to walk outside through a side door to see what is happening outside, and to his surprise, he can see hundreds of people standing outside waiting to enter the funeral home.

Noah sees a friend named Dale and says, "That's a lot of people."

Dale looks at Noah and says, "Yes, they started arriving by the hundreds a few minutes before you came to talk to me. Your dad sure had a lot of friends."

Noah looks at Dale and says, smiling, "Dad had some friends, but the people I see are strangers who are coming from only God knows where."

Dale looks at Noah and says, "Well, look at the traffic jam down the road. This crowd is getting bigger every minute that passes by. I've never seen anything like this."

Noah walks back into the funeral home, and Mr. Clay looks at Noah with an expression of concern. Mr. Clay asks Noah, "What should I do about the crowd in the funeral home?"

Noah is somewhat confused too and says, "There is a bigger crowd outside waiting to come in."

Noah says to Mr. Clay that we will have to extend the time of the visiting to an extra hour and then start the memorial service so that everyone that took time to be here has an opportunity to pay their respects.

Mr. Clay says thanks to Noah for the solution. "I will go make an announcement to let all visitors know we will extend the service."

Noah returns to stand by his family who are greeting everyone by the casket. A large picture of Trent smiling with his children is next to the casket. Noah tells Micah that there are hundreds of people waiting in line outside to come in to give their condolences.

Micah looks at Noah and says, "Why are so many people coming here?"

Noah smiles at Micah and says, "Our dad has shown people what it means to be an American hero."

Micah tells Noah, "I hear you, brother. I heard that from many people today."

Mr. Clay goes to the front of the room where he holds a microphone and asks everyone for their attention. Mr. Clay says, "We will extend the memorial service for one hour so everyone that is here gets to show their condolences. Thank you for your patience."

An hour passes by, and Mr. Clay announces that the last phase of the memorial service will begin. The slideshow of Trent and his life with his family begins. The big TV screen in front of the large room is being watched by hundreds of family, friends, and complete strangers who are in attendance. The slideshow went on for ten minutes, and the people in the large room stand up and applaud for a few minutes to show Trent's family their praise for Trent.

Kelly's oldest daughter, Tammy, who is twelve years old, is passing by Mr. Clay's office to go to the room where refreshments are being kept when the phone begins ringing. Tammy listens to the phone ring, and it sounds different from any phone she has ever heard before. Tammy looks around and sees no one who is going to answer the phone. The phone keeps ringing with its unique tone.

Tammy walks into the office and answers the phone. Tammy can't believe the voice she hears on the phone. Tammy is surprised to hear the voice of her grandfather, Trent.

Tammy loudly says, "Is this really you, Grampsy?"

Trent says, "Yes, it is, my beautiful Tammy. How are you?"

Tammy says, "I really am sad that you died and miss you so much."

Trent says, "I miss you too, and I didn't want to die, but Jesus told me it was time to go to heaven." Then there is a pause on the phone conversation.

Tammy yells, "Grampsy, are you still there?"

Trent says, "Yes, I'm here. Please go tell your family I'm on the phone calling from heaven and would like to speak to them."

Tammy says, "I love you, Grampsy, but there are no phones in heaven."

Trent says, "Yes, there is, because I'm talking to you now."

Tammy shouts, "I'll be right back, hold on." Tammy puts the phone on the table and runs as fast as she can to her family who are greeting people at the front of the large room.

Tammy is out of breath and says very loudly to her mom, "Please come quickly to Mr. Clay's office."

Kelly looks at her daughter with concern and says, "Calm down."

Tammy takes a deep breath and says, "I was walking by Mr. Clay's office. The phone was ringing, and it had a ring to it that I had never heard a phone sound like." Tammy takes another deep breath and says with a smile on her face, "It's Grampsy. I'm telling the truth, Mom. It's Grampsy on the phone. I know it is, and he wants to talk to his family."

Kelly looks at Noah, and Noah, who heard Tammy, says loudly, "Let's hurry to the phone."

This conversation was heard by other people too, and like wildfire the news that Trent was on the phone from heaven has spread all over the inside of the funeral home and outside the funeral home where people are gathered.

All of Trent's family entered Mr. Clay's office with some having their cell phones out, recording a video of what was happening in the office. Noah puts the phone on speaker mode so everyone in the room can hear Trent's voice.

Jackie speaks first in an excited voice, "Hey, Dad, is it really you?"

Trent says in a loud, clear voice, "Yes, Jackie, it's me, your loving dad." Trent continues to speak, "I just want all of you to know that I made it to heaven. Jesus is allowing me to talk to you for a few minutes. Jesus tells me because I saved lives while sacrificing my own."

Mary Ann says in a loud but sweet voice, "Hey, Trent, it's me. I just want to say I miss you and wish you were here with us."

Trent says to Mary Ann, "I recognize your voice, Mary Ann. I wish I could have stayed on Earth many more years, but God had other plans for me."

Micah speaks with enthusiasm in his voice and says, "Dad, have you seen Mom in heaven?"

Trent's voice has a tone of joy with it and says, "Yes, she was there at the pearly gates of heaven waiting for me to enter, and, Micah, I have to say she is looking like the day I married her, so beautiful."

Kelly speaks to her dad and says, "What does your body look like in heaven?"

Trent says, "Kelly, I was surprised to see everyone look to be the same age as Jesus when he was nailed to the cross to be crucified. I would say around thirty-three years of age."

Kelly speaks to her dad with a confused voice of, "But, Dad, what about the children that died at a young age?"

Trent tells Kelly that they have children in heaven, and the parents know who they are, but their spiritual bodies have matured to the age of Jesus when he died and was resurrected.

Leslie asks her dad, "How does it feel to be in heaven?"

Trent says, "It's like heaven," with a laugh. "Leslie, my baby girl, there is beauty all around, and the animals are all as gentle as kittens. There is no one that is in any pain. Our spiritual bodies are as perfect as can be."

Noah asks his dad to describe heaven.

Trent says in a voice of peaceful excitement, "Noah, my son, Heaven has streets of gold that look like you can see right through them. As a matter of fact, the large city has twelve gates, and each gate is made of pearl, so beautiful it's hard to put into words. The walls of this large city we are in is made up of so many different precious stones. It's simply magnificent."

Willis asks his old friend, "Hey, Trent, can you do any fishing in heaven?"

Trent laughs and says, "What you talking about, Willis, of course there is fishing in heaven, with the clearest water you have ever seen, but, Willis, it's a catch-and-release protocol in heaven. You have to understand there is no need for food in heaven, because our bodies are nourished by the joy and love of the Father, Holy Spirit, and Jesus Christ. We all have different jobs to keep us busy, but mostly we glorify and praise God with songs and prayer. I have to go now, but they have a lot of awesome singers up in heaven. I have walked and talked with Jesus, and saw his hands where the nails went through to hold him on the cross."

Trent says with joy in his voice, "Listen, my children, continue to live a Christian lifestyle and keep his ten commandments, and one day soon we will all be together in heaven, I promise. God has mercy and grace that can't be measured. I love y'all, and wish I could talk longer, and by the way, that was a great memorial service that I planned right."

Jackie says, "Yes, Dad, you did an excellent job on that. We had no idea you made arrangements for your funeral service."

Trent says, laughing, "Well, I did that after your mom passed away and didn't want to burden y'all with any more stress than what y'all would be going through already. I love y'all so much. I have to go, but remember, love one another as Christ loves you, and pray for forgiveness often. Goodbye, till we meet in heaven, everybody."

All in the people in the office are saying "I love you," and the tears are falling from everyone's eyes because of the joy of hearing Trent's voice.

CHAPTER THIRTY-FIVE

Everyone in Mr. Clay's office are hugging each other and asking one another how crazy it was to hear Trent's voice in heaven. Noah looks at everyone to tell them, "Listen, I will be having the funeral gathering at my house, so we need to get there to meet the friends and the rest of our family that will be arriving very soon."

Everyone gathers their belongings and go to their vehicles to drive to Noah's house. At Noah's home, many family and friends are having conversations while eating good food and have some cold drinks to wash the food down. Kelly and Noah are talking about the miracle that happened in the funeral director's office.

Kelly says, "We have it on video."

Noah looks at Kelly in a surprised manner and says, "Wow, that's terrific. Can I see it?"

Kelly shows the video, which she recorded on her smartphone while Trent was talking from heaven, to Noah. Noah asks Kelly if it would be okay to play this on his big-screen TV on the patio to show family and friends that it is true, that Trent did talk to them from heaven on the phone.

Kelly smiles and says, "Noah, that would be awesome, because something like this you have to share with people."

Noah takes Kelly's smartphone and connects a wire to her smartphone then connects that wire to his large screen TV. Noah asks everyone to gather around the patio.

"Because we all need to watch this video that was made less than an hour ago."

A lot of curious faces gather around the large screen TV, and Noah turns up the sound on the TV. The look on the faces of everyone watching the video is priceless. Jackie is crying watching the video, listening to her dad's voice seems so bizarre, but as the video is playing, she knows that there is no doubt that it's her dad's voice. The people at the gathering are silent during the playing of the video, listening carefully to every word. The video is finished playing, and many family members request to watch it one more time.

Many people ask Noah if it is okay to record the video on their smartphones, and after he has a short discussion with his siblings, they agree it would be okay. Noah replays the video, and again some people are crying while watching the video, because it truly is a miracle to watch and hear something that is difficult to believe that could happen. The conversations at Noah's home are now alive with joy, laughter, and hope. Noah asks if anyone would like to sing on his karaoke machine, and Mary Ann says she would like to sing a song.

Noah asks Mary Ann, "What song would you like to sing?"

Mary Ann tells Noah, "I would like to sing the song 'I Believe' by Brooks and Dunn."

Noah smiles at Mary Ann and says, "That's a perfect song for this time and place."

Mary Ann starts to sing the song, and everyone turns to listen and watch Mary Ann sing. The tears begin to fall like rain from most of the people watching Mary Ann sing because she is singing with so much heart and soul that her words are giving feelings of hope to people that you have to believe in heaven. Kelly has her smartphone out and is making a video of Mary Ann singing the song. Mary Ann finishes the song, and after the applause from family and friends, she shows the performance to Mary Ann. Kelly asks if Mary Ann wouldn't mind; she would like to put the video of her singing on YouTube.

After pausing for a minute, Mary Ann says with a smile on her face, "Sure, that would be fine. I think it sounded okay."

Kelly says to Mary Ann, "It sounded more than okay. It was great. You really have a gift from God with your voice. Hopefully someone sees this video, and you may get a recording contract from a record producer."

Mary Ann laughs and says, "Yeah, that would be a miracle. A few more people sing with the karaoke machine, but none of the singers sound as good as Mary Ann. Many people at the gathering have talked to Mary Ann after her performance to tell her how good she sings. Mary Ann is gracious in thanking everyone for saying such kind words to her.

Ginger is telling Mary Ann with a grin on her face, "It looks like you are a rock star over here, girlfriend."

Mary Ann smiles at Ginger and says, "You think."

Ginger laughs and says, "Well, you were definitely the best singer here today."

Noah turns on the large-screen TV after no one else wants to sing with the karaoke machine. The local news is on, and the news reporter is talking about a miracle that has happened at a local funeral home earlier today. Noah asks everyone to be quiet and to listen to the news reporter who begins to talk about a memorial service for a local man who recently died from a gunshot wound that was caused by a bank robber.

The news reporter says, "The man that died was a hero in the eyes of all that know the story of how he took the bullet that was meant for a pregnant woman who was walking into the bank at the time of the robbery."

The reporter then tells, "The video you will soon be watching was shot live in the funeral director's office. The video plays the conversation of Trent and his family. The news station has done careful research of voice recognition of the video, and without any doubt in their minds, the voice on the phone from heaven is the voice of Trent, the hero who died for a complete stranger so she may live and have her baby." The news reporter is seen wiping a tear from her eye. She says that a miracle has happened today. "This is one we will never forget."

Noah turns downs the volume on the TV and says, "Wow, good news travels fast." The discussion at the gathering after viewing the newscast was about the cat being out of the bag, which meant how many YouTube views will be seen in the next few months and all the repercussions that will follow.

Micah tells his family that there will be people that believe the video and other people that will say it's a hoax. Micah stands by his wife and says with a smile on his face, "I know my dad, and I know that was him on the phone from heaven, and I'll stand by that till the day I go to heaven."

Everyone at the gathering gives applause to Micah for his statement. Noah is seen beginning to clean up his patio by picking up the food and drinks. Everyone is lending a hand, and Noah is grateful for the help. He tells everyone "thank you" for staying to help clean up. The next day Noah gets a call from Ginger, and she tells Noah that she heard a rumor that ABC World News Tonight with John Kendricks will be playing the video of Trent calling from heaven.

Noah thanks Ginger for the information about the evening news broadcast and would be sure to let his brother and sisters know that the evening news will be reporting on the video that is circulating on the internet. Noah calls his brother and sisters and tells them to watch the evening news, and be ready for the phones to start ringing with people being skeptical to the video being false.

Micah tells Noah, "Let the people think what they want. They always do anyway."

Micah tells Noah, "When he heard about the little girl who called from heaven a few weeks ago, it was hard for me to believe that anyone could call from heaven, but I know it happened, and it happened again with our dad, and that's the truth, my brother."

Noah tells Micah that if he needs to vent to call him anytime. Micah thanks Noah for his concern and tells Noah that he may call him anytime to talk about this matter or any other issues going on in his life.

Noah is surprised at the compassion that Micah is expressing over the phone and tells Noah, "You are the best brother I have."

Micah laughs and says, "Noah, I'm the only brother you have."

Noah laughs and says, "Yes, but you still are my favorite brother."

Micah laughs and tells Noah, "We will be watching the news tonight," and then says goodbye. The evening news is playing on the TV at Noah's home, and Noah is watching with curiosity on how anyone watching will feel about the news of this video being shown for the world to see.

Noah watches as John Kendricks reports that skepticism may run rampant after viewing this video that will be shown and then says, "Let's watch the video together." The video of Trent's call from heaven plays on the news, and after the video, John Kendricks says with a serious voice, "Our investigators have researched this video with all of our resources, and it is our belief that this video is authentic." John Kendricks is saying that this truly is a miracle from God. John Kendricks then talks about another news story that is current. Noah turns off his TV and looks at a picture of his dad and mom that is placed on a wall in his living room.

Noah says out loud, "Dad, enjoy your eternal life in heaven with Mom. I miss y'all."

In a house in New Orleans, a man has been watching the evening news. His brother was killed instantly in a single-vehicle accident. The man who's is in his early twenties turns off his TV and says out loud, "I wish I could talk to my brother one more time. I didn't have a chance to say goodbye and tell him how much I love him."

THE END

ABOUT THE AUTHOR

Gregory Mark Haydel was born and raised in southern Louisiana. In a small town he enjoyed playing sports as a child, especially football, basketball and baseball. After high school hunting and fishing in the bayous were relaxing. He worked at the age of eighteen as a deckhand for a few years and then went to school to receive his United States Coast Guard Master of towing license and has been a tugboat Captain for almost forty years. He started writing poems as a teenager and that led to writing short stories. He is looking forward to his retirement years, and doing more hunting and fishing, and yes writing more novels that he hopes will provide enjoyment for the readers.

CPSIA information can be obtained
at www.ICGtesting.com
Printed in the USA
LVHW030115201119
637819LV00005B/521

9 781645 443414